THE PROBLEM CHILD

Emerson Pass Historicals, Book Four

TESS THOMPSON

Praise for Tess Thompson

"I frequently found myself getting lost in the characters and forgetting that I was reading a book." - *Camille Di Maio, Bestselling author of The Memory of Us.*

"Highly recommended." - *Christine Nolfi, Award winning author of The Sweet Lake Series.*

"I loved this book!" - *Karen McQuestion, Bestselling author of Hello Love and Good Man, Dalton.*

Traded: Brody and Kara:
"I loved the sweetness of Tess Thompson's writing - the camaraderie and long-lasting friendships make you want to move to Cliffside and become one of the gang! Rated Hallmark for romance!" - *Stephanie Little BookPage*

"This story was well written. You felt what the characters were going through. It's one of those "I got to know what happens next" books. So intriguing you won't want to put it down." - *Lena Loves Books*

"This story has so much going on, but it intertwines within itself. You get second chance, lost loves, and new love. I could not put this book down! I am excited to start this series and have love for this little Bayside town that I am now fond off!" - *Crystal's Book World*

"This is a small town romance story at its best and I look forward to the next book in the series." - *Gillek2, Vine Voice*

"This is one of those books that make you love to be a reader and fan of the author." -*Pamela Lunder, Vine Voice*

Blue Midnight:

"This is a beautiful book with an unexpected twist that takes the story from romance to mystery and back again. I've already started the 2nd book in the series!" - *Mama O*

"This beautiful book captured my attention and never let it go. I did not want it to end and so very much look forward to reading the next book." - *Pris Shartle*

"I enjoyed this new book cover to cover. I read it on my long flight home from Ireland and it helped the time fly by, I wish it had been longer so my whole flight could have been lost to this lovely novel about second chances and finding the truth. Written with wisdom and humor this novel shares the raw emotions a new divorce can leave behind." - *J. Sorenson*

"Tess Thompson is definitely one of my auto-buy authors! I love her writing style. Her characters are so real to life that you just can't put the book down once you start! Blue Midnight makes you believe in second chances. It makes you believe that everyone deserves an HEA. I loved the twists and turns in this book, the mystery and suspense, the family dynamics and the restoration of trust and security." - *Angela MacIntyre*

"Tess writes books with real characters in them, characters with flaws and baggage and gives them a second chance. (Real people, some remind me of myself and my girlfriends.) Then she cleverly and thoroughly develops those characters and makes you feel deeply for them. Characters are complex and multi-faceted, and the plot seems to unfold naturally, and never feels contrived." - *K. Lescinsky*

Caramel and Magnolias:

"Nobody writes characters like Tess Thompson. It's like she looks into our lives and creates her characters based on our best friends, our lovers, and our neighbors. Caramel and Magnolias, and the authors debut novel Riversong, have some of the best characters I've ever had a chance to fall in love with. I don't like leaving spoilers in reviews so just trust me, Nicholas Sparks has nothing on Tess Thompson, her writing flows so smoothly you can't help but to want to read on!" - *T. M. Frazier*

"I love Tess Thompson's books because I love good writing. Her prose is clean and tight, which are increasingly rare qualities, and manages to evoke a full range of emotions with both subtlety and power. Her fiction goes well beyond art imitating life. Thompson's characters are alive and fully-realized, the action is believable, and the story unfolds with the right balance of tension and exuberance. CARAMEL AND MAGNOLIAS is a pleasure to read." - *Tsuruoka*

"The author has an incredible way of painting an image with her words. Her storytelling is beautiful, and leaves you wanting more! I love that the story is about friendship (2 best friends) and love. The characters are richly drawn and I found myself rooting for them from the very beginning. I think you will, too!" - *Fogvision*

"I got swept off my feet, my heartstrings were pulled, I held my breath, and tightened my muscles in suspense. Tess paints stunning scenery with her words and draws you in to the lives of her characters."- *T. Bean*

Duet For Three Hands:

"Tears trickled down the side of my face when I reached the end of this road. Not because the story left me feeling sad or disappointed, no. Rather, because I already missed them. My friends. Though it isn't goodbye, but see you later. And so I will sit impatiently waiting, with desperate eagerness to hear where life has taken you, what burdens have you downtrodden, and what triumphs warm your heart. And in the meantime, I will go out and live, keeping your lessons and friendship and love close, the light to guide me through any darkness. And to the author I say thank you. My heart, my soul -all of me - needed these words, these friends, this love. I am forever changed by the beauty of your talent." - *Lisa M. Gott*

"I am a great fan of Tess Thompson's books and this new one definitely shows her branching out with an engaging enjoyable historical drama/love story. She is a true pro in the way she weaves her storyline, develops true to life characters that you love! The background and setting is so picturesque and visible just from her words. Each book shows her expanding, growing and excelling in her art. Yet another one not to miss. Buy it you won't be disappointed. The ONLY disappointment is when it ends!!!" - *Sparky's Last*

"There are some definite villains in this book. Ohhhh, how I loved to hate them. But I have to give Thompson credit because they never came off as caricatures or one dimensional. They all felt authentic to me and (sadly) I could easily picture them. I loved to love some and loved to hate others." - *The Baking Bookworm*

"I stayed up the entire night reading Duet For Three Hands and unbeknownst to myself, I fell asleep in the middle of reading the book. I literally woke up the next morning with Tyler the Kindle beside me (thankfully, still safe and intact) with no ounce of battery left. I shouldn't have worried about deadlines because, guess what? Duet For Three Hands was the epitome of unputdownable." - *The Bookish Owl*

Miller's Secret
"From the very first page, I was captivated by this wonderful tale. The cast of characters amazing - very fleshed out and multi-

dimensional. The descriptions were perfect - just enough to make you feel like you were transported back to the 20's and 40's.... This book was the perfect escape, filled with so many twists and turns I was on the edge of my seat for the entire read." - *Hilary Grossman*

"The sad story of a freezing-cold orphan looking out the window at his rich benefactors on Christmas Eve started me off with Horatio-Alger expectations for this book. But I quickly got pulled into a completely different world--the complex five-character braid that the plot weaves. The three men and two women characters are so alive I felt I could walk up and start talking to any one of them, and I'd love to have lunch with Henry. Then the plot quickly turned sinister enough to keep me turning the pages.

Class is set against class, poor and rich struggle for happiness and security, yet it is love all but one of them are hungry for. ......Where does love come from? What do you do about it? The story kept me going, and gave me hope. For a little bonus, there are Thompson's delightful observations, like: "You'd never know we could make something this good out of the milk from an animal who eats hats." A really good read!" - *Kay in Seattle*

"She paints vivid word pictures such that I could smell the ocean and hear the doves. Then there are the stories within a story that twist and turn until they all come together in the end. I really had a hard time putting it down. Five stars aren't enough!"
- *M.R. Williams*

Also by Tess Thompson

CLIFFSIDE BAY

Traded: Brody and Kara

Deleted: Jackson and Maggie

Jaded: Zane and Honor

Marred: Kyle and Violet

Tainted: Lance and Mary

Cliffside Bay Christmas, The Season of Cats and Babies (Cliffside Bay Novella to be read after Tainted)

Missed: Rafael and Lisa

Cliffside Bay Christmas Wedding (Cliffside Bay Novella to be read after Missed)

Healed: Stone and Pepper

Chateau Wedding (Cliffside Bay Novella to be read after Healed)

Scarred: Trey and Autumn

Jilted: Nico and Sophie

Kissed (Cliffside Bay Novella to be read after Jilted)

Departed: David and Sara

Cliffside Bay Bundle , Books 1,2,3

BLUE MOUNTAIN SERIES

Blue Mountain Bundle, Books 1,2,3

Blue Midnight

Blue Moon

Blue Ink

Blue String

EMERSON PASS HISTORICALS

The School Mistress

The Spinster

The Scholar

The Problem Child

The Musician

EMERSON PASS CONTEMPORARIES

The Sugar Queen

The Patron

RIVER VALLEY

Riversong

Riverbend

Riverstar

Riversnow

Riverstorm

Tommy's Wish

River Valley Bundle, Books 1-4

LEGLEY BAY

Caramel and Magnolias

Tea and Primroses

STANDALONES

The Santa Trial

Duet for Three Hands

Miller's Secret

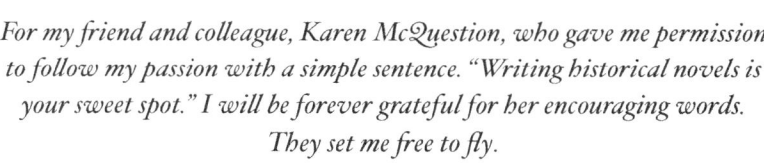

For my friend and colleague, Karen McQuestion, who gave me permission to follow my passion with a simple sentence. "Writing historical novels is your sweet spot." I will be forever grateful for her encouraging words. They set me free to fly.

A note to readers

I'm delighted you've found your way to this fourth installment of my Emerson Pass Historicals Series. Since I first dreamt of the Barnes family (quite literally, they came to me in a dream) I have enjoyed writing Cymbeline most of all. She is feisty and unconventional and absolutely unafraid to be unabashedly herself. As I waited for her to grow old enough for her own romance, she whispered her story in my ear. I've learned a lot from her. She taught me how to find a way to do what I love, even when there were many obstacles in my way. I also learned a lot about the history of ski jumping and how long it took for women to have a place on the slope.

For all the women, past and present, who have fought for the right to compete in any sport, art, academic or business pursuit, thank you for the inspiration. You're all here in Cymbeline.

I hope you enjoy this fourth story in the Barnes family saga. If you do, please consider leaving a review on the retailer of your choice. Also, come hang out with me in Patio Chat on Facebook or sign up for my newsletter so you never miss a sale or new release.

Much love to you and yours,

Tess

THE PROBLEM CHILD

Cymbeline

That November evening in 1925 the wind brought the scent of change. I stood on the porch of my family's home and drew in the smell of woodsmoke and dirt under the layer of newly fallen leaves, but there was something else too. Something unfamiliar. A fragrance I couldn't quite place. One that brought the promise of redemption and transformation. I shivered and drew my coat closer around my slim waist.

Something was coming. What, though? Adventure? Or simply a storm? One which my family would yet again have to weather?

An autumnal setting sun cast an orange gossamer light over the yard. Only a few days ago, the first frost had turned the leaves on the aspens and birches into blazing reds and yellows. Then a howling wind had shaken many of them loose from their beloved branches. They now covered the ground in a patchwork quilt.

This morning when I'd first gone to look out the window of my bedroom, a frost had dulled their dramatic colors. Not for long, however. Like me, their flame couldn't be muted. They'd returned to their vibrant hues to compete with the azure sky.

The sound of a motorcar coming down our driveway drew my attention. My twin brothers and my eldest sister, Josephine, were already inside for Sunday dinner. Did we have a visitor? Strange for a Sunday. Most stayed home with their families.

Squinting into the last of the sun, I waited to see who appeared. I didn't recognize the gleaming black car. But the driver? Him, I knew.

Viktor Olofsson. My nemesis. My competitor. My secret longing.

The man who made my stomach flutter like a silly girl. The object of my admiration.

I hated him.

But I loved him too. How this was possible, I did not know.

His car came to a stop near the horse meadow. What was he doing here? Had one of my interfering sisters invited him to Sunday dinner? My entire family was convinced Viktor was the answer to my restlessness. They should have known I wasn't made that way. Instead, I was an eagle without wings. No man could give me wings. I could only grow them myself.

Recently, I'd discovered I could fly. Not with wings, but with skis attached to my boots that took me soaring off the side of our mountain. After my brothers had built the ski jump for their own amusement, I'd insisted on trying it as well. I'd fallen in love almost immediately. With my strength and lightweight physique, I was able to go longer and farther than even Flynn. Ski jumping had become as much of an obsession and passion as ice-skating and skiing had been. Now I wanted only to fly as long and as far as humanly possible. Farther than the boys who had competed in the Winter Games in France. Faster and higher and longer than any of them. I'd liked to have said I wouldn't care if anyone knew, but that would be a lie. I may be overly competitive by nature, but a liar I was not.

Viktor unfolded from the car like the jack-in-the-box game we had played with as children. He patted the top of his car with the palms of his large hands and grinned at me. "Good evening, fair Cymbeline."

I rolled my eyes but went out to greet him just the same, crossing the driveway in my long, purposeful strides. My sister Josephine had once told me I walked as if I were trying to escape the devil. I'd retorted that I wasn't trying to escape him, simply outrun him.

"Hello, Viktor." I wanted to smack myself for the way my stomach fluttered at the sight of him. Viktor Olofsson was as beautiful a creature as had ever graced the earth, tall and wide-shouldered, with hair the color of sunshine and a smile that weakened knees all over town. Wickedly smart too, which galled me almost as much as his athletic abilities. No matter what I did, I couldn't beat him on the ice or in the classroom. Obviously, I was not immune to his charms. No one with a pulse would be. Unfortunately. "What brings you by?"

"Flynn invited me at church this morning. Said he had something big to announce at dinner that I'd be interested in."

"Really?" Whatever could that be? Why would he want Viktor to know about it?

"I'm curious as a cat, so I couldn't resist coming by." The squared nature of his shoulders and his long graceful neck made it seem as if he were trying to touch the hand of God with his superbly shaped head.

Here I was, running from the devil, whereas he seemed to be reaching for God.

"What are you doing out here in the cold? Waiting for me?" Those darned eyes of his, the color of the creek on a late-summer afternoon, twinkled at me.

"Hardly," I said. "I didn't even know you were coming by, so how could I be waiting?"

"But you're delighted to see me?" His dark jacket and trousers draped perfectly over his slender hips and long legs. Viktor's father was Emerson Pass's one and only tailor. A talented one, given how good Viktor looked in that stupid suit, I thought. He'd always been clean and tidy with impeccable manners. His mother was a fine lady and made sure her boys were honorable and heroic. Isak Olofsson, along with my brothers, had fought valiantly in the Great War. Now he owned the bakery and spent his days making delicious things to eat instead of carrying a gun.

"You may choose to wish it so," I said.

"Then I will." He rose slightly on the balls of his feet, a movement I'd often seen from him. I wasn't sure why or what it conveyed of his inner thoughts, but I liked it anyway. There was something so enthusiastic about him. One couldn't help but feel the world was as sunshiny as his hair in those moments. His shoes shone so brightly I almost expected to see my reflection in the tips.

"You're always welcome here. As Mama's former student, I mean. Not as my guest."

"Right, of course." He smirked, as if I were lying to him. Was I? Could I admit to myself how cheered I was to see him?

"Where did you get this old thing?" I brushed the top of the car with the tip of my index finger, just as Jasper did to check if the maids had properly dusted.

"I bought her today. Right off the floor of the shop."

"Can you afford this?" I pressed my gloved fingers to my mouth. "I'm sorry, that's none of my business."

He brushed aside my apology with a quick and forgiving smile. "You may ask me anything you wish."

"Not about money," I said. "That's not anything to speak of with anyone but your family."

A muscle near his mouth twitched, as if he wanted to contradict me, but instead he said, "I'm a successful banker now. Not the schoolboy you were always trying to beat on the ice."

"Yes, well, I'm happy for you."

"Isn't she a beauty?"

"The car?" I asked.

"Yes, the car. You've made it clear you wish me to remain

silent on the subject of your beauty, so I have turned my affections to this shining piece of metal." He draped his arms over the top of the car. His limbs were so long that I had only to stretch a few inches to cover his hands with my own. I didn't, of course.

"I have to admit, she is."

"You can drive her sometime if you'd like," Viktor said.

"I have my own car."

"Yes, indeed you do. You and Poppy continue to be the talk of the town."

"And why would that be?" I knew the answer, but making him say the truth out loud was akin to picking at a scab. One shouldn't, but one does anyway. Poppy had apprenticed for a veterinarian and upon her return home had asked me to join her. We took care of every sick animal in the valley between our two mountains.

He had the decency to look flustered. "Doing the work of..." He trailed off.

"Doing the work of men." I unbuttoned the top of my coat, suddenly hot. These men and their judgment of Poppy and me. We were darn proud to take care of all the farm animals and pets of Emerson Pass. Did we have to get in some muck and mud? Sure. But it was work we could be proud of instead of sitting around making doilies.

"I admire you for it," Viktor said. "I'm proud to know you both."

Despite the pleasure that gave me, I changed the subject. "How did you get the car home?"

"The road up from Louisville's open now. No more waiting for the train to take us out of Emerson Pass."

"Right, the new road," I said drily. With the clearing of the trees to make a dirt road from here to Louisville, Emerson Pass would be overrun with strangers. Flynn was delighted. He'd been instrumental in getting a road put in. More visitors to the ski runs meant more money in his pocket.

"I'm thinking of naming her Rose."

"The car?" I asked.

"Yes, doesn't it suit her? The most beautiful flower of all."

"That's *my* favorite flower, but not everyone thinks it's the most beautiful. There are peonies, for example."

"We're in agreement, then? Roses are the most beautiful? I believe pink are your most favorite?"

Flushing from embarrassment, I tried to think of what to say. He'd discombobulated me, and I had no idea what we were talking about. "That's a silly thing to name a car. They're not flowers."

"Cars are female, which I associate with flowers." He shrugged his massive shoulders in that playful way I found maddening and attractive all at once.

"So provincial of you, Mr. Olofsson."

He ignored my pointed remark, continuing on as if I hadn't said anything at all. "And she's pretty, like you. It's wrong of me to be so vain, but I'm awfully proud to be able to afford a car."

"What exactly does a banker do, anyway?" I asked.

"Secret money things."

"How did you know I love roses?"

"I've studied you since we were children, devouring every bit of knowledge about you. Not that it's easy. You're quite a study in dichotomy. The stuff of novels."

"That's ridiculous." To prove his point, I couldn't decide if I wanted to kiss him or punch him. I bit the inside of my mouth to remind myself that punching was the better option. "I'm interesting, unlike some of the girls in this town."

"Are you talking about Emma?" His face broke into another of his infectious grins.

I shrugged, fighting against the churn in my stomach as the images of them together floated across my mind. They seemed to be everywhere together of late. "She seems rather dull." Actually, she seemed smart and very pretty. I'd never let him know I thought so.

"Are you jealous?" Viktor asked.

"Wouldn't you like that to be true?" Would he? Or was he as taken with Emma as he used to be with me? Lately I'd seen them together at the club and down at the river where the young crowd socialized. Were they an item or only friends? My throat tickled with my desire to ask him, but my tongue managed to behave.

"Maybe I do."

"Do what?" I'd completely lost the thread of our conversation.

"Maybe I do want you to be jealous." Viktor came around the front of the car, graceful and agile as the elk I'd spotted in the meadow last week. The corners of his eyes crinkled as he brought my gloved hand to his mouth for a quick kiss. "I haven't greeted you properly. Miss Barnes, you're looking lovely this evening, as always. Do you know, I believe you grow prettier every year."

"I'm practically an old lady."

Viktor laughed as his head drifted to the side. His eyes flashed in the last of the sunlight. "Twenty-one is *not* an old lady. I've three years on you, and I know I'm not an old man."

I swallowed and looked away. My legs felt about as stable as a mound of Lizzie's pudding. "I wonder what Flynn's up to?"

"He hasn't told you?" Viktor asked.

"Lately, he doesn't tell me much of anything. I'm a woman."

"Which infuriates you," Viktor said.

"Endlessly."

"He said it was something about the ski mountain, but wouldn't tell me anything more. Whatever it is, it's sure to be a success."

Flynn and my brother-in-law, Phillip, were clever businessmen and kept their affairs between them and my father. The ski slopes and lodge were doing well. Too well, I thought sometimes. Flynn had become as cocky as our rooster. Phillip,

Josephine's husband, on the other hand, seemed to have grown humbler with each success.

"He has the gift of pretty talking, does he not?" I asked, irritated with my brother. "Dropping hints of what's to come only makes us all want to know more." Not that he'd even given me any inclination at all. I was nothing to him now that he was married and a businessman. We'd been close when we were younger. Two rebels. Two troublemakers.

Why didn't I ever know of the changes coming to the ski mountain? Was this the alteration I'd sniffed in the wind? If so, I was disappointed. I'd dared to hope for a moment that my adventure had finally come.

"Do you ever worry about his involvement with bootlegging?" Viktor asked, unusually seriously.

I jerked my head up to look at him. "What have you heard?" There were rumors of bootlegging. I wasn't sure of Flynn's involvement in the making or distribution of product, only that at the very least he flirted too closely with danger. Our family all knew of the speakeasy in the basement of the lodge, but none of us knew where he and Phillip got the gin. Mama didn't want to know. If Papa was privy, he never said a word. Instead, Flynn acted as if the Barnes family were somehow exempt from ordinary rules.

"Not much. I worry, though. So does Isak."

My insides softened to match my pudding legs. His sincerity and love of my brother were irresistible. "I wonder if there are those of us in the world without hope of peace?"

"Are you speaking of yourself or Flynn?" Viktor asked softly.

"Both of us, I suppose."

There was a restlessness and ambition in my brother I knew only too well. He would stop at nothing to become the richest man in town. Richer even than our father, who had continued to increase his wealth by buying property from Boston to Los Angeles. What had been a small fortune when he came to America from England as a young man had become a large one. I suspected Flynn wanted to surpass him as a way to prove his worth to the family. Who could blame him? His twin was a brilliant scholar and now the town's beloved doctor.

"Do you know what you want?" Viktor asked. "Is it wealth, like Flynn?"

"No, it's not that." I pulled the collar of my coat closed. My fingers remained there, clutching the thick wool fabric as if it were necessary for remaining upright. "We both want to win. And we want everyone to know we've won." I hadn't meant to be quite so honest, but Viktor had a way about him that made my weaknesses seem less sharp. Less shameful.

"There's nothing wrong with ambition."

I lifted my gaze to meet his. "But there's no point in wishing for things that can never happen."

"Never give up on your dreams, Cymbeline Barnes. If anyone can do the extraordinary, it's you."

⚬⚬⚬

I WAS SEVEN YEARS OLD WHEN THE FLYING COUNTESS SOARED through the air in Austria for twenty-two meters. My baby sister and I stared at the photograph in the newspaper for many minutes, amazed that she seemed to be suspended in the air as if by magic. Her real name was Paula von Lamberg.

When my brothers built a ski jump as part of their recreational tourist attraction, I'd immediately tried it. The first time I flew through the air, I couldn't get enough.

Viktor

The close proximity and Cymbeline's dizzyingly wonderful scent had gone completely to my head. As if I'd just raced her across the ice as we'd done as children, I was woozy and breathless.

She shivered and stomped her feet. The sun had made its final appearance, leaving us in the somber light of a November evening. This time of year was like Cymbeline, tumultuous and moody. One moment the sky was blue and the next covered with snow clouds. "Are you cold?" I asked.

"A little."

I'd have stood there all night if she wanted to, but dinner and her family waited for us inside.

"Shall we go inside before you freeze to death?" I asked.

She tilted her pointy chin upward and nodded. "I suppose. It's stuffy in there but warmer indeed."

"Shall we then?" I'd have liked to offer her my arm, but I knew better. Even if she wanted to, she'd never have allowed me to escort her into the house when her entire family was just on the other side of the bank of windows that faced the front yard.

We were quiet as we crossed over the rocky driveway to the

front lawn. After our banter, I would have liked to take a nap, but there was no rest when it came to Cymbeline. She challenged me in ways I'd not thought possible and had done so for a decade and then some.

The sound of one of the horses' whinny drifted into the quiet evening. I glanced toward the red barn, a silhouette in the dim light.

"That's Lucy," Cymbeline said. "Trying to coax me back in to give her another apple."

"Should we?"

"No, Mama will be cross if we're late to supper."

Our feet crunched in the fallen leaves. The scent of wet dirt tickled my nose. The Barnes home was nestled between thickets of trees. Lights from their windows cast a cheery glow. Fiona was bent over her piano, and as we drew closer I could hear her music through the window. Lord Barnes and Flynn stood in the frame of the other window talking closely.

We stepped onto the porch. She tugged on my sleeve. "Viktor?"

I turned toward her. "Yes?"

"I wanted to say—" But before she could finish, the light that hung over the door flickered to life and Jasper, the family's butler, opened the door to peer at us with a suspicious expression on his well-groomed face.

"Good evening, Mr. Olofsson," Jasper said.

"Good evening, sir," I said.

Jasper turned his gaze to my companion. "Miss Cymbeline? What are you doing outside? Your mother's been looking for you."

"I was getting some air and ran into Viktor."

"Dinner will be served shortly," Jasper said with a note of disapproval. He didn't like that she'd been out alone in the near-dark with a man. I wanted to assure him I was harmless but wasn't sure how to do so without embarrassing us all.

"Come inside," Jasper said. "The family's all gathered for cocktails and are expecting you."

"Yes, we'll be in shortly," Cymbeline said. "Thank you, Jasper." She was polite but firm, reminding me that this was a house with staff and Cym was one of the mistresses who must be obeyed. It occurred to me that the staff added another element of feeling as if she were always being watched and controlled. Especially for someone like Cym.

His judgmental gaze went from one of us to the other but seemed to decide it wasn't his place to insist we come into the house, and he closed the door.

"What is it?" I asked. "What did you want to tell me?"

She fiddled with one sleeve of her coat. Under the electric light, the wool seemed more green than gray. "It might seem strange to you, but I don't quite know what to say to you. How to say what I want at any rate."

"You can say anything. Ask anything."

"Where's Emma tonight?" She lifted her face upward. Her eyes glittered, and her cheeks flamed pink. "Why didn't you bring her?"

"She was busy this evening."

"Is that the only reason?" Cymbeline asked.

"What other reasons would there be?" I spoke as gently as I could when my instincts wanted to do the opposite. Taking her in my arms and kissing her with everything I had seemed like a better idea than polite conversation.

She looked down at the tips of her boots and mumbled, "I don't know. None, I guess."

My heart leapt with excitement. Flynn had been right. Only this morning at church, he'd told me he thought Cym was jealous of Emma. She needn't have been. Emma and I were friends with absolutely no spark between us. In fact, she had a fiancé back east who was set to move to Emerson Pass sometime before the first snowfall. He'd been working for the better part of the year in Boston to make enough to build a home for Emma here in Colorado.

When the gang had told Emma about my undying and hopeless affection for Cymbeline, she'd cleverly suggested we spend time together in the hope that it would awaken affection in my unrequited love. She understood women, Emma had told me. One way to get them to see their true feelings was to stir up a little feminine jealousy. Fiona had agreed, pointing out that nothing evoked more attention from Cymbeline than a little competition.

"Would you have liked me to bring her?" I asked, acting innocent.

Her lips puckered as if she'd bit into a lemon. "Whether she accompanies you is of no concern of mine. I can assure you no one would care."

"Is that true?" I had the instinct to place my hands around her shoulders to quiet her fidgeting and beg her to look at me. I'd ask her, *Tell me the truth. How do you feel about me?* However, I knew that would result in the opposite of what I wanted. Cymbeline could not be forced into stillness by any man.

A memory of when we'd been schoolchildren flashed before my eyes. I'd sat behind her in our one-room schoolhouse. She'd worn her hair in braids back then, and wisps of hair curled at the nape of her neck. My fingers had practically twitched with my desire to touch them.

Now she wore her hair short. Most of the girls looked all right in their bobs but were more suited to long hair. Not Cymbeline. Her thick curls framed her small face and fell just below her chin to emphasize her slender neck.

From our time swimming at the creek and river, I'd seen her in a bathing costume and knew how the muscles in her arms and legs had been sculpted from her physical activities. My brother had once said with pride in his voice that both the girls we loved did the manual labor of men. His love, Nora Cassidy, had taken over her family's cattle ranch after her father's death.

"Tell me, Cymbeline. Would you care if I were to arrive with Emma on my arm?"

Her eyebrows shot up before her face crinkled into one of her famous scowls. "It seems lately she's always attached to your arm. Does she know how to walk if she isn't hanging on to you?"

I hid a smile behind my hand by scratching a spot on my cheek. "She's delicate."

"Delicate? What's that mean? She's too fragile to walk on her own two legs?"

"Not all women are as ferocious as you."

"I'm not ferocious. You make me sound like a wild animal." She tugged at her gloves, then unbuttoned her coat.

"Fierce, then?"

"If by that you mean I'm not some sniveling, weak little girl, then yes." She shrugged out of her coat and held it close to her chest, causing the silk of her yellow gown to bunch at the collar.

"I didn't think you were weak even when you were a little girl," I said, laughing.

"You don't *think*? You were there. Remember all the times I almost beat you on the ice?" She glared at me.

"I didn't know we were racing." That was a fib. I'd known *she'd* thought we were racing. I'd been merely basking in the glow of the girl I would have swum across the ocean for. Her insistence that we tear across the ice in a mad dash had been one of the ways I could be around her. What I hadn't known was that she thought of me as her nemesis.

I'd been hurt and a little insulted to learn that she'd seen me that way. Until Flynn explained to me that his sister had chosen me as her object of competition for a reason. "There's only one reason a girl is that keen on winning a race against you," he'd said when I was about fifteen. I'd stared at him, not at all sure what he meant. "She has feelings for you. Ones that she doesn't understand, and being Cymbeline, she has to turn them into a race as a way to distract herself from them."

"You knew we were racing," Cymbeline said. "Otherwise you wouldn't have beaten me every time."

"I was trying to impress you." That was the absolute truth. Instead, I'd only made her angry.

"It didn't work."

"I know." I chuckled, shaking my head. "But letting you win wouldn't have, either. What would, really?"

She scowled. "What does it matter now? Aren't you practically engaged to Emma?"

"Is that what you really want to know?" I asked.

She closed her eyes as if her head hurt. "Yes, I suppose I do. Are you serious about her?"

There it was. At last. I chose my words carefully. "I don't think it's serious, no. She's a friend."

All the bluster seemed to leave her body. "I see."

"Why is it that you care?" I asked.

"Who says I do?" She jutted out her chin just as she'd done when I'd beaten her on the ice.

"I say it. I do. And I can't figure out why you can't simply give in and let yourself like me just a little."

"I like you."

"But?"

She shook her coat at me, as if it were a body. "I don't know, all right? I don't know what's wrong with me." Her voice quivered. "But there's something more for me, Viktor. I want more."

"Something that belongs only to you? An accomplishment of some kind. One that gets recognition."

"Yes." She brought her coat back to her chest. "I hate myself for it, but that's the truth. I like you, and I don't know how that fits in with the rest of me."

She needed something of her own. This was as plain as the freckles on the end of her upturned nose. Beyond what most women seemed to want. A quest. A calling. I'd hoped to be her quest and calling, but I had a distinct feeling that until she had quieted her agitation by conquering whatever it was, she would not be able to give in and love me.

"If you found what you were looking for, would it change anything?" I asked. "In regard to me and you, that is."

"I don't know, but I think so."

"Until then, I shall continue to hope that whatever it is you want, you shall find it. And when you're done, I hope to still be here."

"But you may not be. That's what you're saying, isn't it? You might be with Emma, fat and happily married."

I laughed. "I hope I won't be fat."

"You might be. Driving around in your fancy car with your pretty wife. Meanwhile, I'll still be waiting for an adventure that'll never come simply because I'm a girl, and I'll have to see you drive by in that car with her yellow hair glinting in the sunshine and two beautiful babies in the back seat."

The forlornness in her voice caused a shiver to creep up my spine. And just then I understood for the first time how tortured she must feel. To want two lives and unable to choose either one for fear of missing the right one.

Could I help her find what she was looking for? Was it possible there was something out there that would soothe her tortured soul? I felt fairly certain it wasn't me and only me. This was a woman who wanted to live life as big and bold as she was herself.

"If I could give it to you, I would," I said. "I want you to know that."

"Oh, Viktor. Why do you have to be so wonderful?"

I stepped backward, surprised. She thought I was wonderful? A lot of good it did me, I thought. "Let's go inside before you really do catch your death."

This time, she gave me a weary nod and allowed me to open the door. I couldn't help but notice the defeat in the slump of her shoulders. No, no. She mustn't give up.

I shut the door behind me. "Cym?"

She turned toward me.

"Don't let this world—the way it is—stop you. Keep searching until you find it, and then do whatever you need to."

"I'll do my best."

But I knew that every day, she died a little more inside. Someday she would be nothing but dust for all that wanting. If only I could do something about it.

Cymbeline

Every Sunday we gathered as a family for dinner. We were expected to sit down in our formal dining room promptly at seven to a meal cooked by our beloved Lizzie. No one dared be late, not even Flynn.

I gestured for Viktor to follow me. Jasper was no longer lurking in the foyer. He was probably angry with me for staying out with Viktor. I did dislike making him anxious for my well-being, but with Jasper one had to accept a certain amount of overprotection.

Our sitting room was made from dark wood and red velvet, with the stone fireplace as a focal point. Rows and rows of books lined the walls. We had a formal parlor reserved for guests, but as a family we spent most of our time in this space that served as a library, Mama's study, and the central location of family gatherings. In the warmer months, we loved to sit on the screened porch or play on the lawn.

Other than the children, which included my two youngest sisters, Josephine's daughters, and Flynn's baby, my entire family was there. Josephine and Phillip, who always enjoyed a night without their children, sat together on the couch. Across from them Mama, Theo, and his wife, Louisa, were engaged in a noisy discussion of a novel they'd all read and passed around. Papa and Flynn were playing chess at the small table by the window. Flynn's wife, Shannon, large with her second pregnancy, was knitting in one of the easy chairs by the fire. Her fair skin and dark hair glowed in the firelight. Pregnancy suited her.

And my sweetheart sister, Fiona, was at the piano playing a song I didn't recognize. A gentle song, very unlike the raucous jazz she and Li played at the underground club. She nodded at us, but her fingers continued to sweep over the keys.

What did it all look like to Viktor? Did our big, loud, and imperfect family overwhelm him? Compared with his quiet parents and only brother, were we a spectacle?

"Viktor, how nice to see you." Mama stood as we approached.

Viktor took her hand. "And how is my beloved teacher this evening?"

"Very well, thank you." Refusing to succumb to the times, she continued to fix her long hair in a bun with golden tendrils around her face. Papa spoiled her with the finest dresses shipped from Paris. Tonight it was made of purple silk that brought out her brown eyes. "Please come sit. We're delighted you agreed to join us. It's been too long since we've had a proper chat."

"It's my pleasure," Viktor said as he sat in an empty chair across from Shannon.

I took the hardback chair next to the couch. Why did I feel nervous in my family's own sitting room? I knew the answer to my own question. Viktor. And my big mouth spilling my jealousy and the secrets of my heart.

"Cym, where have you been? Did Viktor take you for a ride in his new car?" Mama asked, with enough hope in her voice that I inwardly cringed. Even my sisters and Mama couldn't understand why I wouldn't want Viktor. As accomplished as they all were—Mama's pedigree as a teacher, Jo having organized our first library, Fiona with her musical gifts and discipline—they couldn't imagine a scenario in which I'd choose to hang on to the idea that I was meant for more. They were romantics. All three of them. I was not. I could not be, after all. For to admit that love was the only thing worth having meant that I would succumb to the life of wife and mother.

Yet as my gaze drifted once more to Viktor, my resolve weakened. Was this how it happened?

"I was out in the yard for fresh air when Viktor drove up in his new car," I said to Mama.

"Viktor, you actually did it?" Theo asked.

"Wonders never cease," Flynn said. "Old money-pincher Olofsson actually bought a car."

"Frugality is a virtue." Mama sent Viktor a kind smile. "Don't let Flynn make you think otherwise."

Viktor's cheeks reddened. "I couldn't walk everywhere forever."

"Or ask for rides from your friends," Flynn said.

Shannon's knitting needles stilled as she addressed Viktor. "A young man needs a car. To woo the young ladies."

"Not all young ladies are impressed by a car." Viktor's gaze flickered toward me. "Some of them can drive their own."

I flushed as all heads turned toward me, followed by an awkward silence.

"Would anyone care for a whiskey?" Papa asked, looking up from the chessboard. "Flynn is beating me soundly, which has me contemplating my own mortality. It seems like yesterday I was teaching all of you how to play, and now I can't win a game against Flynn or Cym." He stretched his legs out long under the table. People outside our family said he had a strong English accent, but I couldn't hear it. He sounded merely like my sweet Papa.

"You beat me just the other day," I said.

"Did I?" Fine lines had settled around Papa's eyes and mouth. Silver was now woven into his dark hair. But if anything, he was more handsome than ever. The kind of beauty my father possessed came from inside. He was a man powerful and gentle. A man who loved his family above all else. A man who possessed such great empathy for his fellow humans that he'd dreamt of an entire town in which families could thrive.

Flynn looked up from the chessboard. "Papa, just because I'm better at chess doesn't mean you're declining." He grinned and looked around the room until he found me. "I'm merely the most clever of us all."

"Darling, if you insist on saying it out loud then it must not be true," Shannon said, teasing.

"You're no fun at all, dear wife, but alas, you keep me humble." He winked at her. She smiled back at him. They stared into each other's eyes for a ridiculously long moment. Did they remember we were all here? I almost expected him to sweep her off her feet and take her home. My brother had indeed been tamed by love. We would never have predicted he and pure Shannon Cassidy would be a match. But a match they were. The man who had declared his desire to be a bachelor forever had forgotten all about his pledge after one toss of Shannon's glossy black curls.

"Mrs. Barnes, would you like your drink to be a two- or three-finger pour?" Papa asked from the bar.

"Definitely four fingers," Mama said, and then giggled.

"As you wish." Papa acted as if he would pour her a drink, but at the last second reached for the pitcher of iced tea.

When Mama had first come to us when I was only six years old, Papa had given her a tumbler of whiskey. She'd choked and coughed and swore she would never again touch alcohol. Ever since, Papa had teased her and offered her a tumbler. True to her word, she'd never said yes.

"Viktor? Would you care for one?" Papa asked.

"Yes, please. A small pour. I don't drink much." Viktor's eyes slid to Mama for a quick second. She would always be his teacher, I thought. Even when he was an adult with his own house and car, he still craved her approval.

"Another virtue, dear one," Mama said.

Why was it that the men were offered a drink and not the

women? "What of the women, Papa? Are you offering one to any of us?"

"Would you care for one?" Papa thick eyebrows raised.

"Yes, please," I said more firmly than I felt.

"Don't do it," Mama said. "It'll make you cough."

"It might not," I said. "I'd like to see for myself."

"You're a young lady," Theo said. "Proper young ladies don't guzzle whiskey."

"What does being a woman have to do with it?" Josephine asked. Her mild tone told me she didn't really care one way or the other, but I appreciated her support anyway.

"Yes, what's our gender have to do with whether you take a pint now or then?" Shannon asked. "Not that I would." Her eyes sparkled with humor as she placed her hand over her round stomach. "All of Ireland's done enough drinking for generations to come."

"I'd not care for one. Nothing good ever came from drink," Louisa said softly.

Her father was proof of that. Poor Louisa. How she'd suffered when she was a little girl. Seeing how good she was made me feel worse about myself. She'd had nothing but abuse for the first nine years of her life, and yet she'd devoted herself to Theo. Since Shannon and Flynn's first child, Louisa had found her calling as a midwife, assisting Theo and Dr. Neal in almost every birth of Emerson Pass.

"If you'd like a glass, you may have mine," Viktor said.

"Thank you, Viktor, but I'll have my own," I said.

"Very kind of you," Papa said, laughing. "But in this family, it's best to give the women what they ask for." He poured one last glass and handed it to me. "Here you are, love. Don't drink it all in one gulp."

I sniffed the amber liquid, then swirled it around, almost spilling part of it over the sides. Horrid smell. I'd never actually had whiskey, but I'd made such a fuss that I had to go through with it. I brought the glass of my lips and sipped. The nasty liquid burned my throat and made the hair in my nostrils feel as if they might melt. But I would not cough. No, I would not. I'd not give them all the satisfaction.

"Not to your liking?" Papa shot me a look mixed with humor and kindness. He was always on my side even when I wasn't on my own.

"I loved it." I took another gulp to prove myself. This time I sputtered and coughed. And coughed some more. Blast it all.

"I tried to warn you," Mama said.

"Went down the wrong way, that's all," I said.

Viktor rose from his chair and whipped out his handkerchief. I took it from him without meeting his gaze and wiped the tears from under my eyes.

"May I get you a water?" Viktor asked.

"Yes, please," I mumbled, humiliated. It was bad enough to act like a fool in front of my family, but having Viktor here stung even worse.

"What about you, Fiona?" Flynn asked, his dark blue eyes twinkling. "Do you want a chance to cough like your sister?"

Fiona lifted her eyes from the sheet music from which she'd been playing. "Why would I want to cough?" She obviously hadn't been listening to the discussion.

I groaned and patted the spot just above my bosom that continued to burn. "To prove that women can do anything men can."

Fiona looked at me with blank eyes. She was a thousand miles away, I realized. What could she have been thinking of while we were all talking and carrying on? A niggle of worry came to me. I'd noticed she seemed distracted and forlorn the last few months. Was she feeling as I did? That life was passing her by?

"They certainly drink it at the club," Flynn was saying. "Women toss back as much gin as the men."

Theo shook his head, clearly displeased. "*Illegal* gin."

"A businessman must supply the people with what they want," Flynn said.

"Not if it's breaking the law," Theo said.

"What's that in your hand, brother?" Flynn asked.

"It's different in your own home," Theo said.

"Whatever you say," Flynn said. "But I'm not ashamed of how we run our business, and the police chief sure likes his drink."

Josephine and I exchanged a glance. She'd told me in secret her worries about Flynn and Phillip's illegal business enterprise. We knew our brother. Flynn would do almost anything to succeed.

"Now that we've determined women can have whiskey if they want, I have an announcement," Flynn said. "Or, rather, Phillip and I have an announcement." He looked at his brother-in-law. "Would you like to tell them?"

"No, it was your idea," Phillip said. "You go ahead."

"We're hosting a competition on the mountain," Flynn said. "Something similar to the Winter Games last year in France."

I sat up straighter. "Competition? What do you mean?" My stomach fluttered with excitement.

"Downhill skiing competitions for speed," Flynn said. "As well as ski jumping."

"We hope to attract some of the best in the world," Phillip said. "Along with crowds of watchers."

"We're going to put this town on the map," Flynn said.

"A competition," I murmured as I looked at Viktor. He mouthed the word *you* and gestured at me with his finger.

I beamed back at him, forgetting the world for a moment. He understood. Viktor Olofsson knew exactly where my mind had gone.

My thigh muscles tensed. This was it. I would finally have a chance. The scores of the ski jumpers had been reported in the papers. I'd cut it out and placed it in my stocking drawer. Every day I looked at it and imagined myself beating those scores.

With a little more practice, I might have a chance. *Please, God, bring the snow.*

"I'll have to start training right away," I said to Flynn.

Flynn blinked and glanced over at Phillip as if he needed his partner to answer for him.

"Um, well, this would be for men only," Phillip said.

"You must be joking," Josephine said. "Why? What about Cym?"

Phillip raised one shoulder in a sheepish gesture. "This would be like the Winter Games. Only men athletes."

Fiona had stopped playing. "But Cym could beat them all in the jump."

"Men don't want to compete against a woman." Flynn spoke dismissively and waved his hand around as if he were swatting a fly. "Anyway, this is a business opportunity, not a contest for Cym."

"What about one just for women?" Josephine asked between clenched teeth. "If the men don't want to compete against a woman who can probably beat them, then do a separate contest."

"There aren't any women who want to compete," Flynn said, sounding irritated. "Other than our sister."

"Surely Cymbeline isn't the only one?" Viktor asked.

"If there are, we don't know about them," Flynn said.

"Have you looked?" I asked.

"Well, no, but we haven't even made the announcement yet." Flynn ran a hand through his hair. An impatient gesture he'd been doing since we were children. "We're new at this, Cym. Who knows how it will go? The last thing I need is a controversy while we're still putting together events. Bringing women into it causes nothing but problems. We don't need to bring women into it."

The hair on my arms stood up. *Bring women into it.* As if we were the cause of all problems?

"Perhaps you should think about opening up a competition

for women," Mama said quietly. "You might be surprised by the interest."

"Women don't jump," Flynn said.

"I do," I said tightly.

"It might not be good for you," Flynn said. "Isn't that right, Theo? Couldn't she damage her insides?"

"I don't know if that makes scientific sense," Theo said. "And might be an argument made in order to keep women out of the way."

"Like in many other fields," Josephine said. "Keeping us from the vote for so long was about power and control."

"She's not the only woman to have ever jumped." Fiona came to stand beside my chair. "There was a woman back in 1911 who jumped twenty-two meters." She put her hand on my shoulder. "The Flying Countess."

"That's correct." Cheered by her support, I reached up to pat my sister's hand. "Paula von Lamberg. She was in the newspaper." They'd shown a photograph of her flying through the air, straight-backed with her skirts twirling about her legs.

Fiona and I had stared and stared at the picture of the woman who had seemed suspended in the air by magic. The image had returned to me when the boys first talked of building a ski jump. I'd told Fiona I wanted to try to fly. And fly I did.

I became obsessed. Every afternoon when I returned from whatever Poppy had needed me for, I'd gone up to the mountain. After a few weeks, I'd recruited Fiona to measure my distance. I consistently jumped forty meters but no more. It had been Fiona's idea to have Phillip make a new pair of skis. Ones that were sleeker and slightly longer. He was gifted with woodworking and had spent hours perfecting the scope and curve.

I looked over at Flynn. "The boys at Chamonix didn't clear fifty meters. I have."

He stared at me. "Cym, that's impossible."

"It isn't," Fiona said. "After Phillip made her the new skis, she kept creeping up her distance until she reached fifty."

"The skis made that much difference?" Phillip asked, clearly pleased until Flynn shot him a look.

Flynn let out a long sigh. "Are you all against me?"

"Not against you, son," Papa said. "But we all want Cymbeline to have the chance she deserves."

"You're a businessman, Papa," Flynn said. "Don't you see how this could cause trouble for us?"

"I'm a family man first." Papa spoke gently as he moved across the room to stand by the fire. "I'd do whatever it took to give any of you what you wanted."

Flynn's fury seemed to grow stronger. He turned back to me. "Why can't you be like the other girls?"

"Why do I need to be?" If I'd been a teakettle, steam would have been coming out of my ears. "What's wrong with the way I am? Just because I'm not some simpering damsel having babies and encouraging their husband's careers while they're dying inside." The force of my anger actually made Flynn flinch.

"None of the married women in this family are dying inside," Flynn said.

I ignored that argument, determined to get us back on the subject of the competition. "There's no reason I shouldn't compete. As much as I appreciate the idea of a special category for women, I don't need one. I can beat the men."

Flynn scooted to the edge of the couch as he muttered an expletive. The whiskey glass trembled in his hand. "We don't want you to beat the men. Don't you see, Cymbeline? You'll just cause us trouble. Men won't want to lose to a girl. This is our chance to become known and respected in the ski community— not the opportunity for you to show off."

"Show off?" My entire body tightened with rage. This competition was being planned right here in my own town by my own brothers. For men. For *men* to show off and for Flynn to make more money. "How much money do you need? When will it be enough? You have to ruin our town by bringing all these strangers here and you won't let your own sister earn what I deserve?"

"Stop. Both of you," Mama said. "Stop before you say something you don't mean but can't take back."

"What if we do mean them?" I asked Mama before whipping my head back to my brother. "You have all the power, Flynn. You get more every day. Use it for good instead of for building more wealth. Money you don't even need."

"It's not my job to give you this," Flynn said. "I have my own family to take care of instead of pandering to your outlandish wishes. You need to grow up. A perfectly wonderful man is in love with you and all you can do is think about this stupid competition."

I gasped, mortified, then pointed a finger at Flynn. "You of all people should understand my ambition instead of trying to shame me back into place. We've always wanted adventure. You and me. More than any of the others. It used to be you and me daydreaming of the lives we would have. Do you remember that?"

"I'm a *man*, Cym. That's how I'm supposed to be. You're not. If I were Papa, I'd demand you stop all this foolishness and marry Viktor or be cut off financially. It's not like anyone else would put up with you."

"Flynn, please. Enough." Shannon's eyes glistened with tears. "You must stop this at once."

Theo had left Louisa, who was now crying softly into her hands, to take his twin by the shoulders. "What's the matter with you? This isn't how we do it in the Barnes family. We're a team, always."

Flynn put up his hands as if defeated. "Fine. None of you understand." He marched over to the liquor cabinet and poured himself another drink.

My entire body shook. Flynn, whom I'd always believed to be the most like me, had betrayed me. "I can't believe you just said that." My throat closed with frustration or I might have said more. Instead, I swiped away the tears that ran down my cheeks. *Not like anyone else would put up with you.* Was that true? Would Viktor see that now? Could it be that all this was selfish and foolish? Was I ruining my life by wanting more? I put my hand to my mouth, afraid I might be sick. My brother, for whom I'd had the utmost respect and admiration, was now betraying me? I'd thought he understood me best of all.

Jo rushed over to me and knelt next to my chair, then patted my knee. "It's all right. You've nothing to be ashamed about."

Fiona, still by my side, took her hand from my shoulder and stepped closer to Flynn. "I've known you to be reckless but never cruel. What's happened to you?"

"This isn't my fault. It's Cym. She won't listen to reason." Flynn's complexion had flushed purple, and the thick vein that ran down his neck pulsed. "She can't change the ways of the world by sheer will."

"Son, that's enough," Papa said in a voice that seemed to echo between the walls of the room.

"I think it's time we go." Shannon cradled her stomach and rose heavily from the couch. "Flynn, take me home, please."

He shot me one additional loathing glance before nodding and storming out of the room.

"I'm sorry. I don't know what to say." Shannon stopped to squeeze one of my hands. "He doesn't mean to hurt you. It's just clumsiness on his part."

"You don't have to apologize," I said. "None of this is your fault."

"I'll see you all next Sunday," Shannon said.

Mama had risen and now embraced Shannon. "Take care of him tonight. He'll be upset. His temper got the best of him, that's all."

"I will." Shannon shuffled across the room and out to the foyer. I jumped when the front door slammed.

After she left, we all sat in silence for a moment. I didn't dare look at Viktor. What he must think of us. Of me. Of Flynn, who made it sound as if I were some kind of sick cow being offered to an unsuspecting farmer.

"I shouldn't have pushed so hard," I said, finally. "I'm sorry to have ruined dinner. I'm sorry I can't seem to be like everyone else." I lifted my gaze to Viktor. "I'm sorry if I've embarrassed you."

Viktor jerked up from his chair to fall on his knees in front of me. "Listen to me, Cymbeline Barnes. You're not to make yourself small because you think that would deter a man in any way. If a man wants you to be something other than your splendid self, then he has no right to be in your life. Your dreams and ambition are part of what make you special. Special to me. To everyone in this room and our town. Do you understand?"

"I think so," I said, meekly, overwhelmed by his declaration in front of my entire family.

"With all due respect to your family, your brother's wrong. Half the men in this town wish you would choose them, including me. But if it's not me you want, please, I beg you, don't ever let a man make you feel ashamed for wanting more than what's expected of you. I'd never be ashamed, only proud, to see you conquer all your dreams."

I once again teared up, making the large Norwegian man in front of me blur as if I were looking out a window dripping with water.

Viktor

The idea had come to me earlier in the library. All through dinner, I pondered my outlandish idea further and had decided by the time pie and coffee were served that I would propose my solution to Cymbeline.

As we finished our dessert, Lord Barnes asked Cymbeline and his wife if they would follow him into his study. "We'll only keep her for a moment," Lord Barnes said to the rest of us. "You young people go and enjoy the firepit. We'll send Cym out shortly."

"Yes, Papa," Fiona said.

Jasper entered the room with a note in his hand, which he gave to Theo. My brother read it quickly and then looked over at his wife. "No more play for us, my love. Mrs. Coughlin's in labor."

Louisa's eyes lit up. "It's about time. The poor woman's at least two weeks late by my calculations."

"Yes, please go," Mrs. Barnes said. "We'll pray for a healthy baby and mother."

I was pleased when Cymbeline glanced my way and gave me a smile. "I'll see you all later."

Phillip helped his wife to her feet. "I apologize, but I need to look up something in the library but will join you shortly."

"Of course, darling. Don't be too long though," Josephine said. "I don't want to be out too late."

"I won't dally," Phillip said.

A few minutes later, Fiona and Josephine led me down the hall and through the back porch to the stone firepit. We each took one of the wooden chairs. The flames were robust and warmed my cheeks.

"Thank you for this evening," Josephine said to me. "Your support of our sister means a lot to us."

"She will always have my undying affection," I said. "Even if she doesn't want it."

"We shall see about that, won't we?" Fiona said. "After your speech tonight, how could she resist you?"

"She's done well thus far," I said.

"Don't give up on her yet," Josephine said. "Sometimes people surprise us."

Josephine hadn't changed much over the years. She still wore her golden hair long and pinned at the back of her neck. The fabric of her gown was a soft pink, which complemented her fair skin.

Fiona, who wore a dark blue dress that matched her eyes and a sparkly band in her curly brown bob, had only recently turned eighteen. Regardless, she had a maturity and serenity beyond her years.

"It's good to see you, Viktor," Josephine said. "Since the babies came, it seems I never get out anymore. How are you?"

"I'm doing well and enjoying my new home." I'd moved into a cottage not far from the Barnes property. The twins and my brother Isak and I had all agreed long ago to help one another build houses. Being the youngest of the four of us, my cottage had been last. Now I was in the process of furnishing the four modest rooms and making plans for a garden come spring. "I planted roses over the summer. My brother built some furniture for the lawn. I'm going to have a garden party next summer and invite the lot of us from school. I'm thinking of building a firepit in the back just like this one." I blushed at the sound of my eager voice.

"That sounds lovely," Fiona said. "I'll play music for your party, if you'd like. Li and me, that is."

"That would be a treat." I shifted my feet closer to the fire. The night air was frigid but refreshing. "Fiona, what are your plans? Will you attend music school as Li did?"

"Oh, no. I like being home too much for that. Everything I need is right here."

"My little sister's quite busy," Josephine said. "Playing at the nightclub, for example."

"Josephine, if you'd ever gone there, you would see that it's nothing terrible." Fiona played with a long string of black beads that hung around her neck. "My sister doesn't approve of me playing there. Or of the music."

"You're too young," Josephine said. "Playing blues and jazz in a place with drunk men terrifies me."

"If you ever came to hear me, you see that I'm perfectly fine," Fiona said. "Papa and Mama don't mind. You shouldn't either."

Josephine shook her head. "Despite my husband's reassurance that it's not different from one of our church dances, I have my doubts."

"You're right that there are some differences. There's moonshine, as you said. The music's a bit scandalous as well," I said, teasing.

Fiona laughed. "Li and I enjoy ourselves very much. Playing all those saucy tunes."

"Li and whoever from the old gang is there that night take good care of Fiona," I said. "You shouldn't worry." I cleared my throat. "I have a thought—an idea about the competition."

"Yes?" Josephine asked.

Both of the Barnes sisters gazed at me with their intelligent, discerning eyes.

"It's important that Cym has her chance. We're all in agreement with that, yes?" I asked.

"I have my music," Fiona said. "Without it I might feel as she does."

"I have the library and my family, of course." Josephine looked over at me fondly. "If it weren't for you, I might be resting in the family plot at the cemetery."

Fiona visibly shivered. "I don't like to think about that night or what would have happened if Viktor hadn't saved you."

At the memory, prickles of discomfort traveled up my spine and raised the hair on the back of my neck. The insanity and desperation in the man's eyes before I took him out would be forever conjured in a split second. Like Fiona, I hated thinking about those terrifying moments. I'd transformed in seconds into a man capable of killing another. "Ladies, it was all a long time ago. Let us think of it no more."

"Tell us, dear Viktor. What's your idea?" Josephine asked.

"It's a bit outlandish, but it might work."

They both sat forward, watching me.

"I thought of it earlier in the library. Do you remember the plot to *As You Like It*?"

"I think so," Fiona said. "Is that the one with the storm?"

"No, that's *The Tempest*," Josephine said. "He's referencing the one where Rosalind pretends to be a boy."

"Right, yes." Fiona looked perplexed for a moment before comprehension swept her features. "Oh my. You think she should dress up as a boy."

I nodded, watching them closely. Would they think me foolish?

Josephine stared into the flames, obviously thinking through my proposal. "Your father could make her an outfit that would disguise her figure."

Now that she mentioned it, who better than my father to help us? "He would keep our secret."

"Could he pad the pants and coat to make her look bigger?" Josephine asked.

"No," Fiona said firmly. "Weight would slow her down. She needs an outfit made of the smoothest materials."

"Yes, that makes sense," I said.

"But what happens if she's discovered?" Fiona asked.

"What if she was discovered?" I asked. "Would it be so bad?"

"She might be publicly humiliated," Fiona said. "Which would be embarrassing to her and Papa. To our whole family, perhaps."

"What if we don't care?" Josephine said. "Maybe we care more about proving that anyone who can compete shouldn't be cast aside."

Fiona clasped her hands together. Brow furrowed, she nodded her head slowly as if growing accustomed to the idea. "It could work. As long as she wasn't discovered until after she'd won. If not, they won't let her compete."

"We have to keep it a secret until after it's all over." I smiled, imagining the moment when it's revealed that a woman has beaten them all.

"It's scary," Fiona said. "I'm frightened for her. The repercussions might push her right back to where she was before. Given Flynn's attitude tonight, he's surely not the only one who wishes to keep women away from sports."

Josephine turned toward her sister. "Yes, but think of all the other women in her position who would benefit from her bravery."

"It will be her decision," I said. "But if she wants to try, we'll all be there to help her along the way."

"You two better be right that she can beat the men's scores," Josephine said.

"I'm right," Fiona said. "I've seen her with my own eyes."

"Who wants to ask Cym?" Josephine asked.

"Ask me what?" Cymbeline said from behind us.

I jumped at the sound of her voice, but Fiona jumped up to

give her sister a hug. "Nothing of consequence, dearest. Just that he'd like to take you for a walk under the lovely moon."

Josephine stood as well and took Fiona's hand. "Therefore, we will leave the two of you to it."

Fiona and Josephine exchanged a conspiratorial look before heading toward the porch, leaving me alone with the object of my affection and my big idea.

❦

"WOULD YOU MIND IF WE WALKED?" CYM ASKED. "THE moon's come up, and I'm feeling too antsy to sit."

"Whatever you want," I said.

She nodded toward the barn. "Let's walk out to the pasture. I love the way the moon hangs over the meadow this time of year."

"Lead the way."

"Let's go together," Cym said. "You may take my hand."

I grinned at her in the light cast from the fire. "That would be my pleasure.'"

We walked in silence for a moment. She'd taken off her gloves, and her hand was small and warm in mine. From somewhere far away in the woods, the hoot of an owl whispered into the night.

❦

AS WE ROUNDED THE HOUSE AND OUT TO THE DRIVEWAY, I gasped at the beauty of the autumn moon that hung low and large in a purple sky. "I see what you mean about the moon."

"On nights like this, I think I shall never want to leave here," Cym said. "But I wonder if I should?" We came to the fence that encircled the horse pasture. She loosened her hand from mine and leaned against the top rung. I stayed close to her, marveling in the warmth of her body next to mine, as I rested my elbows on the rough railing.

"Why do you say such a thing?" I asked. "Where would you go if you left here?" The very thought made my blood feel as if it cooled in my veins.

"I've no place to go, and I don't want to anyway." She lifted her face toward the moon. Her skin, white and radiant in the moonlight, reminded me of a bowl of cream.

Without realizing what I was doing, I brushed my knuckles against her cheek. She turned to look back at me.

"I can see the moon in your eyes," she said.

"I can the stars in yours."

"My mother and father want me to go to college."

"Oh, I see. Why?" My blood further cooled until I was nothing but ice.

"They think it'll tame me if I'm at a women's college learning, using my mind, instead of fretting over things like races."

"Do you want to go?"

"No, I don't. I can learn anything I want in the library of our home. I don't need to go to college where I'll study books I've already read. But they're at a loss as to what to do with me. I cause so much trouble. The problem child."

"What did you tell them?"

"I told them no."

"And?" I asked. There was more. I could tell by the way she hesitated.

"And they said that it was either I settle down with a man or I go to school. There was nothing else."

I swallowed back the panic that rose from my belly. "A man?"

"You, in fact."

"Me?"

"They seem to think I'm in love with you. And of course, in their eyes, there's no one better than you that walks the face of the earth. They're afraid I'm missing my chance for happiness."

I didn't know what to say. "What do you think?"

"I think you could do better than me," Cymbeline said.

"You know my thoughts on that." I was quiet for a moment, thinking through how to approach her with my idea. "I've an idea about the competition. What if you dressed up as a man?"

Her eyebrows shot up her forehead. "A man?"

I warmed under her glare. "Like in Shakespeare. You could disguise yourself and enter the ski jumping race."

She continued to stare at me, frozen other than a twitch at the side of her mouth. Bats from one of the trees swooped low, then back up again, distracting me for a moment from my lovely companion. "Shakespeare?"

"Yes. *As You Like It.*" I rubbed my sweaty palms together.

"Rosalind," she said, "fleeing persecution, must disguise herself as a man."

"Correct. You're not persecuted, of course, and your life isn't in danger." I cleared my throat. "Obviously."

"Sometimes it feels that way," she said.

"I know," I said softly.

"That's a play, though. A man playing a woman playing a man."

I had to laugh. Mrs. Barnes would be proud to hear both of us conjure the plot and characters of the play we'd studied in school. She'd told us that in Shakespeare's time, female characters were played by twelve- to twenty-four-year-old boys. Essentially, Rosalind would have been an actor pretending to be a woman who then pretended to be a man. The other boys and I had looked at one another in wonder at such an idea. After that particular lesson we'd gone out to the schoolyard and pummeled one another with snowballs.

"How could I possibly disguise myself well enough that my own brothers wouldn't recognize me?"

"My father's a very clever tailor."

"Yes, true." She seemed to mull this over, glancing upward at the sky, then back to me. "Eventually the truth would come out, wouldn't it?"

"Would you want it to?"

She seemed to contemplate this for a moment. Her brow furrowed before she turned to face the direction of the house. "Does it make me a bad person to admit that I'd want everyone to know?"

"Not at all. Part of the fun of competition is winning in public." I turned slightly to get a better look at her.

She sighed, forming clouds in the air with her warm breath. "I can't stop thinking about what Flynn said."

"What part?"

"About me wanting to show off," Cym said.

"That bothers you? Do you know why?"

"I suppose because it's true."

❦

"YOU'VE THREATENED THE WAY OF DOING THINGS THE WAY they've always been done. That's disconcerting for a man."

"Yes." Her gaze slid toward the house. "Flynn's stubborn. Like me. We're alike, you know."

I nodded. The words *headstrong, wickedly intelligent,* and *ambitious* came to mind when I thought of either of them. They were mountains ahead of the rest of us but at times were blinded to the right path by their aspirations.

"Flynn's dream was to bring skiing to Emerson Pass. His heart is in that mountain. He wants badly for it to succeed. Ambition can make a man short-sighted."

"*Macbeth*," Cym said.

"Lady Macbeth," I said. "It's her in the end, you know."

She laughed. "Yes, it was. Like me, maybe?"

"You're not murdering anyone. You're simply asking to compete in a sport."

Nodding her head, she turned back to face me. "I think that's what it feels like to Flynn. I'm murdering a way of life. Tradition even."

"Sometimes we have to do so—for change that's necessary."

Her face crinkled into a dozen skeptical crevices. "Do you think I'm spoiled and ungrateful? Should I just take what's offered me?"

"You already know what I think. I said it before, and I'll say it again. There's nothing wrong with you. It's the rest of this that's not right. The world's set up for men, not women. You should be able to do whatever it is you want to do. Don't ever let anyone tell you otherwise."

"Oh, Viktor. Do you really think these things?"

"I never say anything I don't mean."

The night settled in around us as I waited for her response. A breeze rustled the fallen leaves, making them dance along the stone pathway. From the back porch came the sound of laughter.

"Do you really think this plan will work?" Cymbeline asked. "Or is it simply a way to get everyone really mad at me?"

"I'm not sure, but it's worth trying, don't you think?"

She laughed. "Perhaps. The whole idea seems like something that could land me in the asylum."

"Your sisters think it's a good idea."

She jerked back to look at me. "You talked to them about this?"

"Yes, just now."

"What did they say?"

"That you could beat any man, most likely, and why shouldn't you? They're going to help us in any way they can."

She blinked as if a gnat had flown near her eyes. "What if I'm wrong and I can't beat them? Then what?"

"At least you would have tried. You don't want to be an old lady thinking back with regret that you passed up this chance."

"I never thought it would be you." Cymbeline's voice reached out to me in the darkness, as soft as a goose feather against the tender skin of my cheek. "I never thought it would be you who would offer to help me. All this time I imagined you thought of me as something to conquer."

"Conquer? Why would I want to conquer you?"

"I didn't understand anything for too long." She rested her elbows on the top of the fence. "You're the one who wants to see me shine."

"As brightly as the stars. Or the sun. Maybe the sun. It's brighter."

I reached for her hand. Surprisingly, she let me take it. Her skin felt soft in my rough, large hand. I ran a thumb over the pads of her palms. "Is it impossible for you to think of me as someone to go through life with?"

She moved closer. I twitched as she placed the cool fingers of her other hand against my cheek. "If it's to be anyone who will tame me, it will be you."

"I don't want to tame you." I brought my hand to my lips, unsure if she'd really touched me or if I'd imagined it. "I'll bask in your triumph, Cym. If you let me."

She inched closer. "Viktor, thank you."

"For what?" I could barely breathe.

"For tonight. For being my champion." Then, to my utter amazement, she drew up on her tiptoes and kissed me on the mouth.

I didn't dare put my arms around her, fearing she would feel trapped and run away from me. But I did lean in and take another kiss from her sweet mouth.

"Do you remember when I kissed you that night?" Cym asked.

"Yes, I remember." I'd played that moment over and over in my mind ever since.

"I felt so foolish afterward and embarrassed. That's been part of why I've shunned you. You've made me feel like a girl."

I laughed. "Is that bad?"

"I used to think so."

"And now?"

"And now I find that I quite like kissing you." Cym drew away from me, taking the warmth with her, and turned back to look over the fence into the pasture. A sudden breeze brought the scent of dry grasses. "What about Emma?"

For a second, I wasn't sure what she meant. So wrapped up in Cym, I'd forgotten she believed us to be an item.

"Would you still care for me if there was no Emma?" I voiced the fear that threatened my joyfulness in this glorious moment.

"I believe so," she said. "But I can't know for sure. I know only what I feel now."

"There's no Emma. There's only you. Let me take you out to dinner tomorrow at the club. If nothing else, we can talk about how we're going to prepare you for this race."

"I will, yes."

"I'll pick you up at six," I said.

"Fine." She lifted her face toward the moon that hung behind my head. "You may kiss me again."

I did as she asked, lingering against her soft lips for a second longer this time. When I lifted my face from hers, she smiled up at me. "Is kissing always so delicious?"

"I don't know. I've not kissed anyone else."

"That can't be true," Cym said. "You're too good at it."

"I promise."

"Maybe we should keep it that way."

Before I could answer, she pranced away and ran fast across the yard and disappeared into the house. I touched my fingers to my lips, as dazzled by her kiss as if she truly were the sun itself.

Or the moon. I turned to look at the giant silver ball in the sky. Had he sent magical dust down to me tonight? Was it the moon who had brought Cymbeline to me at last?

Cymbeline

For hours that night, I tossed and turned as I tried to find a comfortable position before falling into a fitful sleep. I dreamt of Viktor holding me and then dancing me across the floor of the club. When I woke the next morning, my eyes felt as if they had sand in them. For a few minutes I lay curled up on my side, thinking of Viktor. Our time in the light of the moon seemed almost as a dream.

After a few more minutes of luxuriating in the memory of his kisses, I pulled back the covers and padded across the cold wood floor to the windows and pulled back the curtains to reveal blue sky, a backdrop to the bright leaves. I went to the fireplace and poked the few remaining embers back to life before tossing in a few pieces of dry kindling. Once they caught fire, I put a few logs on top and closed the grate.

After the room had warmed a bit, I dressed in trousers and a sweater. This morning Poppy needed me to accompany her out to the Fredericks' sheep farm. There were no dresses for Poppy and me on a day when a farmer suspected worms had infested their flock. A dull headache accompanied me to breakfast.

Papa and Mama as well as the little girls were at the table

when I entered the dining room. I said good morning as I poured myself a cup of coffee from the silver pot on the buffet.

"Good morning, sweetheart." Papa had the newspaper spread out in front of him and only briefly looked up at me. Steam from his coffee cup swirled in the cool air of the autumn morning.

Mama gave me a wave. She had a book open next to her but at the moment she was listening to Delphia's tale of the eagle she'd spotted that morning.

"He swept low, Mama, looking for his breakfast, and then up he came with a mouse. I know it was a mouse because I saw his tail."

"Disgusting," Addie said, not looking up from the book she was reading. Her plate of scrambled eggs and a slice of Lizzie's thick sourdough bread appeared untouched.

"Addie, eat your breakfast," I said to her before planting a kiss on the top of her blond head. She was too thin and as pale as the whitewashed wainscoting.

"Your sister's right," Mama said. "Here, give me your book. You can read it after you have your eggs and toast."

Addie did as asked, sliding her book over to Mama obediently before lifting her fork. She stared down at the plate and sighed before setting aside her utensil and picking up the toast.

"Aren't you hungry?" Mama asked her.

"Not really." Addie took a small bite from the corner of her bread.

Delphia had finished her meal and was now staring out the window lost in thought. "Hello, pet," I said to her.

"Hi, Cym." She flashed me one of her smiles that seemed to warm the room. With their blond locks and fair skin, my little sisters looked like Mama.

"Do you want me to take the girls into school this morning?" I asked. "I'm headed over to Poppy's so I could drop them on my way."

Delphia was only nine and still at the primary school. Since I'd been at school, the town had grown big enough that we now had a high school and a primary school. They'd expanded the original schoolhouse, adding a second story for the younger grades. The high school was now in a new brick building next to the library.

"That would be lovely, darling. Thank you." Mama gestured toward the buffet. "Have breakfast first. You have fifteen minutes before you'd have to go."

I filled a plate with eggs, chunks of potato, and two slices of toast. I'd have to eat quickly if we were to get out of the house on time. Papa allowed me to drive one of the cars whenever I wished. He only went into his office in town a few days of the week, preferring to be at home with Mama.

"Did you sleep well?" Mama asked me.

"Not particularly. Do I look horrid?"

"You could never look horrid," Addie said before taking another small bite of her toast. "It's impossible."

"Even though you're wearing trousers." Delphia's tone rose an octave in obvious glee. Unfortunately, my youngest sister had the same affinity for rebellion as yours truly.

"Mr. Frederick suspects the flock has worms," I said in way of an explanation. "I can't help Poppy in a dress. But you, little missy, are going to school and must look decent."

"Yes, I look decent." Delphia didn't care for decent, given her scathing tone. "I can't wait to wear pants."

"Whatever for?" Mama's brow furrowed.

"To be like Cym," Delphia said. "A woman of the world."

I laughed. "Where do you get these ideas? What do you know of the world?"

Papa set his paper down to look at his youngest daughter. "Cymbeline is not a woman of the world. She's a woman of Emerson Pass."

"What's the difference?" Delphia's light blue eyes danced with excitement. "Do you know, Papa?"

"The difference is obscure." Papa lifted his brows in a gesture of mysteriousness. "What do you think it could be?"

"The world's big and Emerson Pass is small," Addie said, as if to herself, before taking another nibble of her toast.

"That's obvious," Delphia said.

"I think she means it symbolically." We all turned to see Fiona entering the room. She looked like a newly budded pink rose in a light blue dress. She stopped near the buffet. "As in, the world is hard to understand in its vastness—its lack of familiarity and mysteriousness. Whereas our town is a community. No one is anonymous."

Addie's mouth lifted in a rare smile. "I suppose that's what I meant."

Fiona plopped a spoonful of eggs onto a plate and sat next to Addie. "Good morning, family. How's everyone today?"

"Cym has to pull some worms out of a sheep's bottom," Delphia said.

"Delphia, goodness." Mama placed both hands over her cheeks pretending to be appalled, but I knew from the twitch at the corners of her mouth that she was trying not to laugh. "Not at the table."

"Or anywhere." Papa coughed into his fist. "Love, we don't talk about bums at the table or anywhere else for that matter. We'll have to send you to live in the barn with the rest of animals."

"Really?" Delphia sat up straighter, clearly excited by the idea. "Will I spend the night out there? I already thought about how I could make a bed with hay and sleep next to Lucy." Lucy was her favorite of our horses. She was a gentle mare, although getting older. These days, she lived a life of mostly eating and getting pets on her nose.

"I'm not sure the barn is the punishment we're looking for," I said.

"If only we knew what to do with you, Delphia," Fiona said.

"What are you doing today?" Papa asked Fiona.

"I've several care baskets to take to the sick," Fiona said.

"Theo left me a list last night, and Lizzie and I put them together this morning."

"Before breakfast?" Delphia shook her head as if this were the most outlandish thing she'd ever heard. "You really are a saint, Fiona." She tapped the side of her head and spoke with a strange accent. "Myself? I couldn't do it. Me old head needs food straightaway."

I covered my mouth, afraid the spoonful of eggs I'd just put in there were going to fly out from my bark of laughter.

"*Me head* is not proper English," Addie said, not unkindly, but merely stating a fact.

"I know that," Delphia said. "I only said it to make Cym laugh."

"When have you heard a cockney accent?" Papa asked.

Cockney? Apparently Papa was familiar.

"One of the kids in my class. His family just moved from there," Delphia said. "I imitate him and make everyone laugh."

"Delphia Barnes, you are forbidden to do that ever again." We all jumped slightly at Mama's raised voice. She hardly ever spoke a harsh word to any of us. However, the one thing she wouldn't tolerate was unkindness to others.

"But why?" Delphia asked. "Everyone thinks it's so funny."

Mama leaned over the table and spoke sternly to Delphia. "I can assure you that the little boy you're imitating doesn't think so. You should be ashamed of yourself. You're a girl with everything, which means you have to be even better than everyone else. Kinder. Gentler. More sensitive to others' feelings. Do you understand me?"

Delphia's bottom lip quivered. "Yes, Mama."

"The other children look up to you and will do what you do. If you're mean, they will be too."

"Why do they look up to me?" Several tears caught in Delphia's thick lashes.

"They just do," I said. "You're that kind of girl."

"That's right," Mama said. "You have a responsibility as a Barnes to make sure that all new children feel welcome here."

For once, Delphia knew better than to ask another question. She nodded, then lowered her head. A tear traveled down her cheek and landed in her lump of eggs.

"You'll march right in there today and tell him you're sorry," Mama said. She looked over at Papa. "We'll send them something. A welcome gift."

"I could take something out to them today during my rounds," Fiona said.

"Good idea," Mama said. "Does Lizzie have any cakes down there?"

"She does. One of her white ones," Fiona said.

"Take that one," Mama said. "I'll write a quick note before you leave."

"But that's *my* favorite cake," Delphia said.

Mama whipped her head around to glare at her youngest offspring. "You, young lady, wouldn't be having a piece even if cake were served to us tonight," Mama said. "As a matter of fact, you'll have no dessert for the rest of the week."

Delphia looked crestfallen but again was wise enough to remain quiet.

"Come along," I said to my little sisters. "Let's get you to school. It's going to be chilly all day, so you should wear your hats." I turned to Mama. "Does Florence need a ride?" Florence was Jasper and Lizzie's daughter. The same age as Addie, she often rode to school with us.

"Not today. Jasper wanted to take her," Mama said. "He had to go into town anyway."

I swallowed one more bite of eggs and then ushered the two of them out the door and into the hallway. Lizzie had placed their lunch buckets by the bench next to the door. I helped them into their coats. "Wipe your eyes," I said to Delphia. "Time to start our day, and it's best to shake off our mistakes before we go."

"All right," Delphia said in a meek voice. "I'm going to be good like Addie all day."

"Good for you," I said. And good luck, I thought. She was too much like me to be able to keep that promise.

A few minutes later, we were headed down the rocky driveway to the road that took us into town. Usually Delphia chattered away, but she was subdued by the tongue-lashing of her mother and looked out the window with a forlorn expression.

"Delphia, do you understand why Mama got angry with you?" I asked.

"Not really. I thought she liked it when I made people laugh."

"She likes it when you make *me* laugh," Addie said. "But not at the expense of others."

"What does expense of others mean?" Delphia asked as she brushed another tear from her black lashes. The child was way too pretty for her own good. With her golden hair and blue eyes, she looked like a toy doll.

"It means you made someone feel bad in order to make others laugh," I said.

"I didn't mean to hurt his feelings," Delphia said. "I didn't even think about it."

"That's Mama's concern. You must think before you do things. Think about who it might hurt. Do you understand?"

"I guess so." She didn't say anything for a moment. "How do you tell if it will make someone feel bad?"

"If you want to make people laugh, it's better to make fun of yourself rather than someone else," I said. "That way you know you won't hurt anyone's feelings."

"Did you like to make people laugh when you were my age?" Delphia asked.

"No, I didn't care about that. I just wanted to win everything."

"Did you?" Addie asked.

"Not all the time. Viktor Olofsson had a nasty habit of always beating me on the ice. I used to get very mad." Saying this, an image of him from the night before played before my eyes. His earnest eyes and warm hands and surprising softness of his lips. A delicious shiver went up the back of my spine.

"I like to win too," Delphia said. "I like everyone to pay attention to me."

"We know." Addie smiled as she looked over at her sister with fondness.

"Do you hate it?" Delphia asked. "That I'm always getting attention?"

"Not at all," Addie said. "I prefer they look at you and ignore me completely."

"Why do you want to be ignored?" I didn't like the idea of her being ignored simply because of her vivacious sister.

"I like to be left alone to read my books," Addie said.

"Or write in that silly journal," Delphia said.

"It's not silly." Addie's fair skin flushed. "I write about life in there."

"If your nose was ever out of a book, you'd have more to write about," Delphia said, sounding suspiciously like me and my big, bossy mouth. I made a vow to be more careful around my little sisters. They were impressionable. Giving them ideas about how to be sassy served no one, especially them. Why did everything bad about my family always lead back to me? Would they all be better off if I disappeared?

We were in the main part of town by then. A sleeping town waking up. Shopkeepers were outside their front doors sweeping the wooden sidewalks. Mrs. Johnson was outside her dry goods store watering pots of yellow mums. She raised a hand when I beeped the car horn. Mr. Olofsson was already hard at work, bent over his latest project in the window of his tailor's shop. Several men were getting a shave in the barbershop. My uncle Clive seemed deep in thought as he put the open sign in the window of Higgins Brothers Butcher Shop. Aunt Annabelle was going to have a baby any day now. After years without children, they'd been quite surprised by the pregnancy. Mama had told me her sister and Clive had resigned themselves to a childless marriage. They'd always been so in love, and Annabelle had her own successful business making wedding gowns for the elite of Colorado that their lives had been full. Still, my aunt and uncle were thrilled that a baby would come sometime around Christmas.

I pulled into the lot next to the school and turned off the engine. "Do you want me to walk you in?" I asked, already knowing they would decline my invitation. Last year, Delphia loved when I walked her up to the front doors, but she'd announced on the first day this year that she would be escorting herself into school. "I'm not a baby," she'd told me.

"No, thank you," Delphia said.

I caught her eye in the rearview mirror. "Don't forget what Mama said about teasing."

Delphia's face sobered. "I won't."

"Have a good day," I said as they climbed out of the back seat.

For a moment, I sat in the car, watching them walk up the steps of the schoolhouse. How different it was now from when I'd been Delphia's age. Our little town had grown up.

⟡

POPPY AND I SPENT THE MORNING WITH THE FREDERICKS' sheep, who were indeed infested with worms. We prescribed our usual remedy, which Poppy had concocted from tar and vinegar. By noon we were on our way down the dirt road in Poppy's truck. The air was crisp but sunny, and we decided to stop by the river to have our sandwiches. Lizzie always packed two of everything, knowing that Poppy would need a lunch as well. Having grown up with us, Poppy was practically another of the Barnes siblings. When we were young, she and Josephine had been best friends and remained so to this day.

We sat at one of the picnic tables on the lawn that over-looked the river. During the warm weather, this was a popular location for the youth of Emerson Pass to congregate. We often had bonfires on the sandy beach. In the summers, children swam and played in the water. Today, however, the park was empty other than us and the ducks.

While I unpacked our lunch, Poppy took off her hat. Her glossy brown hair had grown out a few inches from the shorter bob she'd come home with a few years ago and nestled just shy of her shoulders.

Poppy tilted her face toward the sun and closed her eyes. Her skin was a few shades darker than my own alabaster complexion and looked luminous under the blue sky. She stretched her legs out and yawned. A dried piece of mud fell from the sole of her boot.

"Are you tired?" I asked.

"A little. I was out late with Neil last night. We drove out here to look at the giant moon."

"It was a nice evening." I handed Poppy one of Lizzie's ham-and-butter sandwiches and took one for myself. There were two apples and several cookies as well. We would not starve on Lizzie's watch.

I studied my friend before taking a bite of my sandwich. Small and strong, she moved with ease and speed but was grace-ful, too, like a dancer. Today, she'd been fidgety and distracted. She'd barely said two words all morning. "Everything peachy?" I asked.

"What? Oh, yes." She pulled her hat back over her glossy hair. As modern as we were, we still coveted our complexions and didn't want to get too much sun. "I've news. I suppose you could call it that. But I'm nervous to tell you."

"Yes?" I braced myself for what was coming.

"Neil has asked me to marry him. Can you believe it? An old maid like me? Getting married at twenty-eight?"

"You said yes, then?" Neil Hartman was Emma's brother. A

perfectly nice man and not hard on the eyes, but this was our Poppy. The Hartman siblings had opened a feed store in town. Poppy had met Neil when she went in for supplies for her horses. She'd been smitten almost immediately. I'd not predicted it. Not at all. I'd imagined that she and I would be the last women standing. The only ones in this town who would resist convention. Would Neil stifle her? Keep her from her work?

"I said yes." Her dark eyes sparkled. "Isn't love the most remarkable thing? Turning an old workhorse like me into a blushing bride?"

"I suppose." I took another bite of my sandwich, which now tasted of river rocks. What would happen to me if Poppy stopped working to stay home and raise babies?

"Don't be like that." She nudged my shoulder with her elbow. "Nothing's going to change."

"You say that now."

"He understands about my work," Poppy said. "We've agreed I'll keep working."

I nodded as if I believed it all to be true. However, I wasn't so sure everything would go as planned. Married people had a habit of having babies.

"What about you?" Poppy asked. "Have you come to your senses about Viktor yet?"

"It depends on what you mean."

"What happened?" She nudged me again. "Spill it. I know he was at dinner out at your house last night."

"How did you know that?"

"He mentioned it yesterday after church."

"Were you at church with Neil and Emma?" My real question was if Viktor had been there with Emma. Jealously reared its ugly head once more. What was she to him really? Was I in jeopardy of losing him if I didn't figure out my own mind?

"I was there with Neil. Emma wasn't there. She had something else to do."

I felt immediate relief.

"How was last night?" Poppy asked me.

"Let's say I caved under the moon."

Poppy squealed. "Did you kiss him?"

"You could say that. It was the silly moon. Who could stay sane with it overhead like that?"

"You're the most infuriating girl in the world. Why didn't you tell me first thing? Did you like it? Isn't kissing the bee's knees?"

I couldn't help but smile. "It was surprisingly pleasant."

"You're impossible. Why are you resisting giving in to love?" Poppy asked.

"I'm afraid to lose myself." That was as honest as I could be.

"What if you find another part of yourself? One that makes you even better?"

"Is that what you believe?" I asked.

"I don't know. I'm in love, that's all I know for now."

Despite my worry about the future, I smiled. "I'm happy for you."

She tucked her arm into mine. "I'm happy for me too."

We ate our lunch and watched a group of ducks bobbing in the shallow parts of the river. "My parents think I should go to college."

"What? Do you want to? You've never said anything about that. I'm not holding you back, am I?"

"No, no. I love working with you. I don't want to go, but they think it would help me to get away from here for a while."

"But why?"

I sighed and told her about the competition as well as my argument with Flynn. "It was a terrible row. He said if he were Papa he would make me marry Viktor."

"He said that?"

"In front of everyone, including Viktor."

Poppy brought her napkin to her mouth. "You must have been mortified."

"I was. Anyway, after dinner, Papa and Mama asked me into their study for a talk. They asked how I felt about Viktor, and I couldn't lie. I told them I was in love with him but that I didn't feel ready to be a wife and mother."

"What did they say to that?"

"They suggested college and some time away."

"But that's not what you want?"

"I don't want to take the chance that he gives up on me and marries Emma. My parents are smart. They know that and are trying to push me into a decision. This whole ski jumping thing brought everything out into the open. Maybe they're right. Should I just leave and let Viktor get on with things?"

"That's not what you want."

"You should have heard what Viktor said to me after Flynn stormed out." I summed it up as best I could Viktor's declarative speech that I was not to make myself small. "He said I should shine and he'll bask in my glow."

"Oh, that Viktor. He's one of a kind. What a good man he is. One who understands and accepts you as you are." Poppy beamed as she squeezed my hand. "You two are the perfect match."

"Maybe." Were we? Or did he deserve better? A woman like Emma? "I believe Papa's pushing me a bit to see if I'll make a decision about Viktor. They all seem to think I have to be tricked into things."

"Well, you're as stubborn as a mule."

"I'm more like a goat, wild and unruly."

"At least you don't eat hats," Poppy said. "I'm sorry about the competition. I wish you could compete."

"My own brother won't open the races to women. I wanted to punch him I was so angry."

"I understand why you'd feel that way, but it's not surprising. I'm not sure why it would be to you."

"I thought Flynn would see my side."

"He's a man in a powerful position. They don't have to see our side of things." Poppy squinted out to the river where a breeze made ripples in the water. "Cym, at some point, you have to accept what is and decide where you can find joy within the parameters of conventional society. And your father's right. It's not fair to Viktor to string him along."

"I'm not doing that."

"Are you sure?" Poppy asked.

I debated for a moment about whether to tell her Viktor's idea that I dress up as a man. She could be trusted, of course. But the more people knew, the less likely I could keep it a secret. Plus, she would be Neil's wife soon. If my siblings' marriages were any indication, spouses shared everything.

"Enough about that," I said. "When will you and Neil marry?"

"As soon as possible. Something small out at my brother's place."

Her brother, Harley, and his wife, Merry, had worked for Papa when we were all young. Now, he and Merry bred horses out at their farm. Poppy's house was on the same piece of property not far from them. "Will Neil move into your home?"

"Yes, since he and Emma are living in rooms above their feed store, it's our best option."

At the thought of Emma, I tossed the rest of my sandwich back into its wrapper and got up to walk down to the water's edge. A hawk screamed and swept over the water looking for his lunch. Poppy came to stand beside me. We stood there quietly for a moment. The rush of water over stones upriver soothed my nerves. Whatever happened would happen. I would not shy away from any of it. Not the race or Viktor.

Poppy turned and walked back to our picnic table, leaving me there to watch a poor fish get pulled from the river by the hawk.

Viktor

During my lunch break from the bank, I crossed the street to have a meal with my parents. They closed the shop every day from noon to one. At least a few times a week, I dined with them. I took the back stairs up to their apartment above the shop. Before I reached the top of the stairs, the aroma of chicken soup filled my nose.

"Mother," I called out as I entered through the unlocked door. "Father?"

"In here," Mother said from the kitchen.

I walked through the front room, as spare and neat as it had been for the last two decades. We'd come here when I was only nine. Father had rented the building from Lord Barnes for what he said at the time was a very fair price. He'd seen in an advertisement in the Boston paper where we were living after coming over from Norway that a frontier town was in need of a tailor. Father, as requested in the advertisement, had written to Lord Barnes with his qualifications. What came in the return post was an offer to assist with moving costs and reasonable rent on one of the buildings in town where we could have a shop and an apartment. We'd come that summer before I'd started school with the others in the first class of Emerson Pass.

I kissed my mother's cheek before joining Father at the kitchen table. Their apartment was small, only two bedrooms, a kitchen, and the sitting room. However, we'd always found it to be just the right size. What we lacked in imagination, the Olofsson family had made up for it with a natural gratefulness about our circumstances. From the very first day we arrived, my parents had made sure we knew how blessed we were to have been given the chance to come to such a beautiful place and open a business. And school? My mother valued education above all else. When I'd attended college, it was the only time my stoic parents had ever expressed pride. I knew it was there, always. However, it was seldom expressed verbally.

"Smells good, Mother," I said.

"Nothing special." She set a steaming bowl in front of my father. "But it will warm your bones on a chilly day."

"Thank you, dear." Father tucked his napkin into the collar of his shirt.

After placing a bowl in front of me, Mother fetched another for herself, along with a loaf of crusty bread. Other than the appreciative slurps and clanking of spoons against the ceramic bowl, we ate in silence. When I'd finished my soup along with two pieces of bread, I pushed the bowl away and leaned back in my chair.

"I talked to Mrs. Johnson this morning," Mother said. "Have you heard about the competition?"

"Yes, I was over at the Barneses' last night," I said.

"Will you compete?" Father asked between bites. He ate as he did everything, slowly and methodically.

"No, I'm not fast enough. Skiers will be coming from all over the world."

"How exciting," Mother said. "Our little town be famous."

"You'd like that, Mother?"

"It would be nice for Lord Barnes." Mother got up to clear the dishes, but I put a hand on her shoulder.

"Let me, Mother." I gathered the dishes and took them to the sink for washing. We'd had running water for at least five years, but we never got tired of commenting about how much we enjoyed the convenience.

Mother put a pot of coffee on the stove before returning to her chair and pulling out her accounting book. She ran all of the shop's finances, keeping a close watch on receipts and expenditures. I had loved helping her when I was a child. Now I worked at a bank, so it had come full circle. Nothing made me happier than a row of numbers adding up correctly. I'd known back then that I'd like to do something of the sort for work.

The coffee percolated and filled the room with its pleasant aroma. I finished washing up and drying, then poured us all a cup. Mother liked cream in hers, but Father and I drank ours black.

By the time I delivered his mug, Father had tucked his chin into his neck like a nesting bird and closed his eyes. The man woke every morning at dawn. By lunch he was tired.

"Your brother came by earlier," Mother said. "He brought us some cookies. They're in the cupboard if you'd like some."

"No, thank you." I patted my stomach. "I'll save room for later. I'm taking Cymbeline to dinner at the club."

"What about Emma?" Mother asked.

I looked at her, surprised. "Emma?"

"People tell us things when they come in for fittings or whatnot. There's nothing the ladies in this town love more than gossip. They have you two married off already."

"Emma and I are only friends," I said. "She has a beau back east."

Mother's thin eyebrows raised. They had always been fair, but lately I'd noticed they'd turned white, as had her once-blond hair. Emerald eyes peered at me from over her coffee cup. "Back east? Well, how will that work?"

"He's coming out here eventually," I said.

Father untucked his chin from his neck. "You could do worse

than Emma Hartman. She has a very small waist. Although her torso-to-leg ratio is strange. Very long legs. Like a stork."

"Anders, she looks nothing like a stork. More like a graceful swan," Mother said.

I laughed. "If we're talking about waists, there's nothing wrong with Cymbeline's." She didn't look like a stork or a swan. Cym was more like a Thoroughbred horse like the ones Harley and Merry Depaul raised. "She's the only woman for me. Always has been. I'm slowly wearing her down."

"Ah, I see," Mother said. "Emma is supposed to make Cymbeline jealous."

"Would I do such a thing?" I asked.

"Clever," Father said. "That Cymbeline loves to win."

"I should've known," Mother said with a hint of approval in her voice. She and my father loved the Barnes family.

"Speaking of winning," I said, "she wants to participate in the ski jump at the competition. She believes she has a chance to win."

"But no girls are to complete." Mother frowned. "Mrs. Johnson said so this morning when reading to me from the newspaper."

"Yes, well, I have an idea. She would dress as a boy," I said, glancing at Father. "I thought perhaps you could sew her something to disguise her gender."

Father's bland expression did not change as he set aside his fork. "Legend has it that sometime in the mid-eighteen-hundreds, a young Norwegian woman jumped six meters."

"The year was 1862," Mother said. "Her name was Ingrid Olavsdottir Vestby. In Trysil."

"Mother, how do you know that?" I gawked at her in surprise.

"Back then, in Norway, all the girls knew of the legend of Ingrid," Mother said. "There were some in my circle who wanted very badly to compete. They'd ski jumped right along with their brothers and wanted the chance to show what they could do. In 1892, some organized their own competition."

"Yes, yes. I haven't thought of that in years," Father said. "Not recognized, of course. But compete they did."

Mother's eyes shone at the memory. "Then, in 1904, Miss Strang jumped fourteen and half meters. We were very proud. I'll never forget it."

My parents rarely talked of their time before coming to America. I longed for more of these gems. "What else do you remember?"

"Not long after, we left Norway," Father said. "We don't know what happened to her after that. Or any of the girls we grew up with."

"If Cymbeline wants to jump, we'll make her a costume," Mother said. "Right, Anders?"

"Do Quinn and Alexander know?" Father asked.

I shook my head. "Only Jo and Fiona."

"They might be angry at us for helping," Mother said.

"No, they'll see once it all unfolds that this was a good thing for Cymbeline. She needs this...to feel at peace."

"Do you think this will do it?" Mother asked. "Give her the contentment she's craved?"

"I hope so," I said. "And then she'll be willing to settle down finally."

"Yes, I can see why you think this is a good plan," Mother said. "But what if it does the opposite? What if she tastes the glory of winning and never stops? Back home, the girls were in shows for carnivals." She shuddered. "We can't have Cymbeline running off to the carnival."

"She won't run off. Not from her family. Or from here." I looked back at my father. "What do you think? Will you help us?"

He didn't say anything for a moment. I could see him weighing the decision. To be involved in the ruse or not? What culpability would he have in it all if Lord Barnes were displeased? Finally, though, his sense of adventure won. "I would do anything for any of the Barnes family. But this—well, this is a job worthy of the finest tailor. And Miss Cymbeline is a fine woman. Brave and talented. A woman who deserves to compete in whatever sport she desires."

"Thank you, Father."

"I have her measurements from the last time she was in for a dress. I have just the right kind of wool to make her pants. She'll need a wool sweater. Made from the lightest yarn we can find."

"Yes, but yarn that makes her look bulkier than she is," I said.

Mother nodded. "I'll have Mrs. Johnson order something for me. In gray so she doesn't stand out."

"What about her face?" I asked. "Mother, would you be able to knit a cap that covered everything but her eyes?"

"Yes, yes. With a hole for the mouth. She must breathe," Mother said.

"Almost like a mask," Father said. "In a dull color. Quite the opposite of what I would make her if she were going as herself. Cymbeline is the type of girl who can wear any color. The brighter the better." He picked up one last piece of bread and slathered it with butter. "I shall take it as a challenge to make a disguise. What about her hair?" He gestured in the air to indicate her thick curls. "The hair will need to be stuck up into the hat or she'll be uncovered. From what I've seen, that hair seems to go every which way."

"Whatever gave you the idea?" Mother asked me.

"Shakespeare." I'd read out loud to them on many a winter's night. We'd completed the entire works of Shakespeare over time.

"Ah, yes. Rosalind," Mother said.

❦

THAT EVENING, SEATED AT THE CLUB, I STOLE GLANCES AT Cymbeline as she perused the menu. She wore a dark blue dress made of silk and taffeta. Her curls were covered with a stylish cloche hat of the same color with a sassy feather sticking up from one side.

She looked up, catching me staring at her.

"I forgot to tell you how beautiful you look. I'm clumsy at all this."

"Don't be silly. I can see in your eyes that you think I look nice."

The club was quiet tonight, with only locals dining. Come ski season, the restaurant would be packed with tourists. I preferred it quiet.

The server brought a basket of bread made by my brother. As of last year, he provided all of the baked goods to the club.

Cymbeline took a piece of thick crusted bread and handed me the basket. "Are you hungry?"

"Famished," I said. "You?"

"Yes, very hungry. Poppy and I had a busy day today. Lunch seems forever ago already." She buttered her bread with quick, efficient strokes.

"Have you thought any more about my idea?"

"I have. I've thought about it all day." Her upper arms and shoulders were bare. I wanted to stroke her soft skin.

I lowered my voice to make sure no one else could hear us. "I talked to my parents, and they've agreed to help us."

"Really? That's great news." She broke off as the server reappeared to take our orders.

We both asked for the trout, caught in our very own creeks and river, served with buttery potatoes and squash. My mouth watered just thinking of the meal to come. "Do you know I've never been here," I said after the server left.

"You haven't? I had no idea. What do you think?"

I looked around at the opulent room with the glass chandeliers and tall ceilings held up by wide beams. Tables with white cloths and shiny silverware and multiple sets of glasses waited for guests.

She glanced out the window. Night had fallen. All that we

could see in the glass was our own reflection. I liked what I saw —the two of us dining together as if we were a couple. She turned back to me.

"Do you think I should shave my head?" Cymbeline asked without a hint of humor.

"What? No." Shave her head. Good Lord, the lengths she would go to. "Why would you do such a thing?"

"To make me more slippery when I come down the slope." She made a gesture with her hand to imitate her jumping-off point.

I looked around to make sure no one was looking at us. "Be careful. There are folks everywhere."

"Right, yes," she whispered. "I must be careful."

"Absolutely no shaved head. It would be a shame to destroy your pretty curls, but a shaved head would be a sure giveaway that something was afoot. Even Cymbeline Barnes wouldn't be excused from that."

"Excused? What does that mean?" Her nose wrinkled as she leaned closer.

"I mean that people know you have your own mind. Your own way of doing things. Regardless, I believe a shaved head might be too much."

She laughed. "All right, I suppose that's true. But you know, once they learn what I've done, I might be run out of town."

"You won't be run out of town. You're a Barnes."

"Yes, but one can be ostracized and feel as if people will think you're…" She trailed off and lifted her hands in the air as if to conjure the right word.

What was the word people would use? *Disturbed? Insane?* Or did others see her as I did? Brave, unconquerable, unconventionally brilliant? "You've never worried about what people think of you," I said.

"I care a little." She looked down at the table. A frown line appeared just above her eyebrows. "It doesn't seem that way, but I do."

"You shouldn't."

"I feel bad that I embarrass my family," Cym said.

"You don't embarrass them. They're proud of you."

She tilted her head and smiled. "You look nice tonight too. I like your suit."

I brushed a hand over the dark gray material. "My father does good work."

She lifted her gaze. A softness in her eyes seemed to reach out as if she'd caressed me. "You wouldn't mind, then? Being with someone like me?" Her voice had lowered, husky and slightly breathy.

"I think you know the answer to that," I said.

The server came with bowls of pea soup. She picked up a spoon.

"Do we pray at a place like this?" I asked.

"Would you like to?"

"It would be best, wouldn't it?"

She nodded and put down her spoon. "Would you care to say it, or shall I?"

"You, please."

Cym tented her hands and closed her eyes. I did the same.

"Dear Lord, thank you for this meal we're about to receive. And thank you for sending Viktor to me."

The back of my throat ached. "Amen," I said.

"Now can we eat?"

"Yes, now we can eat."

"Does your family always pray before dinner?" Cym asked.

"Every night, yes."

"Isn't it funny that I've known you all these years and never knew the answer to that question?"

We ate for a few more minutes, chatting about various subjects, including my parents' immigration from Norway and that until Isak and me, all Olofsson men had become tailors.

"Was he upset that neither of his sons wanted to follow in his footsteps?" Cym asked.

"No, he was glad. *We're in America*, he always says. *You can do whatever you wish.* He was proud for me to attend college."

"I've wondered what they thought about Isak and his bakery."

"They knew that's what he wanted. He'd been baking since he was small. When we were young, my parents worked long hours downstairs. Isak and I often made dinner for them."

"Really?"

"Not everyone has a Lizzie," I said.

"Do I seem spoiled to you?"

"Not spoiled. Rich, maybe."

She laughed. "Papa's rich, not me."

"Now the snow needs to fall," Cymbeline said.

"Have you considered training before the snow falls?"

"How?" Her eyes widened with obvious interest.

"Strength regimens. I could put a plan together for you," I said.

"How do you know what I should do?" She didn't ask this with skepticism but seemed truly interested. Her fingers tightened around her spoon.

"At university, I had a good friend on the track team. They did more than just run to improve their times."

"What else?"

I thought back to the times I'd seen Marcus training. Squats and lunges, sprints, jump rope sessions. I shared with her what I remembered. "I could train you," I said.

"You?"

"Why not me? Who else would motivate you more?" I grinned, remembering how angry she used to get when I beat her on the ice. "I'll train with you. That way you'll have someone to compete with."

"I *would* like the chance to prove to you once and for all that I'm tougher than you."

I knew it to be true already. "We could meet in the mornings before work. Do you think you could come out to my house without arising suspicious?"

"No one gets up too early," Cym said. "Usually Fiona's the first one up, and she already knows."

"How's six? Tomorrow morning? I have to be in at work right at nine to open the bank."

"I can do that." Her eyes sparkled with excitement. "You think you can break me, don't you?"

"I would never be so bold."

Her gaze flickered to the front of the restaurant. "Oh dear."

"What's wrong?" I asked.

"Emma's here."

I'd not talked to Emma in a few days. She wouldn't have had any idea I'd be here with Cymbeline. Was she here with her brother? If so, it would be quite the splurge. They were living on pennies, putting everything back into the feed store. I looked over my shoulder. Emma stood next to a tall, dark-haired man in a perfectly draped suit. The out-of-town beau? Had he arrived early? Emma had told me Peter wanted to marry as soon as he arrived in Emerson Pass.

They made a beeline over to us, ignoring the host who wanted to lead them to one of the empty tables. Cymbeline planted a fake smile on her face and lifted her chin up to fix her dark eyes on my friend.

"Good evening," Emma said, flashing her pretty smile. "May I introduce you to Peter? He's come from Boston just this morning."

I stood to shake Peter's hand. He was a good-looking man although slight and pale, as if he never left the confines of an office. Perhaps Colorado could change that. Emma had told me he came from money and had been delayed in Boston taking care of his father's estate. She'd met him while working as a maid for his family. The whole affair had been quite the scandal, which is why they'd agreed to start fresh out here.

The ladies exchanged greetings. Cym acted friendly enough. To an outsider, she would seem polite and welcoming. However, a twitch in the side of her face told me she was clenching her teeth. I knew this particular expression. She'd had the same one every time I beat her in one of our skating races.

"Do you fish, Peter?" I asked, still standing.

"Fish? No. I mean, I haven't," he said. "But I'd like to."

"All in good time," Emma said. "We mustn't scare him away, Viktor, by taking him out to the wilderness too soon."

"I can't be scared away from you," Peter said. "Not ever. Show them your ring, darling. We've made it official."

Clearly Emma hadn't known I'd be here, because a ring sparkled on her left hand. I sneaked a glance at Cymbeline. She was staring at them, looking a bit like a man who'd just caught a fat fish. I'd get an earful on the way home. Of that I was certain.

"You're engaged?" Cym asked.

"As of this morning," Emma said, with a quick glance in my direction. "Peter and I've known each for a long time, but we were separated by many miles."

"Thanks, old boy, for taking care of my girl until I could get here. She tells me you've been quite the friend to her."

"Sure thing. It was a pleasure." I gestured toward the table. "Would you care to join us?"

"Not tonight," Emma said. "We're celebrating, but some other time? Cymbeline?"

"Some other time," Cym said. "Have a nice evening, and congratulations."

Cymbeline

The moment Emma and Peter walked away, I turned to Viktor, who had sat back in his chair. A flush had reddened his cheeks. In general, he appeared chagrined, which only gave me further joy. He deserved to be uncomfortable. It was clear to me now that he'd orchestrated a courtship of Emma to make me jealous. Obviously, her fiancé had been back east all this time. I suddenly liked this Emma more than I had only moments before.

"Emma's engaged?" That's all I said. When we were kids and Papa wanted either Flynn or me to confess to something, he always started with an innocuous question to see how fast he could get the truth out of us.

"Yes, well." Viktor straightened a fork and avoided looking at me.

"Yes, well, what? Are you devastated? Do you need my shoulder to cry on?" I grinned at him.

He dabbed at the corners of his eyes in an overdramatic fashion. "I'm crushed. I had no idea her heart belonged to another."

I laughed. "You're quite the actor. Did you concoct the whole thing up to make me jealous?"

He grinned back at me. "You think a lot of yourself, Miss Barnes."

"I don't know if I should be flattered or angry." For months now, he'd played me perfectly. Knowing my competitive nature, he'd planted the idea in my mind that he was courting someone else, thus forcing me to confront my feelings. If I weren't so disgusted with him, I'd have felt admiration. He knew me. Knew how I would respond.

"Was it working? Were you jealous?"

"Obviously not," I said.

"Liar. Why can't you admit you were jealous?"

"I might have been a tiny bit. Just this much." I held up thumb and index finger to indicate about a half inch.

He laughed. "I knew it."

"Don't be smug." I waved my napkin at him. "You should be ashamed of yourself."

"Why? Have you lost sleep pining away for me?"

"I sleep like a baby every night," I said.

The server appeared with our main courses. He set them in front of us and then swept away bread crumbs before walking away backward as they were trained to do. Flynn and Phillip put their staff through a vigorous schooling before they were allowed to interact with customers.

I sipped from my water, then picked up my fork. Inside my chest, a warmth had come. Like warm tea with honey on a cold day. Viktor didn't love Emma. He still loved me.

"Your mouth just curled up like a satisfied cat after a saucer of milk," Viktor said. "It's not becoming." The way he was smiling at me made me think otherwise.

"That was a dirty trick," I said.

"I was spending time with a friend. I can't be held responsible for your assumptions."

"Don't act innocent with me. You knew exactly what you were doing."

"What if I did? What if I knew the way to your heart was to fire up your competitive nature?" Viktor asked.

"You do seem to have a good understanding of my terribleness."

"Yes, indeed." He raised both eyebrows. "And?"

"And you don't seem to mind, which I don't really understand. I'm beastly, and everyone knows it."

"I welcome a challenge, like our hero in *Taming of the Shrew*.'"

"I'm not like Kate. Am I?"

"You're a bit like her, which is one of the many qualities I admire about you. You and Kate have your own minds and no patience for the ways of convention."

Despite what many women might have thought about being compared to Kate, I was flattered. I grinned at him. "You and your Shakespeare. I might be wild, but you're odd."

"I'm myself," Viktor said.

"Unapologetically so."

"Thank you."

"That wasn't a compliment," I said, teasing.

"Ah, too bad, because I would say the same about you. You're you, and no one has ever made you deviate from your convictions."

I'd never thought of it before, but he was right. We were uniquely the same that way. Unapologetically ourselves. Could we be thus while together?

"Can you just give in and admit you like me a little and allow me to court you?" Viktor asked.

"You've gone to all this trouble to make me jealous. I suppose I owe you for that. We can't have all that effort go to waste."

"How generous of you."

"You're welcome." I poked at my trout, pleased. Again, a warmth washed over me. Was this what it was to be in love? "May I ask you something?"

"Anything."

"Will we still be ourselves if we're together?"

"Is that what you're worried about?" Viktor asked, soberly.

I nodded. "Quite a lot actually."

"I believe so. In fact, together we might become even better than we were before. Regardless of the answer, there's only one way to find out."

"Eat your fish," I said.

"Whatever you wish, Miss Barnes."

THE NEXT MORNING, AS THE SUN ROSE IN THE EASTERN SKY, I pulled up to Viktor's house. I'd dressed in an old pair of knickers I'd found in the back of the closet that had been left behind by one of the twins. They were too big, but I held them up with a leather belt tied like a bow around my hips. I'd pulled a sweater on over my undergarments. Over it all, I wore Papa's man's flannel peacoat he used for outside work. It dwarfed me but would be warm.

A layer of frost crunched under my leather boots as I made my way to the front door of Viktor's cottage. The boys had done a good job on the place. Situated between trees and painted white with black shutters, I had the sensation of walking into a fairy tale. A gurgling from the creek to the left of the house accompanied the call of a flock of geese who flew overhead in a vee shape in the pale blue sky.

Viktor opened the door before I had the chance to knock. He smelled of shaving soap and wore a white sweater with a collar that nestled near his ears. An orange scarf hung loosely around his neck. My breath hitched at the sight of his green eyes, still puffy from sleep. What would it be like to wake next to him each morning? To turn over and see his face every day of my life?

"Good morning." He frowned at me. "You're late."

"I'm not. It's exactly six a.m." I lifted my leather glove away from my wrist to show him my delicate watch.

"Early is on time. On time is late."

"What's late then?" I liked this bossy side of him. He'd always been so unflappably pleasant that I often found myself wishing I could goad him into a fitful state.

"Late is inexcusable," Viktor said as he stepped out to his front porch, closing the door behind him. I couldn't tell if he was teasing or not. "As in, don't bother showing up at all." He held out his hand. "Give me the watch. You'll break it with what I have planned for you."

I gulped. "What've I gotten myself into?"

"You want to win?"

"Yes."

"Then don't ask questions."

Unlikely, I thought. I was full of questions. "How early is early?" I followed behind him, feeling momentarily like a small dog following behind its bigger, faster friend.

"Ten minutes or more." He stopped under a maple tree where a rope had been looped around a thick branch. I guessed the branch to be about fifty feet up. Rocks of various sizes were set about the grass.

Tomorrow, I vowed to myself, I'd be thirty minutes early and roust him out of bed.

"Did you eat?" Viktor asked.

"An apple on the way over."

"Tomorrow eat eggs. You're going to need the energy."

"But Lizzie doesn't have breakfast ready that early." I stopped myself, realizing how spoiled I sounded.

He raised one eyebrow. "Do you really not know how to boil an egg?"

"Um, not really." I'd never even peeled an egg for myself. Lizzie would have to teach me these things if I were to ever survive on my own. Or be someone's wife.

"Put that on the list of tasks to learn then," Viktor said. "An athlete must know how to feed herself."

"You're an entirely different Viktor this morning. What happened to the one who admires me?"

"It's for your own good." He tugged on the rope. "The goal is for you to be able to climb this rope by the time the first snow falls."

"Climb it? What's that to do with skiing?" Not that I didn't like the idea. Climbing trees had been a passion of mine as a child.

"I told you—you need strength if you're going to beat the men."

"Will strength help?"

"I believe so, yes."

"Then I'm here and ready to work."

He instructed me to take off my coat. "We'll get warmed up first."

We started by running as fast as we could to and from the rocks he'd set up. After that, we moved on to using the rocks in various ways: thrusting them overhead, squatting with them held to our chest, curling them in one hand up to our shoulder and back down again. We did push-ups and more sprints. Finally, it was time to try to climb the rope.

"Here's what you do." He held the end with his feet and used his bare hands, one after the other, to inch up the rope. I couldn't take my eyes off him. The muscles of his legs bulged under his denim pants.

When it was my turn, I looked down at my hands. I'd grabbed a pair of worn leather gloves from several seasons ago, not wanting to wreck my good ones. "Better with or without?" I asked.

"As long as you can grip, then I'd recommend them."

"Why don't you have any?"

"I'm tougher than you," Viktor said.

That was enough. I tore the gloves off my hands and tossed them under the tree.

I stood next to the rope and looked all the way to the top. I wasn't intimidated by much, but conquering that rope looked daunting, especially after seeing Viktor climb as if it were nothing.

He told me to bring the rope between my legs and anchor it with my feet. "Then, go one hand over the other until you get to the top."

I did as instructed. Once I had the rope between my legs and held loosely with my feet, I clenched my stomach and tried to pull myself up. I managed one hand over the other and then one more. That was as far as I got. I let go and plummeted to the ground. Fortunately for me, it wasn't but a foot to drop.

"Do it again." Viktor picked up my gloves from the ground and slapped them against my shoulder. "But for goodness' sake, put on your gloves. Your hands will be so torn up by the end of the day you won't be able to try again tomorrow."

"Fine." My hands were raw, chapped, and cold after only one attempt. After I had the gloves back on, I faced the rope once more.

I tried five more times with no more success than the first. Finally, I had to admit defeat. "It's as far as I can get." I sat on the cold ground and leaned against the tree, panting.

"We'll try again tomorrow."

I might have changed my mind about his bossiness being attractive. At the moment, I wanted to smack him. If I'd been able to raise my arm, that is.

My muscles burned by the time we were done with the rope. For having gone no higher than when I'd started, I was exhausted, mentally and physically.

"Come inside. I'll get you some water," he said. "And some eggs and toast."

I grabbed my coat from where I'd hung it on the bush and hobbled behind him. How would I endure another day of this?

"Is this really going to help me?" I asked.

"Perhaps you don't want to work this hard?"

I gave him a scathing glare and handed him my coat. He

hadn't even seemed to break a sweat. However, the perspiration under my clothes had cooled on my warm skin. I shivered and hugged myself. "I'm a little cold. Do you have any tea?"

"I'll make us some." Viktor hung both our coats in the closet. I liked the look of them together. "You need to bring a change of clothes from now on."

"Good idea."

His cottage was bare, other than a chair set close to the stone fireplace and a rickety-looking table in the dining room with two more chairs. The kitchen, situated at the back of the house, had a decent-sized stove and icebox. A cup was overturned, drying on a towel, as well as a lone plate and one fork. He'd cooked and washed up, all for one. What would it be like to live alone? I might never know, given the size of my family.

"You need furniture," I said. The room smelled pleasantly of wood shavings and was empty enough that our voices echoed.

"You don't find my furnishings adequate?" Viktor asked.

"Not if you plan on marrying."

"Do I plan on marrying?" Viktor's mouth curved upward in a smile.

"I suppose it depends on the girl. If the right one came along, for example."

"Indeed."

"Indeed," I said.

He told me to sit on the floor and reach for my toes. "You need to stretch after such strenuous exercise."

Wincing, I dropped to the floor in front of the fire. "Are you trying to kill me?" I bent over my legs and groaned. "Everything hurts already."

"Give it a few weeks. You'll be fine." His usual affable tone had returned. He set the table with two napkins and two forks. "Just give me a minute and I'll get some food in your stomach."

"I like you better when you're not barking out orders."

He set a teapot on the stove. "You'll thank me later."

"We'll see." I continued my stretching until my legs seemed

less tight. By that time, Viktor had scrambled up eggs and cut slabs of bread.

"Shall we eat?" He pointed at the table. "Sit. I'll serve us up."

"I don't know any men who can cook." I sat in one of the spindly chairs at the table.

"When we were young, my parents worked a lot. Isak and I had to learn how to do household tasks." He placed a steaming plate of eggs and one of the pieces of bread in front of me.

My stomach growled. "This looks very good."

He sat across from me with his own plate, and we said a quick prayer before tucking into our breakfast. This was nice, I thought. Natural. Would this be what it was like if we were married? Eating in compatible silence?

"Will your father be upset to learn you're spending time alone with me?" Viktor asked as he pushed away his empty plate.

"I don't know. I've not thought about it." Young ladies weren't supposed to be alone with young men. But this was Viktor. My family trusted him. "I don't think he would, because it's you. Like Li and Fiona. He knows you two take good care of us." I stretched and got up from the table. "I have to get back. Poppy and I have a few stops to make today."

He reached into his pocket and pulled out my watch. "Don't forget this."

I gingerly got to my feet and held out my hand. "Thank you."

He placed the watch in my hand but instead of letting me go, covered mine with his and pulled me gently toward him. "May I have a kiss?"

He circled one arm around my waist.

A girlish squeak escaped. "Now? But I'm wearing knickers and I must smell atrocious."

"No, you don't." He yanked off my hat and tossed it to the floor. My curls, happy to be free, bounced back into place. "You're a little dirty, but you smell as lovely as you always do."

"One before I go?"

"Yes, just one." He leaned down and brushed my lips with his.

A shiver ran through me. I wrapped one arm around his neck. "You're much more likable now than you were a half hour ago." He smelled of coffee and the outdoors.

"Enough of that. Off you go." He tucked a curl behind my ear. "Even your ears are beautiful. Like shells."

"Just one more couldn't hurt anything, could it?" I asked.

"It might, but we don't care." He leaned down and captured my mouth with his. I reached up with my fingers to touch his hair. That hair! Like a down feather.

I deepened our kiss, opening myself to him.

A faint groan rose out of his chest. I'd have thought it would scare me, but instead it made my skin tingle. My legs felt as if they were made of liquid. A fog settled between my ears. What was happening to me?

He seemed to come to his senses first, letting me go and walking over to the window. With his back to me, he took in several deep breaths. I could almost see the muscles under his shirt as his back expanded and contracted. My fingers tensed. What would it feel like to run my hands down his back?

"Viktor?"

He turned slowly from the window, wearing an expression I'd never seen before. His features twisted into various shapes as if something pained him. What was this? Fear? Wide-shouldered, tall Viktor Olofsson afraid? The man who had bravely saved my sister from her captor without a second thought? Yes. And it was me he feared. "I've never known you to be afraid of anything, Viktor Olofsson."

"I'm not afraid," he said.

"You are. I can see it in your eyes."

He shook his head, then dipped his chin. "Cymbeline Barnes, if you break my heart, I might not recover. When it comes to you, I have no way of saving myself. You can't toy with me if you don't mean it. I've waited too long. I'm too in love with you." He lifted his eyes to mine. They blazed as if he were feverish. "Do you understand what I'm saying to you?"

I stood there, frozen for a moment. This was a choice, I thought. Whether to be brave or run away like a spoiled little girl. No, I would meet him here in this place of courage. That was it, after all. Love wasn't a game, as some of the great poets had suggested. Not with Viktor, anyway. Not with anyone who let themselves be as vulnerable as he was now. "I understand."

And I did. I had the power to break this giant man. But I wouldn't. Not now. Not after the way he'd carved that confession from his chest and handed it to me. "I won't hurt you." I almost added, *not if I can help it.* But for the first time, I understood that I *could* help it. All of this was in my command.

"I'd do anything for you," Viktor said. "Anything you wanted."

"But what do *you* want?"

"You. Just you. Love's the only adventure I've ever wanted."

I went to him and let him take me into his arms. We did not kiss this time. Instead, our hearts beat together as we stood in the room with only one chair. Would there soon be two? "I'm a lot to take on."

"I know. Believe me, I know."

I smiled against the fabric of his shirt and nestled closer.

Viktor

Every morning for a week, Cymbeline showed up at ten to six ready for her training session. I kept upping the regimen but as I suspected, there was nothing I could do to break her. If she ever wanted to complain, I certainly never heard it from her. My adoration and admiration for her grew to new levels. Ones I wasn't entirely certain were reciprocated.

Other than the way she kissed me.

We ended every session with a few kisses. Ones that kept me awake at night despite my physical exhaustion.

After the end of an hour of intense exercise, we were inside my house having coffee and pieces of Lizzie's bread and cheese. After the second day, Cym had started to bring a basket of food with her that Lizzie had put together for her the night before.

I tore a chunk of bread from the loaf. "What have you told Lizzie about why you need breakfast in a basket?"

"She didn't ask," Cymbeline said. "My family seems to have accepted my eccentricities. No one questions me much these days."

"What about your clothes? Do they wonder about that?" Today, she'd dressed in a flannel shirt and one of the pairs of knickers that she said she'd found in the back of a closet.

"I told them I meet a friend for sport to prepare for the upcoming ski season."

"Do they know it's me?" I asked.

"Oh, goodness no. They'd have us married by Christmas if I told them that."

I laughed. "Would that be so bad?"

I put a slice of cheese between two pieces of bread. "I feel as if I need two breakfasts these days."

"Me too." She took a bite of her bread and chewed before speaking. "After this, I spend the day working with Poppy. By the time lunch comes, I'm hungry enough to eat for three men."

I looked out the window. The sky had the close, white feeling that came before a snowfall. "Looks like we'll get our first snow today."

"I hope so. I can't wait to get on the slopes." She took a big sip of milk, then wiped the mustache away with her napkin. Just then, she looked like the little girl I'd first known. God, I loved her. "I overheard Phillip tell Papa that the new jump is finished."

"New? What was wrong with the old one?" They'd built it last year after Chamonix, hoping to attract jumpers to the mountain. From what I could tell, the idea had worked. Word spread throughout Colorado that the Emerson Pass ski mountain had a slope, bringing daredevils excited to try something new. None of them could beat Cymbeline. However, the men coming from afar might.

"They wanted to make sure it's good enough for the competition." Cymbeline sat back in the chair and placed her arms over her midriff. "That was the best cheese and bread I ever had."

I nodded in agreement. "It's the fresh air and hard work."

She'd taken off her cap when we sat down for breakfast. The perspiration from the exercise had made her hair even curlier. I reached across the table to put a finger through one for a second. A smudge of mud streaked one of her cheeks. "I'm a mess, aren't I?" Cymbeline asked.

"Not to me."

She placed her cheek in one hand and looked over at me. "They announced the official dates and sent it out through the newspaper. Papa said it will be in all the papers across America." A slight tremor in her voice caught me by surprise. I'd never heard her admit any nervousness or apprehension about our scheme.

"No. No you don't." I waggled a finger at her.

"What?"

"No nerves. We're in this far. We're going to do this."

She brushed a crumb from the table into her hand and let it fall onto her plate. "I started thinking about Papa and Mama. What if I embarrass them?"

"You won't. They know how you are. What you want. It shouldn't even surprise them."

"True. But this feels different somehow. Deceitful. I've never done anything my family didn't know about."

"Your sisters know," I said. "Your family hasn't seemed to mind when you girls want to do something. Josephine opened the library. Fiona plays music."

"Yes, but I'm pretending to be someone I'm not."

"Is this nerves or conscience?" I asked.

Cym shook her head. "I don't know. It's just that I'm a Barnes. I hate the thought of making anything difficult for my parents."

I smiled. "What about Flynn?"

She rolled her eyes. "He's fine. Flynn's like me. He bounces. And nothing makes him mad for long."

"This is for yourself," I said. "And to prove to the world that women can jump. Even if it doesn't mean anything in our lifetime, someday it might."

A fleeting smile crossed her face. "That's true. Like the women you told me about."

"That's right. You keep your eye on the prize."

THAT AFTERNOON, I WAS COMING OUT OF THE BANK TO HEAD to my parents' for lunch when I saw Addie Barnes sitting on the steps of her father's office building. Slumped over her legs, I thought at first she might be asleep.

"Addie?" I asked as I approached. "Why aren't you at school?"

She lifted her head to look at me. My stomach clenched at the sight of her wan face and purple smudges under her eyes. She blinked a few times as if trying to remember who I was.

I drew closer. "Are you all right?"

"Yes, I'm waiting here until lunch is over. At school," she added, as if I were unsure about where she should be at this very moment.

Was that allowed? When we were in school, Miss Cooper would never have let us leave the premises unless one of us had to go home to help our parents. "Does your teacher know?"

She looked away, evasive. "I don't think she noticed."

I sat on the steps near her. "Why wouldn't you want to stay at school for lunch?" Had one of the children done something to her? Driven her away?

"I'm not feeling well. I don't want to be around food."

"Your stomach hurts?" I asked.

She nodded and then folded over, resting her forehead on her knees.

I scooted closer. "How about if I take you home? You should be in bed."

She made a listless sound and then fell over onto her side. My pulse raced as I scooped her up in my arms and headed back across the street to where my car was parked in back of the bank. She weighed no more than one of the rocks Cym and I had used for training that morning.

Mrs. Johnson was outside her store sweeping the sidewalk. She stopped what she was doing to come scurrying toward me. "Viktor, can I help?"

"Can you call out to the Barnes house for me? Tell them I've got Addie and she's not well. I'm going to take her over to see one of the doctors."

"I saw both doctors head out earlier on house calls," Mrs. Johnson said. "I'll call around to see if I can find one of them after I call out to Quinn's house. Take Addie home. She'll be more comfortable there. As soon as I get either Theo or Dr. Neal, I'll send them out to the house."

"How will you know where to look for the doctors?"

She waved me away. "I know everything that goes on around here."

I knew this to be true. Mrs. Johnson was one of the mothers in our town. All of us obeyed her without question, as we would have Mrs. Barnes, Mrs. Cassidy, and my own mother.

The ground was frozen in the parking lot behind the bank. My nice shoes had slippery soles, so I walked with care even though my instinct was to run as fast as I could.

I put her in the back seat and covered her with a blanket I had in the back. Her pink scalp showed through her thin hair. She was sick. Very sick. If I didn't know better, I'd think she was starving to death.

By the time I reached the Barneses', both Lord and Mrs. Barnes were waiting by the front entrance. I parked and got out to help them carry Addie inside but Lord Barnes beat me to it, lifting Addie up out of the back and heading across the driveway with his wife following at his heels. It's not a scene I would soon forget, I thought, as I traipsed behind them. Tall, powerful Lord Barnes with his tiny daughter in his arms seemed as helpless as the sick child he carried.

Once inside the foyer, I ripped off my hat and told them what I knew as quickly as the words would come out of mouth.

"She was just sitting there?" Mrs. Barnes asked.

"Looking dazed," I said. "We might want to call the school. I'm not sure her teacher knows where she went."

"I'll do it, if you can take her upstairs," Mrs. Barnes said to her husband.

I stood there, awkward, unsure if I should stay or go, then remembered that Mrs. Johnson had said she would try to find one of the doctors. "Did Mrs. Johnson tell you she would call around and send one of the doctors out immediately?"

"Yes, she did. I can't thank you enough, Viktor. You seem to always be right where we need you when we need you. Will you do me a favor and go down and tell Lizzie and Jasper what's going on?"

"Yes, of course."

She turned away to use the telephone. I knew my way and took the stairs two at a time down to the kitchen. Lizzie and Jasper were there, eating lunch at the table in the corner. Scents of herbs and butter made my stomach growl. Steam rose from a pot on the stove. The small window on the door that led outside was covered in fog.

"Viktor, what on earth's brought you around?" Lizzie stood, wiping her hands on the front of her apron.

"I'm sorry to interrupt your lunch, but Mrs. Barnes sent me down to tell you that I've come home with Addie." I shrugged out of my coat, hot in the warm room. "She's sick." I once again gave my account of what had happened.

Jasper had risen by now as well and gone to the stove to put the kettle on. He moved silently, like a stealth animal. I'd not seen or heard him move.

"The wee girl. She needs to eat more," Lizzie said, fretting. "I make all her favorites, but lately she just pushes it all away. There's something wrong."

I nodded but didn't say anything further. What was there to say? I knew nothing of the situation, only that it was dire. They already knew that.

Jasper excused himself to go upstairs to help Mrs. Barnes with whatever she needed.

"My poor husband. He worries himself sick over all the children." The teapot whistled, and Lizzie scampered over to take it from the stove. "He thinks of them as partly our kids, you know."

"You've been with the family a long time," I said. "It's understandable."

"Have you eaten lunch?" Lizzie wore her silver-and-brown hair in a bun at the back of her neck. There was always something a little messy about her, as if she were in too much of a hurry to worry about tidiness. Today, she had a smudge of flour on her neck and what looked like berry jam in her hair. Her round cheeks were pink, and a sheen of perspiration shone from her forehead. As she grew older, she grew plumper and jollier. Soon, she would look like Mrs. Claus from one of the picture books I'd enjoyed as a child.

"No, ma'am. I was headed to my mother's when I saw her."

"Oh dear me. Have a seat. I'll put a plate together."

Mere minutes later I was seated at the table with heaps of potatoes, carrots, and roast beef on my plate. "This is very kind of you," I said. "But I feel terrible imposing on you this way."

Lizzie patted my shoulder. "Think nothing of it, young man. You've done enough for this family that you're welcome anytime. Would you like a biscuit?"

"I couldn't pass up one of your biscuits." I picked up my fork and dug in. The meat melted on my tongue. "Lizzie, no one cooks like you."

"Bless you," Lizzie said. "I wish little Addie would think so."

"How long has she been like this?" I asked.

"Months now. Lately she's worse." Lizzie poured herself a cup of tea and sat down across from me. "I can't help but feel it's my fault. If only I could tempt her with a recipe."

I swallowed a soft, sweet carrot. "I'm sure it's nothing to do with your cooking. She must be sick."

"Theo will fix her. He has to. We couldn't bear to lose her." She scooped another spoonful of sugar into her tea and stirred. "Do you know she was the sweetest of all the babies born in this house. Barely made a peep. Never cried. Mrs. Barnes used to go into the nursery at night to make sure she was still breathing. The little angel would be fast asleep. She was the prettiest baby, too. Fat with those big blue eyes. I don't understand what's happened."

What words of comfort could I provide? From what I'd seen today, we all had reason to worry.

Cymbeline

Snow had started to fall by the time I headed home late that afternoon. My heart leapt with excitement as it began to stick. If it kept going like this, I'd be on the slopes soon. Finally, I would get to start actually training for the event instead of tossing rocks about with Viktor. Pulling into our garage, a shiver went through me. A feeling of worry overcame me. Something wasn't right.

I sprinted across the yard and into the house. "Hello? Anyone home?" I called out as I hung my coat in the closet.

"In here," Mama said.

I found her in the sitting room. She seemed to have shrunk in size from when I left in the morning, and her eyes were red and puffy. "Mama, what's the matter?"

She tapped under her eyes with a lacy handkerchief. "It's Addie. She's not well."

"What's wrong with her?"

"We don't know. Viktor found her outside your father's office, just sitting there, disoriented. He brought her home. Theo's up with her now."

"Viktor did?"

"Yes, he seems to be in the business of taking care of all the Barnes sisters."

Bless Viktor. Always there when we needed him. I put that aside to focus on my sister. "How bad is she? What's wrong with her?" I thought back to that morning. I'd not taken them to school. But at breakfast, she'd seemed her usual self—pale and quiet.

"Your father and Theo sent me down here. My fussing was making everything worse."

"But isn't it just one of her colds? She'll be fine." Wouldn't she?

"She's not strong. Not since she was about two years old. She's too thin but never seems to have an appetite. I've seen her drag herself out of bed in the morning and then is listless and disinterested in most everything. Even her studies have worsened. Last night, I peeked in on them before I went to bed. She was still awake, lying there in the dark."

"How strange." Last evening at dinner, she'd seemed as though she could barely keep her eyes open.

"She said she was tired but couldn't sleep. I don't know what to do."

I patted Mama's hand and tried to think of something to say, but the boulder on my chest prevented me from thinking of anything helpful. My little Addie. Had we all been avoiding the truth? Was there something truly wrong with her? Would she not make it to adulthood? No, that couldn't be. She had to get better. We'd gotten the twins back from the war. We couldn't lose Addie right here at home where we were supposed to be safe.

"I knew better than to send her to school this morning. She's missed so many days, though," Mama said. "She looked so weak and tired."

"Don't blame yourself."

"The rest of you have always been so robust. I've never had to worry about your health, but Addie's fragile."

From the foyer came the sound of the front door opening and closing, followed by footsteps. Seconds later, still in her overcoat, Delphia appeared. She stomped across the wood floors to stand before us. "What's wrong with Addie? Tell me, please. Now."

"We're not sure," I said.

Delphia looked at me and then to Mama. "How can you not be sure? You're grown-ups."

"Theo's with her," Mama said. "He's going to help us understand better."

Delphia's bottom lip trembled. "One of the girls at school said she's probably dying. Is that true?"

"No, that's not true. She's going to get better." Mama held out her arms to our little ball of fury and took her in her lap.

Delphia laid her cheek against Mama's chest. "I hate Celeste. She's the one who said it. She was telling everyone how she saw Addie fall and how she's going to be dead before spring."

I gasped. "She said that?"

Delphia raised her head from Mama's chest to look at me. "She's a pig with a lying mouth."

An image of a pig with an apple stuffed in its mouth came to me. Maybe a little girl named Celeste needed an apple in her mouth to keep her quiet.

Fidgety, I put another log of wood on the fire. Outside, the light continued to fade. I shivered, cold. Last week, every muscle in my body screamed out to me every time I moved. Apparently, I'd grown accustomed to my morning exercise, because today it had lessened to a dull ache. I was strong. If only I could give Addie some of my strength.

Hugging myself, I went to the window. A chiffon-like layer of snow covered the front yard. The tracks from my car were still evident but would soon be covered as well. Fluffy flakes tumbled from the sky. As I'd done since I was a child, I sat in the window seat and followed a single snowflake as it fell onto the ground.

What could I do for Addie? What could any of us do? Cut

open our veins and pour our healthy blood into her? Fill her with the robustness of the rest of us? Each of us would if we could. Even if it meant having less for ourselves.

Theo came into the room, carrying his medical bag. "Papa's with her," Theo said.

Delphia jumped from Mama's lap and ran to him. She wrapped her arms around his legs. "Did you make her well?"

"She's resting," Theo said. "When she fell, she knocked her head on the railing. She has a bump the size of an egg."

He came to sit across from Mama. Delphia shuffled over to the window seat. I helped her take off her coat and patted the cushion. She hopped up and snuggled beside me.

"Theo? Do you have any idea of what could be wrong with her?" Mama asked.

"Her main ailment is malnourishment," Theo said. "She's so thin her ribs show even through her nightshirt. I noticed tufts of her hair on the pillow too. How long has that been going on?"

Mama flushed and looked down at her hands. "About a month now."

"She needs nutrients," Theo said gently.

"I've begged her to eat more," Mama said. "She always says she's not hungry."

"I try to get her to eat too," Delphia said, sounding older than her eight years. "It's no use."

We'd all noticed how she picked at her food or pushed it around her plate to make it seem as if she'd eaten more than she had. I'd thought she needed more exercise. She was always curled up with a book, even when we were down at the creek in the summer for a swim. The rest of the Barnes family ate with gusto, but we were active. Maybe that's all she needed? But without energy to do so it was a vicious circle.

"She needs more outside time." I didn't know if it were true but I wanted it to be. "More fresh air."

"I wish it were that simple," Theo said. "Or that I had better answers for us."

He had told me many times that there were still many things we didn't understand when it came to human health.

Theo stood and wandered over to the fireplace, warming his hands above the flames. "I'm bewildered. She won't talk to me, either. I feel there's more to this than she's telling me, but she buries her head when I ask questions." He turned slowly to face Mama. "But I'll not give up until I figure out what's wrong with her."

"You don't think it's an emotional reason?" Mama asked in a small voice. "A reason why she won't eat?"

"Like what?" I asked. "What would make a person not want to eat?" I couldn't fathom one idea.

"Sadness," Theo said. A shadow crossed his face. "Like our mother."

"No, that can't be it," I said. "She has nothing to be sad over."

"Sometimes it doesn't matter," Theo said. "Brains are complex."

Furious at the idea of madness touching our Addie, I shook my head with such violence that it felt as if my brain were full of glass balls smashing into one another. "She's not sad."

"She is," Delphia said. "I hear her crying sometimes at night."

"What?" Mama turned to her, obviously astounded by this information. "Often?" Her tone sharpened as she fixed her gaze on my little sister.

Delphia folded over herself, as if she wanted to shrink and disappear. "I don't know. I'm sorry."

I put my arm around her and held her tightly. "It's all right. You don't have to remember exactly."

"I don't want Addie to know I know," Delphia said. "She would be mad at me."

Mama took in a deep breath and stood. "I'm sorry, darling. I didn't mean to sound sharp."

"You're not mad at me?" Delphia asked.

"No, absolutely not," Mama said. "Why would I be?"

"Because she's sick instead of me," Delphia said. "I'm naughty, so it should be me."

Mama strode over to the window seat and knelt on the floor next to Delphia. "I don't want either one of you to be sick. And you're not naughty, darling."

"I'm not?" Delphia's big blue eye filled with tears.

"You're spirited and full of life," Mama said. "I wouldn't want you any other way."

Delphia took in a shaky breath and thrust herself into Mama's arms.

Mama kissed the top of her head. "Do you want to go down and see if Lizzie has something for you to eat?"

"Yes, Mama." Delphia loosened her grip around Mama's neck, and together they stood.

"Off you go," Mama said, patting the small of Delphia's back.

Once my little sister was gone, Theo gestured for us to come closer. Mama and I sat together on the couch.

"There's something I need to tell you that I didn't want the little one to hear," Theo said. "Addie's stomach is distended. She's starving...quite possibly to death."

"Is it really that bad?" I asked as panic dried the inside of my mouth. *To death.* How could this be? If she didn't start eating, we would lose her.

He turned to me. "Cym, I think you should try to talk to her."

"Me?" I asked.

"He's right, Cym," Mama said. "She might tell you things she wouldn't tell me or Papa."

"I'll try," I said, inwardly wincing at the pinched look around Mama's mouth. I hadn't seen her like this since my brothers were away at war. Were we about to begin a war of our own? One in which we raced against time to save my sister? "I'll do my very best to understand what's behind this." Even as I said the words, I knew in my heart I was inadequate for the task. But try I would.

❦

I RAN INTO PAPA IN THE HALLWAY ON MY WAY TO SEE ADDIE. He greeted me with a grim smile. "Hello, sweetheart."

"They've sent me up to talk to her," I said quietly.

"If anyone can get her to open up, it's you. She looks up to you."

"Papa? I'm scared," I whispered.

He embraced me, smelling of pipe smoke and shaving soap. My papa. Once upon a time I thought there was nothing in the world he couldn't fix. If only I'd been right. "I'm scared too. But we mustn't give up hope."

I took in a deep breath and asked God for courage, then walked into my sisters' room.

Addie was sitting up in bed, propped against pillows. I had to fight tears. She looked small and tired, like someone who wanted to give up on life and be done with it. "Hi, baby sister. I heard you're feeling poorly."

"A little, yes." She nodded and drew the covers closer to her neck. "Is it your turn to watch over me? Did I take you away from helping Poppy?"

I sat in the chair next to the bed. "No, we had a short day today."

"I don't need all of you looking at me every minute of the day." She turned her face away from me. "Like I've done something wrong."

"We're all worried, that's all. You've done nothing wrong." I knelt on my knees close to the bed and pushed back a strand of her wispy hair from her clammy cheek. Her pink scalp reminded me of the underbelly of one of our piglets. How had I not noticed how thin her hair had become? I smoothed the bedcovers over her legs. Even through the thick quilt, I could see they were no rounder than twigs. "Tell me what's going on, Addie. Why aren't you eating?"

She slid further into bed, bringing the quilt up to her chin and staring at me with her big blue eyes. Her face seemed almost skeletal, with her once-golden-tinted skin taut over the bones. "I can't tell anyone. I'm embarrassed."

"You can tell me anything."

"Not this." She moved her gaze to the ceiling. A tear slipped from the corner of her left eye.

Papa had left one of his embroidered handkerchiefs on the bedside table. I took it and dabbed the dampness from her cheek. How could I get her to talk to me? A secret for a secret? "What if I told you something scary and embarrassing? Then we'd both be the keeper of each other's secret."

"You don't have any secrets. Do you?"

"I do. A big one." I folded Papa's handkerchief into a square. "Do you want me to tell you?"

She nodded. "But I don't know if I can tell you mine."

"All right, that's fine." I'd tell her anyway, hoping that it would open her up to sharing hers. I glanced at the doorway and got up to close it. One could never tell when another Barnes was lurking around a corner to eavesdrop. I sat on the side of the bed. "I'm dressing up as a boy so I can compete in the ski-jumping competition."

She blinked, as if she didn't know if she'd heard me correctly. "Oh. You're lying?"

"They won't let women compete, so I have no choice." I told her about Viktor and how he was training me every morning. "I want to get as strong as I possibly can before the competition."

"Aren't you afraid you'll get in trouble?"

"Nah. I've been in trouble a lot, so I'm accustomed to it."

"I want you to win," Addie said. "To show them all you're as good as any of those boys."

"I want that too." I placed my hand on her clammy forehead. "Can you tell me why you won't eat?"

She turned onto her side. The covers drew back so that I could see under her cotton nightgown. As thin as her arms and legs were, her poor tummy was as round as a ball.

I drew in a deep breath, fighting against the panic that swept over me. "Addie, you have to eat."

She covered her face with her hands. "I can't."

"Why? Sweetheart, tell me why."

She pressed her lips together as if the words might fall out of her mouth.

"If you tell me, maybe I can help. Please." The desperation caused my voice to rise. I had to be careful. Gentle. She must feel safe or I'd never get her to talk.

"Whenever I eat, my stomach cramps. Then I have to run to the toilet....and I have to go really bad. All day long, I feel like this. But only when I eat. If I don't eat, then my stomach doesn't hurt. Today I had breakfast. Mama made me, remember?"

There had been a battle at breakfast. I'd forgotten that, preoccupied with Viktor. Finally, Addie had given in and eaten the piece of bread Mama had insisted upon.

"Do you have an appetite?" I was starting to understand what she was saying to me. The consequences of eating were keeping her from eating, not a lack of hunger.

"Yes, I'm hungry all of the time. Until I eat, and then I'm sick."

"Why didn't you tell Theo?"

"I'm too embarrassed. I don't want anyone to know...about the bathroom. At school, I'm miserable unless I don't eat break-fast." She turned back to her side. Tears streamed from her eyes. "I would rather die than feel like this any longer. What if no one can help me?"

"Doctors heal people. Theo can fix you."

"I don't think so."

I dabbed at her cheek with the handkerchief. "Do you trust me?"

"Yes," she whispered.

"Then you have to let me help you. I'll tell Theo what you told me. With more information, he'll be better able to diagnose what's wrong. It's the only chance you have of getting better."

My eyes stung with tears. Was I right? Would Theo be able to figure it out if he had more information? "You've not told him anything?"

"No. I told them all the same thing—that I'm not hungry."

"You poor baby," I said.

"I'm sorry, Cym." She began to sob. "It's awful at school. Girls started noticing I was in the bathroom a lot. One day, they told everyone that it was me who had made the toilet smell bad."

I got onto the small bed and pulled her into my arms and stroked her hair. "I'm sorry, baby. We're going to make you well. None of this is your fault. Of course you haven't wanted to eat. No one would if they immediately felt sick afterward."

"Am I dying?"

"No. You're not dying. You're a Barnes. We're tough. We'll figure out what all this is about and you'll be well again. Do you hear me?"

"I hear you." She shuddered against me. "I don't want to go back to school. Everyone talks about me behind my back. I have no friends. Delphia's probably humiliated by me."

"Delphia loves you. She just wants you to get better. Don't think about those girls right now. You're to concentrate on getting better. Mama and Papa won't make you go back there ever again if you don't want to."

Her tense little body relaxed against me. "I'm so tired, Cym. And cold. Always cold."

"I know you are. Close your eyes. I'll stay with you until you fall asleep. But let's fix your pillows first." I got out of the bed and took one of the stacked pillows away so that she could lie down without craning her neck.

"You have to jump, Cym," Addie whispered. "For all the girls who can't. Or are too afraid."

"I'll do whatever you ask of me." I kissed her forehead and then sat on the edge of the bed and stroked her back until her even breathing told me she was asleep. After I put another blanket over her, I got down on my knees to pray. *Please, God, heal my sweet little sister. If one of us has to be sick, make it me.*

❧❦❧

FIONA WAS HOME BY THE TIME I WENT BACK DOWNSTAIRS. She'd been out all day teaching her piano students. By the worried expression, it was obvious she'd been filled in on the situation. Mama, Papa, and Theo were also there, talking quietly. They looked up expectantly when I approached.

"Anything?" Mama asked.

I sat down next to my brother. "She told me why she won't eat." I gave them the description as delicately as I could. "So, as you can imagine, she doesn't want to eat and then be sick. It's especially embarrassing for her when she's at school." I told them what she'd said about the other girls.

"Poor Addie," Fiona said. "How awful for her. I had no idea."

"She hasn't said a word about any of it," Mama said.

"Son, do you have any idea what could be ailing her?" Papa asked.

"No, I don't. But my guess would be something environmental," Theo said.

"Something around us?" I asked.

"That's correct. Something she's breathing or eating that's making her sick. I'll put a call in to some colleagues in the city and see if anyone has seen a patient with these same symptoms. I can't think of anything from my textbooks, but I'll go over them tonight. It can't be in our water or food, or the rest of us would be sick too."

"Unless it's something that just Addie is bothered by," Fiona said.

Theo nodded. "An allergic reaction of sorts."

"Like Mrs. Cassidy and the mold," I said. Last year, Theo had figured out that Mrs. Cassidy was being sickened by mold on a box of old letters. Since his diagnosis, she'd made a full recovery.

Theo had began to pace back and forth in front of the fireplace. We all felt the urgency to find out what was making her sick now but perhaps no one more than the doctor of the family.

"There's only one thing to do." Mama brushed her skirts. "We must pray with all our might."

"Yes, Mama," Fiona said. "We will."

"I'm going to sit with her," Mama said.

"I'll go with you." Papa embraced Theo. "God's by our side through this. The burden's not yours alone."

"I know, Papa." Theo set his jaw the way he did when he was determined to do something. "I'll figure this out if it's the last thing I ever do."

When the three of them were gone, Fiona sank into the big armchair. "Cym, I'm scared."

"Me too." I plopped down next to her. She tucked a throw blanket around our legs. We snuggled as we had when we were little and would read together by the fire. For a long time we remained thus, wrapped together for warmth and comfort. I don't know if she prayed as hard as I but knowing my angelic Fiona, she probably did.

Viktor

The morning after I'd delivered Addie to the Barneses, I didn't expect to see Cymbeline. For one thing, at least twelve inches of snow had fallen overnight. In addition, I assumed she would be too worried about Addie to want to leave the house. However, she arrived around eight but without the pink glow of excitement that typically graced her cheeks. She'd come on skis instead of by car.

I was outside clearing a pathway to my cottage when she arrived. The snowplow had not yet come through. Typically they didn't get to me until midmorning. Being Saturday, I didn't have to worry about getting into work. Setting aside my shovel by my front porch steps, I trudged though the snow to greet her. "I didn't expect you," I said.

"I couldn't stay in the house this morning. I needed to see you."

My stomach clenched, fearing the worst. "How's Addie?"

"The same. Which means, not good." She hugged her middle as if she were cold. "Thank you for bringing her home to us yesterday."

"Of course. I'm only sorry she's unwell."

"Viktor," she said in a small voice. "I'm terrified we may lose her. It's something with her stomach. Theo says she's starving to death. There's nothing I can do. That's the worst part of it. I want to *do* something. I'd take it all on myself if I could."

"We can't give up hope." I took both her hands. "Let's get you out of those skis and inside to get warm."

She nodded, then reached down to unbuckle the skis from her boots. Once she was out of the skis, I flung them over my shoulder. "What did you do? Leave at the first morning light?"

"Yes. The minute it was light enough to see, I headed out."

"Does your family know you came here?"

"They know. No one could sleep, worried about Addie. I fell asleep at some point and woke this morning terrified. But Addie was sleeping peacefully. Mama hadn't left her side, so Papa made her go to bed. It's all a mess." She gestured toward our training area under the trees. "Can we take a break today? My heart's not in it."

"One day of rest won't hurt you." I drew her into my arms and rested my chin on the top of her head. "It's cold out here when we're not moving."

"I guess not."

"Come inside." I took her by the hand, leading her into my cottage. I'd anticipated giving her a happy surprise this morning. My furniture had finally arrived yesterday. Delivered before the snow began to fall that morning, I'd imagined her delight at seeing the pretty pieces I'd picked out for my home. Last night, restless and anxious about Addie, I'd spent the entire evening arranging them in different locations around the room, settling finally on setting them around the fireplace.

She took off her jacket and handed it to me, then walked farther into the front room.

"Oh, Viktor, it looks nice. You didn't say they'd come." She went to the back of the sofa and ran her hand along the velvety material. I'd ordered it in dark blue from a fine shop in Denver. They'd taken months to finish. I'd been excited to show her, but now it seemed unimportant.

"They came yesterday morning, but now it doesn't seem as wonderful as I'd thought it would," I said.

"I know what you mean," she said. "Nothing seems as important as it did yesterday at this time."

I put a few more logs on the fire. "Sit, anyway. I'll pour you a cup of coffee. I've just made some."

"Thank you. Hot coffee sounds good."

A few minutes later, I returned with coffee and a few scones I'd picked up at Isak's bakery before the snow fell. I set the tray down on the new table and handed her a cup. "Scone?"

"No, thank you. Just coffee for now," she said.

I joined her on the couch. The cushions were so new that it seemed as though I was sitting on a large ball.

We sipped our coffee, and I ate a scone that seemed dry in my mouth. For once, I was at a loss as to what to say. Seeing her upset had quite undone me. Finally, I thought to ask if Theo had diagnosed Addie with anything specific. "Did your brother have any ideas?"

"No, he doesn't know what's wrong with her," Cymbeline said. "He's always known everything. All our lives, even when we were little, if we didn't know the answer to a question, we'd turn to Theo. He could always find the answer. I don't know what to think. The whole world has tipped on its side and nothing makes sense." She went on to describe Adelaide's symptoms—weight loss, listlessness, thinning hair. All of which I'd seen for myself, but she seemed to need to talk through it all with me. If it had been under different circumstances, I would have been delighted.

"Her stomach, Viktor. It's like this." She stretched her hands in the air across her midsection to indicate a roundness to her belly. "Theo said that's an indication of severe malnourishment. She says that when she eats, her stomach cramps. The other girls at school have been so cruel to her. They've said terrible things." Cym's fists clenched in her lap. "I want to kill them."

I almost smiled. Violence and aggression over despair were

Cymbeline's natural tendencies. "Theo and Dr. Neal are a great team. They'll figure out what's wrong and come up with a treatment."

She looked over at me. "Do you really think so?" The desperation in her eyes—this desire for me to be right—made my chest feel as if it were hollowed out by a rough blade. "What if it's cancer?"

Cancer. For which there was no cure. "Did Theo think so?"

"No. He didn't say so, but I lie awake all night thinking about it. There's cancer of the stomach, you know. What if that's it?"

"Theo would have suggested it," I said. *Please, God, don't let it be that. Not sweet Addie.*

"Yes, I suppose you're right." She rounded her shoulders and bent over to put her hands over her knees. "I'm frightened, Viktor. And suddenly, all this nonsense about the competition seems just that—selfish, self-centered drivel. I'm the silliest person in the world."

"You're passionate about sports. There's nothing silly about that."

"For the first time in my life, I'm wondering why I haven't focused on education instead of all this stupid obsession with being outside. Should I go to college? Maybe I would learn something that would actually help other people. Instead, I stayed here thinking only of myself."

I thought for a second about what to say. Although for some, finding their true purpose wasn't as obvious as others. However, I knew deep down we all had one. Each of us possessed a particular gift bestowed upon us by God. Our work was to find that talent and use it for good. Cymbeline's contributions would not come from scholarly pursuits. She was an athlete. A competitor. Being true to her dreams and aspirations would encourage other young women to do the same. It was only people like Cymbeline, who had the courage to try what hadn't yet been done, even at the expense of their personal lives, who moved society forward. I inched closer to her, catching one of her curls with my finger.

"Cym, pursuing what you're passionate about will have positive repercussions on others—in ways you'll never fully understand. You're a brave warrior and an inspiration to anyone who has been told they're not allowed to use the gifts God gave them."

She tilted her head in my direction. I put my arm around her slumped shoulders and pulled her close. "How come you're so wise?"

"I'm not, really," I said. "You've made me a better person."

"How could I make anyone better?" She brushed her fingertips against my knee, then rested her cheek against my shoulder.

"By being unapologetically you and never acquiescing to how the world wants to mold you."

She sniffed and wiped under her eyes with the heel of her hand. "You're full of so many words today. All the right ones."

"We have to trust that Theo will do what God put him here to do. Find the answers to questions. He'll figure out what's wrong with her. I truly believe it to be so."

"Addie told me I should jump," Cym said. "She said it was for all the girls who couldn't or wouldn't."

"She's right. You know that."

"Do I?"

"You do," I said.

We sat for a moment, listening to the crackle of the fire. The aroma of coffee wafted up from the pot and mingled with the woodsmoke. "What do you think your purpose is?" Cymbeline asked.

"Encouraging you to be as bold as you want to be?" I asked it as a question even though I knew there was no answer.

She nudged my ribs with an elbow. "For your sake, I hope that's not true."

I drew in a deep breath, taking in the sweet smell of her hair. "If it were, I'd be satisfied. To be by your side while you conquer the world would be more than enough for me. I'm a simple man, Cym. For better or worse, my dreams will be forever wrapped up in yours. That is, if you'll allow them to be."

"I'm here, aren't I?"

"True enough," I said.

"When I woke today, you're the person I wanted to talk to most. Isn't that strange?"

I smiled to myself. Not strange. Glorious.

৩৯৩

AFTER OUR TALK, CYMBELINE SEEMED SOMEWHAT rejuvenated and suggested we head out to the slopes as soon as the snowplow had come through. I agreed, eager to distract her.

A little after nine, Cymbeline and I stood on the patio of the lodge, taking in the beauty of the freshly fallen snow. When Flynn had first built the resort area, he'd put three ski runs down the middle of the mountain. Last year, inspired by the games in France, he'd added the ski jump, which consisted of the run itself along with the wooden platform. Steps from the bottom of the mountain led up to the starting area, whereas the other runs had pulley ropes.

Flynn came out, greeting us with a friendly wave. "Fancy seeing you two here."

"We came to ski," Cymbeline said. "You might be able to keep me from the competition but not the mountain itself."

"We're not officially open, you know," Flynn said. "But I have no intention of keeping my sister from the slopes."

"Why aren't you open?" Cymbeline frowned at her brother. "The snow's perfect."

"We plan on opening the runs tomorrow. Phillip wanted to give the pulley machinery a good check before people came."

"You don't mind if we try out the run?" I asked.

"Be my guests. Let me know what you think of the spectator stands we made." Flynn gestured toward the wooden platforms perched on either side of the jumping slope.

"Do you really think people will come?" Cymbeline asked.

"That's what we're hoping for," Flynn said. "I've put advertisements in all the major papers across the country."

"Where will people stay?" Cymbeline asked. "The lodge can't accommodate big crowds."

"They'll stay in Denver or Louisville and come up for the event," Flynn said. "It's going to be great business for Emerson Pass. Papa will be pleased."

"He's already pleased with you," Cymbeline said.

"I wonder sometimes," Flynn said.

I studied my friend for a moment. Was that what all this was about? Trying to please his father?

"I don't know why you think you have all this to prove," Cymbeline said.

Flynn tugged on her hat. "Are you still mad at me?"

Cymbeline shrugged as if she'd forgotten all about their argument. "Doesn't matter. As long as I can ski all winter then I don't really care."

"The mountain is yours." Flynn squinted up at the sky. "I'm going out to see Addie later this morning. Papa came by earlier. He and Mama didn't sleep much last night. He didn't look too good."

"None of us slept much." Cymbeline's voice wobbled.

"Theo will cure her," Flynn said. "I'm not worried."

"I am, but things always go your way, so maybe I should take your cavalier attitude." Cymbeline looked down at her boots.

"I refuse to go down the worry hole. It does no one any good." Flynn scratched his neck, obviously irritated. "Enjoy your morning. I should go."

He disappeared into the dining room, where staff were setting up tables for this evening's dinner.

"Let's go," Cym said. "I don't want to think about him today."

"Lead the way."

The snow was as soft as powder today. Carrying our skis on our shoulders, we started up the steep steps to the platform from which she would begin her speedy descent to the jumping-off point. Built into the side of the mountain, the wooden structure jutted out a good twenty meters before a steep drop-off.

As we climbed to the starting place, our boots made deep tracks. When we reached the top, we stopped to put our skis on.

"You ready?" I asked.

She pursed her lips as she looked out over the horizon. "You know what I read in the paper?"

"What's that?"

"There are people jumping at carnivals. As entertainment, not sport. There are women too. Sometimes they jump holding hands with a man."

"Are you suggesting we do that?" I laughed.

"It's embarrassing to all women."

I chuckled under my breath. "Some might think of it as romantic."

"It implies we can't jump by ourselves."

"No one thinks that of you," I said. "Go on. Show me how it's done."

I watched her as she glided gracefully onto the snow. "I won't get much speed in this powder," she called back to me.

"Is that an excuse?"

"Ha! Never." She sent me a sassy look before tearing down the hill. From where I stood on the platform, I had a good view of the jump itself and could watch her fly through the air like a bird with her skis in parallel and her body upright. A few seconds later, she landed smoothly on the snow below.

I'd never actually gone off the jump before, and standing here I was fairly certain I didn't want to. "Maybe I won't come down?" I called out to her.

She put a hand over her eyes and peered up at me. "Are you afraid?"

"Yes."

She laughed and gestured for me to come toward her. "It's fun. You'll like it."

I had a feeling I wouldn't, but I slid from the platform on the ski run and started down. Seconds later, I too, was flying. For a terrifying few moments, I was sure I would die. My landing was not as elegant as the lady's. I crashed into the snow and on my back like a bug.

"Viktor, you can do better than that." Cymbeline stood over me, laughing.

"I need to work on my landings." One of my skis had come off, and my hat was missing. Righting myself, I stood and managed to gather my ski. "But I don't think I will. I'll prefer watching, thank you very much."

Cymbeline squealed with glee. "At last, I've found something I can do that you can't."

"You do other things better than me." I grunted as I struggled to remain standing on my shaking legs. My heart continued to race, and sweat rolled down my back. Ski jumping was the worst sport ever invented.

She placed her hands on both hips. "Think of one thing. You were better at school. Skating, obviously. You're faster on the slopes."

"Actually, I'm not faster. And you're much, much prettier than me."

Expecting her to toss a snowball my direction, I braced myself for an onslaught. Instead, a dazzling smile lit up her face. "I couldn't agree more. I *am* much prettier than you."

"If I could get to you, I'd give you a big kiss to punish you for being so much better than me."

"Who says it would be a punishment?" She tilted her head flirtatiously.

"I see. I've now nothing to hold over you then?"

I unfastened the other ski and then trudged through the snow to the steps. By the time I arrived, Cymbeline had found my hat. She skied over to me and tugged it over my head. A gloved finger teased my earlobe. "Your ears are pink from the cold. You must keep your hat on at all times. And why is it that I can't kiss you?"

I swallowed as I rose to my full height. "No one said you couldn't. No one here, anyway."

"Good." She leaned over and kissed me soundly on the mouth. "Your lips are cold, too. We better head back up before I have to take you back to the lodge and give you hot chocolate like we do the little ones."

"Very funny." I brushed the snow from my sweater and knickers. Leaning against my skis, I peered at her, overcome by her beauty and energy. She belonged here. A creature made of sky and mountain air. And lo and behold, I was here with her. I was the man she wanted to kiss.

"What is it?" Her nose scrunched up as if she smelled something bad.

"Nothing. Just you."

"You too," Cymbeline said.

We smiled like a couple of children for a moment before she got back to the business at hand.

"What do you think? How did I do?" Cymbeline asked.

"Not bad, but you can do better."

"I know." Her brow wrinkled as a thought seemed to occur to her. "What if I bent over toward the skis slightly? Make myself more like a bird?"

I pondered that idea for a moment. It *would* make her more birdlike. Standing straight worked against the natural momentum. Almost like a bird fighting against the wind.

"If you're able to, it might help," I said.

"I'm going back up."

I watched her as she took the stairs up with her skis slung over one shoulder. Whatever anyone wanted to say about her decision to race as a man, no one could fault her work ethic.

While I waited for her to reach the top, I brushed snow from each step, working my way up one stair at a time. Not wanting to miss her next jump, however, I stopped midway and returned to my coaching seat.

During the subsequent jump, I could see her thinking about bending over, which might have distracted her from keeping her skis straight. She was shy of her first run because of it. Although I was hopeless at doing so myself, I could see that style was important to get the distance she wanted. I'd been right to have her training. She'd need strength to arrange her body and skis in the right ways.

We chatted about this for a moment before she trudged back up the stairs and tried again. For the rest of the morning, jump after jump, she worked to better her distance and technique. Her scores improved with each one. Finally, just before noon, she told me she was too tired and hungry to climb the stairs one more time and wanted to return home.

"You did well," I said.

"Not well enough, but I will."

Cymbeline

❧❧❧

I woke with a start when we pulled into our driveway. I'd fallen asleep in a car? In the middle of the day?

"I'm sorry," I said to Viktor. God, I hope I hadn't snored or drooled. "Did I do anything embarrassing?"

"Besides looking like a sleeping angel?"

"I'm sure that's not true." He made my tummy feel all warm when he said things like that. Love had turned me into a simpering fool already. "Thank you for this morning. I'm sure you had better things to do with your Saturday morning than spend it watching me jump."

"I can't think of anything more important."

"I'm not sure I could do this without you. How ridiculous I've become. Relying on a boy."

He smiled and reached over to caress the side of my face. "You're doing very well."

"We could go back up tomorrow afternoon," I said. "But there will be others on the mountain."

"You should ask your brother if we can have an hour before he opens to the public," Viktor said.

"Will that give us away?"

"No more than anything else will." Viktor turned to the

front window of his car. Snow had began to fall. "I should probably get home before the roads get bad again. I hate to leave you."

"I don't know if we'll be at church tomorrow. It depends on Addie."

"You're going to be the strongest jumper on that mountain. Or at least we'll try, right?" His green eyes were clear as he gazed across the seat at me.

"Thanks again." I looked around to make sure there were no prying Barnes eyes and gave him a quick kiss. "See you soon."

"Yes. Addie's in my prayers tonight."

I gave his hand one more squeeze before jumping from the car and heading inside to my family. It was nearing one, which meant everyone had probably eaten. Hopefully, Lizzie had something for me downstairs.

No, she wouldn't. She had Saturdays off, a tradition we'd always had. Staff had the entire day off, and the Barnes family took care of themselves. When I was a child, we'd loved Saturdays because it meant time in the barn with animals. Flynn and I especially had loved being outside doing physical activity.

I stopped in the foyer, listening for the sounds of my family. An eerie silence greeted me. My heart beat in my throat as I climbed the stairs. Grimacing from my already sore and stiff muscles, I hesitated at the top of the stairs before heading down the hallway to Addie's room. The door was ajar a few inches. I peeked my head through the space and was surprised to see Addie sitting up in bed looking surprisingly well. Mama was reading on the window seat.

"Hello?" I bustled into the room, buoyed by the sight of Addie with a slight pink in her cheeks. A history textbook was open on the bed. She was well enough to be studying? Surely this was a good sign?

"Hi, Cym," Addie said.

I rushed over to perch on the side of the bed. "Are you feeling better?"

"Yes, my tummy's been fine all day. I had some of Lizzie's broth and it didn't hurt me."

Mama had come to stand on the other side of the bed. "Theo wants to see how she reacts to certain foods. So far, we've only had broth. We're going to try the blandest of foods first."

As glad as I was that she was feeling better, having only broth wasn't enough food to make a full recovery. She needed to put on weight. "I'm so glad, pet," I said out loud. "What food will we try next?"

"Lizzie's working on some potato soup," Mama said. "She insisted on coming in on her day off to make it for Addie."

"Can I help?" I asked. "Where's everyone else?"

"Delphia and your papa are working in the barn today," Mama said. "Fiona had errands in town but should return any moment. She had to pick up her new dress for the dance next weekend."

The fall dance. Every second Friday in November, we had one to celebrate the start of our winter activities. If the pond in town had frozen over by then, we followed up with a skating party the next day. The dances had been Mama's idea. Skating was fun for all ages, but the dances were an opportunity for men to have an occasion to take their love out for a special occasion. I'd forgotten all about it with all the worry over Addie.

"Are you going, Cym?" Addie asked.

"I don't know," I said. Would Viktor like to take me? He hadn't said anything about it.

"Will Viktor take Emma?" Addie asked. "Are you going to be jealous if he does?"

"What do you know about all that?" I asked.

"I have ears," Addie said. "People talk."

"Well, little missy, if you must know, we've had a surprise twist in the story of Viktor and Emma."

Both Mama and Addie seemed to perk up with excitement. They both loved a good story.

"Viktor was only taking Emma around to make me jealous." I

sounded like our rooster crowing. "She has a fiancé who has arrived in town. I met him at the club the other night. Viktor had to confess that they were only friends and had hoped rile up my competitive nature."

"Did it work?" Mama's brown eyes sparkled.

"Yes, it did," I said, sounding less like the rooster. "I'm ashamed to say, I was terribly jealous and have had many dark thoughts about Emma Hartman."

Mama tutted. "Cymbeline, if you'd simply admit to your feelings, you'd save yourself a lot of troubles."

"Yes, Mama."

"Where have you been? You smell a bit ripe," Mama said as if she were only just noticing me.

"I've been practicing my ski jumps," I said. "With Viktor." I added this last part for dramatic effect.

"Really?" Mama asked.

"Didn't Flynn mention it?" I asked. "He saw us this morning."

"No, he hasn't been by," Mama said.

Strange. He'd said he was on his way to see Addie. Had something waylaid him?

"Shannon came by." Addie plucked a bookmark of a pressed violet from her study book. "She brought me this."

What had happened to Flynn? Had something come up after I'd seen him at the lodge? A spark of fear caused the hairs at the back of my neck to stand up. I could not seem to shake this worry that Flynn was involved with something he shouldn't be.

"Where did you get those knickers?" Mama asked. "Where have you been going every morning?"

"Out. For exercise." I hadn't thought anyone noticed my early-morning activities. Perhaps I was wrong? "I haven't woken you, have I?"

"My love, there's nothing that goes on in this house that I don't know about." Mama's voice was gentle, but a trace of concern gave it a slight edge.

"I'm sorry if I've disturbed you."

"You've woken me, yes. It's a mother's instinct. I always wake at the slightest sound. I've seen you leaving in the car every morning very early. I assumed you were meeting someone. Fiona reassured me that it's only Viktor. She said you two are tossing rocks about to get stronger. I can't imagine why."

"I'm training for skiing," I said.

"Skiing? " Mama's forehead crinkled in evident confusion. "Why would you need to prepare for skiing? Don't you just put the skis on and head down the mountain?"

I glanced at Addie. She hadn't yet returned to her history reading and seemed engrossed in our interchange.

"I'm building my endurance," I said. "For ski jumping mostly. Viktor's very good at coming up with ideas to make me stronger."

"It's so romantic," Addie said.

"Romantic? What's that to do with anything?" I tried not to smile but was unsuccessful.

"Have you finally fallen for Viktor?" Mama peered at me with narrowed eyes. The same look she'd often given me when I was little and she knew I'd been up to no good.

"Don't look so surprised. Isn't that what you've all wanted me to do?"

Mama smiled. "It is indeed. I've been waiting for a long time for you to come to your senses. There's not a finer man than Viktor."

"Why do you sound sad then?" Addie asked.

Mama did sound somewhat forlorn.

"Because I'll be losing another one. Another of my birds flying from the nest."

And flying off the edge of a mountain.

"Will you be married to him soon?" Addie asked in an excited voice, followed almost immediately by a dipping of her head. Tears gathered at the corners of her eyes.

"Addie, what's the matter? I'll still visit all the time. Like Jo."

She shook her head. "I might not live to see you in your wedding gown, and that makes me so very sad."

"Oh, darling." Mama crumpled like a tissue.

"Addie," I said. "This is utter nonsense. You're not dying. Theo and Dr. Neal are very good doctors, and they're going to make you better. Look how much better you're feeling today."

"But people need food to live," Addie said. "What if I can only eat chicken broth? I'll not grow round and strong like the rest of you on that alone."

My sister might be ill, but she wasn't feeble-minded. She knew the risks and the reality of her illness.

"Your sister's right, darling." Mama seemed to have recovered somewhat. She dabbed under eyes. "You simply mustn't think about anything but how much better you'll be soon."

"I'd like to live." Addie spoke in a small, soft voice that trembled with emotion. "But I've always thought I'd leave the world sooner than all of the people I love. Except for Grandmother, of course."

"You're not leaving this world before me," I said. "Or Mama or Papa. You're going to get strong and outlive us all. How about that?"

"I do so want to live. I want to become a teacher like Mama was. Then I'd like to have a beau and get married and have babies."

"You're going to," I said. *Please, God, let it be so.* I decided to change the subject and return to Viktor as a way to distract them. "Viktor's awfully mean to me. You should see the things he makes me do."

"Like what?" Addie asked.

I described the sprints and the stacking of the rocks. "Today, I had to climb the stairs to the jump at least a thousand times while he sat and watched."

"That's funny." Addie giggled.

"He's having his revenge on you for tormenting him all these years." Mama wiped away the remnants of her tears.

"Actually, he's helping me get strong so I can win." Why had I said that? Win what? That would be the inevitable question. I was such a big mouth.

"Win?" Mama asked sharply. There it was.

"If I can't compete in Flynn's competition, at least I'll know myself that I could. Viktor's measuring my jumps."

Mama touched her fingertips to the bottom of her chin. "I can understand why you'd do that. You'll have the satisfaction of knowing you could beat them all."

She *did* understand. I could see it in her mother eyes that peered at me with unconditional love and acceptance. From the very start, Mama had understood me. She'd never tried to make me be someone I wasn't. "It's important to me that I know."

"Yes, I can see that," Mama said.

"Was there something like that for you, Mama?"

"Teaching. Coming out here all alone. Saving my mother and sister. Doing something only men did. I was quite frightened, but I knew I had to do it."

"You did. Splendidly," I said.

"If I hadn't braved it all, I'd never have found all of you and the life I was meant to live. You keep jumping, my darling. Someday the world will catch up."

If she only knew what I had planned to shock the world.

Mama got up from the window seat and went to the door. "Cym, come downstairs with me. I'd like a cup of tea. Addie, will you be all right for a moment?"

"Yes, Mama. I'm fine." Addie returned to her reading.

I followed her out to the hallway.

"I've been distracted with Addie and not paying enough attention to you." She took my face between her hands. "Should I be worried for your virtue?"

"Virtue?" I flushed, remembering our kisses.

She scrutinized me with such intensity that I had to look away. "You do know how it might look to some if they knew you were spending all this time alone with Viktor at his home."

"I promise, Mama. It's nothing like that. He's the perfect gentleman."

"Do you plan on marrying him?"

"He hasn't asked." I studied my hands.

"If he does?" Mama asked.

"Then I will say yes."

She sighed with what I could clearly see was relief. "Cym, you've no idea how I've worried about you. Finding a man who understands you and doesn't try to change you? This is a rare thing."

"And especially for a girl like me?" I couldn't help but laugh. She was right. That Viktor loved me was nothing short of a miracle.

"Not that. I mean, finding a man special enough for you," Mama said. "That's what I've worried about. One who would hold your interest."

"He does hold my interest, and he makes me laugh."

"During this life, you need to laugh as much as you possibly can," Mama said. "The other thing I wanted to say…I'm sorry you can't compete. I know it bothers you, and I wish the world was different."

"But it's not. I've accepted it." Being dishonest did not come easily to me. However, I couldn't let her know my plans or she would worry. Would she disapprove? Strangely enough, given how old-fashioned she was, I didn't think she would. I couldn't take the chance, though. If she didn't want me to continue and expressed this to me, I would not be able to carry through with our plan.

"I'm proud of you," Mama said. "Whether you win a race or not."

"Thank you." I hugged her quickly and tried to squelch the guilt inside me.

LATER THAT AFTERNOON, ADDIE DID WELL WITH THE BLAND potato soup Lizzie made for her. When she'd finished her bowl, I took the tray down to the kitchen. Lizzie was there with her daughter, Florence.

Lizzie greeted me with her usual cheery hello. She was kneading bread on the wood-slab island in the middle of the kitchen. Florence was at the table reading. She and Addie were the same age, but they couldn't have looked more different. Florence was fair-skinned like her parents and as healthy as a blooming rose. With copper hair and freckles, she was lovely to look at, but heavens the girl was clumsy. She brought to mind an enthusiastic but uncoordinated Irish setter puppy. She even had the large hands and feet—ones that seemed too big for the rest of her. I suspected she would eventually grow into them, but for now they seemed to cause her a great deal of trouble, for she was always tripping or knocking items off her mother's counters.

Not that any of her accidents caused us to love her less. She was like Fiona, impossible not to love. She'd inherited her mother's vivacious and feisty traits and her father's precision when it came to her studies. Lately, she'd talked often of going to college when she was done with high school. I had no doubt she would.

"Lizzie, Addie ate the whole bowl," I said as I set the tray near the sink. "So far, she's feeling well." I turned, leaning my backside against the chill of the ceramic sink. "I'm much cheered about her situation."

"I hope it remains that way," Lizzie said. "I'm sick myself thinking about her."

"She usually feels sick right after she eats. So we might have found at least one thing she can eat."

Lizzie pushed back stray strands of hair that fell over her forehead with a flour-dusted forearm. "I've been poisoning her. Do you think it's my spices? I've learned to add flavors to my bland English recipes over the years. Perhaps I've made her ill?"

"Lizzie, you've done nothing wrong. Goodness knows you've dedicated your life to making sure we're all well fed."

"I'm beside myself." Lizzie smacked her dough like it was a naughty child.

Florence looked up from her book. "I've told Mummy it isn't her fault, but you know how she is."

"Yes, I do." I went over to give Lizzie's rounded shoulders a quick squeeze. "You mustn't worry, Lizzie. Theo will figure out what's wrong with her."

"He told me I can only feed her one type of food at a time. How's a person supposed to do that, I'd like to know?" Lizzie's English accent was as thick as the day she'd arrived in America over two decades ago.

"The potato soup was a wonderful idea," I said. "But we don't even know if food is the problem. It might be something else making her sick."

Florence set aside her novel and picked up a notebook instead. "I've got something to show you." She scooted out of the bench seat that curved around the table with no troubles. However, as she bounded toward us, the toe of her shoe caught on the wood floor and she stumbled. I thought she was going down, but she righted herself before she tumbled over completely. Seeming to barely notice her mishap, she bounced on her tiptoes the rest of the way over to the island.

She slapped the notebook down too close to the pile of flour, causing a cloud of white dust to billow several feet over the island.

"Love, please be careful," Lizzie said.

Ignoring her mother, Florence tapped a finger on top of the notebook. "I've been studying the patterns to Addie's illness. And making notes on what she ate and the reactions."

"What made you think to do that?" I asked.

"Theo asked me to."

The pride in her voice touched my heart. "He's lucky to have such a good helper."

"Thus far, we have only two items. The broth and the soup. I'll list them all, though, don't worry." She opened the notebook to show me her list. "Mummy, what did the potato soup have besides potatoes?"

"A little salt and pepper and water," Lizzie said. "Theo told me no milk or flour until we see how she did with the potatoes.

"He said I could try bread next. No sugar in in it, though. Only my sourdough mix and flour." Lizzie gave her dough one last ferocious knead and stuck the ball into a buttered bowl. "Nothing blander than sourdough bread."

"We all love your freshly baked bread," I said, trying to make her feel better. "Save a little for me?"

"You eat like a man," Lizzie said. "I don't know where it goes."

"It's all my outdoor activities," I said.

"Addie has to get better," Florence said as she wrote down the words: *sourdough bread*. "She's my best friend."

"She *will* get better. Especially with you and Theo working together."

I was rewarded for my kind words with Florence's smile worthy of any dog's best tail-wagging.

Viktor

N one of the Barneses showed up to church Sunday morning. A feeling of dread became a stone in my stomach. Addie must have taken a turn for the worse. That had to be the reason for their absence. Mrs. Barnes made sure they were all in the front pew every Sunday.

After church, I drove toward home but decided at the last second to turn the other way and head out to the Barnes estate. I wouldn't bother the family, but Jasper could give me an update on Addie's situation.

Snow had fallen again the night before, but the plow had come through to clear the road. However, the Barnes driveway had not been, so I was careful to stay within the tracks made by whoever had driven to and from earlier in the day.

All seemed well, however, when I parked the car behind the one Cym and Fiona usually drove. I knocked on the front door to the tinkling sound of Fiona's piano. That was good, surely?

Jasper answered the door. "Mr. Olofsson, how are you?"

"I came by to see how Addie was faring." I stuck my hands into my overcoat and balled my fists, hoping for the best.

"Come in. Miss Cymbeline and Miss Fiona are in the sitting room."

I followed Jasper inside and let him take my coat. The melodious notes of Fiona's playing continued. Was it my imagination, or was it a mournful song?

She stopped when we entered the room. Cym, who was at the desk, looked up and then stood, coming over to greet me. Jasper disappeared to go do whatever butlers did, leaving me alone with the women.

"Viktor, what brings you by?" Cym asked.

"I wanted to inquire about Addie." I drew her hand to my mouth for a light brush. *Please don't scold me for my rudeness*, I thought. "I worried when you weren't at church."

"She's not well." Upon closer inspection, I could see that Cym's eyes were puffy. "Yesterday, we were encouraged, but today she's quite ill."

Fiona approached, welcoming me with a sad smile. "How kind of you to come by. We've been beside ourselves."

"After she had her dinner of bread and more potato soup, she became ill," Cym said. "She's refused to eat at all today."

"We're afraid she's given up." Fiona's face contorted as she tried not to cry.

"I'm so very sorry to hear this." The boulder in my stomach grew heavier. "What can I do? Anything?"

"Mama and Papa are with her now. Theo's just left," Cymbeline said.

"Does he know what's wrong?" What a stupid question. Of course he didn't, or he would have done something by now. "I'm sorry. That was dumb."

"It's all right," Cym said. "In fact, he has a suspicion. She became sick after eating Lizzie's bread."

"Bread?" I blinked, confused. "How could bread make a person sick?"

"I don't know," Cym said. "But that's what we saw. If she'd try to eat something else, we could see if she was all right without bread."

"She won't, though," Fiona said. "It's like a hunger strike."

"Poor Addie," I said.

"None of us had the heart to go to church," Fiona said. "I couldn't stand to hear that pontificator Pastor Morris. There hasn't been a time I've missed Pastor Lind more than now."

"He'd be a comfort to us," Cym said. "That flaming red ball of a preacher is another matter altogether."

Our new pastor wasn't well-liked by those of us who had grown up listening to Pastor Lind's gentle and encouraging sermons. Pastor Morris was bombastic and verbose, and preached about an angry and vengeful God.

"Would you like to stay for lunch?" Cym asked. "It's only sandwiches. Lizzie was too upset to cook much."

"I would, but I promised Mother I'd come by later," I said. This was a lie, but I didn't want to stay and be in the way. Their family didn't need an outsider lurking about.

"I can't ski this afternoon," Cym said. "I don't want to leave Addie."

"I understand completely," I said. "I'd figured as such."

She escorted me to the door and helped me on with my coat. "Shall I walk you out?"

"I'd like that," I said.

I followed her down the steps and out to my car. The day had darkened. Given the smoky-colored sky, snow would come again before long.

She placed her fingers on the lapels of my jacket. "Viktor, thanks for coming by. And caring about my family."

"I hope I wasn't intrusive," I said. "But my car seemed to drive itself here."

"You could never be that. Especially after how often you've saved us."

I drew her close and kissed the top of her head. "You have to keep the faith. God is good."

"Only the good die young, though. Isn't that what they say?"

"That's a saying. Not truth," I said.

She lifted her gaze to me, and I kissed her gently on the

mouth. "I won't expect you tomorrow morning," I said. "But come if Addie's better. I'll be on my knees tonight."

"Thank you." She stepped aside so I could get into the car. As I backed up and drove out of the driveway, she remained in the yard watching me. Just before I turned the corner, she lifted her hand in one last wave.

SUNDAY EVENING, I SAT AT MY PARENTS' KITCHEN TABLE. Mother had made a beef stew, saying it was only right since Nora was coming for dinner. The Cassidys' farm had provided most of the beef for Emerson Pass for as long as I could remember. Since Mr. Cassidy's death, Nora had run the farm by herself. Now that she and Isak were engaged, they were actively looking for a buyer. So far, they'd not had any luck. Until she could sell the farm, Nora felt stuck doing the hard work of running a small ranch. Isak was anxious to marry her and have her and her mother move in with him. Until the farm sold, however, that would be impossible.

Mother served us all heaping bowls of stew before joining us at the table. Isak had brought a loaf of his crusty bread. I took a chunk and spread creamy butter over it.

Isak lifted his water glass. "We have something to celebrate."

"The farm sold today." Nora smoothed a hand over her corn silk–colored bob. "To a family from Denver. They want to move in as soon as possible."

"Did you get a good price?" Father asked.

"We got what I asked for," Nora said. "After some concessions."

"My fiancée was a shrewd negotiator," Isak said.

"It helped that you were there," Nora said. "Otherwise, he would have thought he could get away with more since I'm a woman."

"Does this mean we will have a wedding soon?" Mother asked softly. "You've had to wait a long time."

"With your blessings," Isak said. "We'd like to do it at the end of the month."

"The new owners will take possession on the twenty-seventh," Nora said. "Then I'm free."

"And I'll be the luckiest fellow breathing." My brother beamed. He'd been patient, but I knew he was more than ready to start this new season with his beautiful bride.

We raised our glasses. For the rest of the dinner, we discussed their plans for the future. I could see from the gleam in my mother's eyes she was already thinking about the babies who would come to bless us. The offspring of my large Nordic brother and tiny Nora Cassidy, of good Irish stock, would surely be pretty. I had to confess to being excited by the idea of some little nieces and nephews. Under normal circumstances, I would have been overjoyed, but my worry over what was happening at the Barnes estate had me less than my usual jocular self.

"What is it, brother?" Isak asked. "Is something troubling you?"

"It's little Addie Barnes," I said. "She's ill. The family's worried sick." I explained to them what I knew and that she was refusing to eat. "Yesterday, they were encouraged because she was feeling better. Theo's idea was to take away all foods and start adding them in one by one. She was fine until last night when she had bread for dinner."

"Bread?" Isak asked, sounding offended. "What could bread do?"

"I don't know," I said. "After she ate it, she was very sick. She doesn't want to feel that way any longer. Thus, she's refusing to eat." I looked over at my mother. "They're afraid she might not make it."

"Oh, dear me," Mother said.

"That's terrible," Nora said. "What can we do?"

"Not much we can do, other than pray," I said.

"We'll get the whole town to pray." Isak swept his hand across the table. "I'll ask all our customers to pray."

The Barnes family would be touched at the thought of the whole town praying. "It'll give them hope, I think." Hope. Such a massive idea within one small word. What would we do without it?

Mother's brow had creased the way it did when she was thinking hard.

"Mother, what is it?" I asked.

"I just remembered something. There was a little girl back in Norway. A class chum of mine. She'd been sick for a few months and not able to go to school. Her family owned a bakery. They discovered, finally, she couldn't eat baked goods. Bread and muffins made her sick. My mother told me once that there were others like her too. Anything that had flour in it made them sick." She lifted her gaze to me. "What if Addie has the same thing?"

"Was your friend cured?" Isak asked.

"No, not cured, but the symptoms stayed away as long as she didn't eat bread."

I leapt from my chair, knocking my water glass over. Fortunately, it was empty. "I've never heard of such a thing, but it could definitely be what Addie has." Couldn't it? I looked wildly around the table at the others. They were all nodding in agreement.

"It was rumored to be a Scandinavian ailment," Mother said.

I pressed my hands to my mouth and looked at the door. Should I go out to the Barneses' house now? *Yes*, a voice seemed to whisper in my ear. *Go now.* "I'm going out there now to tell them what you've told me. Maybe this will convince Addie to eat."

"Godspeed," Mother said.

I DROVE DOWN THE DRIVEWAY TO THE BARNES ESTATE AS THE snow began to tumble from the sky. As I went around the sharp turn, a shadow appeared in the distance. I squinted into the darkness. Someone was walking toward me. The figure wore a pair of boots and a flannel nightgown. The meandering, slow gait made me think at first glance she was drunk, but I dismissed this idea when I realized it was a child. Addie. She stopped, staring into my headlights.

I slammed on my brake but left the engine going before jumping out and running to her.

She appeared like an angel, with the snow falling around her. For a split second, I imagined she had wings attached to her back.

"Addie?"

"Viktor?" Her eyes shone in the glow of the car's headlights. She sounded surprisingly strong and clear.

My instincts told me to stay calm and approach slowly, as if she were a frightened animal. I forced myself to speak evenly, almost conversationally. "What are you doing out here?" Was I seeing her ghost? Had Addie become an angel? I tried not to cry, but tears fell anyway, warm on my cheeks.

"I'm a cat, looking for a private place to die."

I took one step closer. "Addie, no. Not that."

"I'm going to find a cozy nook, like our cat did. They like to die alone. I have to do that too."

"Where is everyone? Didn't they see you leave?" This was said out loud but more to myself than her.

"I had to sneak away. They were all sleeping. I can't be here any longer, keeping them all from living."

I reached her just as her knees seemed to buckle and caught her in my arms. Lifting her, she seemed to weigh even less than the day I'd brought her home. "You want to live, Addie. You said so to Cym." I carried her to the car. Snow caught in my lashes and made it hard to see, but I managed to get her into the passenger side.

She leaned over and grabbed my coat collar in her small white hands. "I want her to jump, Viktor. Promise me you'll make her."

"You're going to be here. You're going to see her with your own eyes."

"I don't want to live like this any longer. Each day is worse than the last. I'm not going to get better."

"You don't know that." I hesitated, worried to say too much.

"I'm so very tired," she whispered. "I'm a burden, too. All of them should live and laugh, and I'm ruining all of it."

I had to tell her what my mother had said. Hope was all I had to offer. If she could just hang on for a little bit longer. "I just had dinner with my parents. I told them you were sick and refusing to eat. My mother said she knew a girl when she was young in Norway. The girl was like you. Sick all the time. Her family were bakers. There was always a lot of bread around. Just like Lizzie makes at your house. When she stopped eating bread and muffins and whatever else was made with flour, she stopped being sick."

Her eyes fluttered, as gently as a butterfly's wings. "Is that true?"

"Do you remember yesterday when you had the bread? Afterward you were sick."

"Mama thinks it's the bread too, but that's such a silly idea." She sounded about a hundred years old. "Bread is nothing but flour."

"That's right. You're a smart girl. What does that tell you? Flour makes you sick."

"Flour is wheat. Wheat comes from the earth."

"What if you try eating something without any flour in it again? Like the potato soup? It didn't make you sick, remember? Isn't it worth trying?"

She clutched my collar again. "I'm scared, Viktor. I'm scared to live and scared to die."

"I know, sweetheart. I know." My throat ached so badly I could hardly speak.

"Sometimes having hope is worse than just giving up." Unshed tears shone in her eyes.

"Can't we give it one more try, though? Have just enough hope for one more bowl of that soup?"

"Maybe." A slight lilt told me she wanted to try. Hope. That word again. The one that had sustained many a sufferer.

"Do it for Cym and all of your family," I said. "They all love you so much. They don't want you to leave them."

"I'd not had any more hope left in me," Addie said. "Even the angels couldn't convince me to return. I could feel them, Viktor. All around me. They whispered to me—go home—but I couldn't listen any longer. And then I saw your car."

"An angel brought me here to you," I said. "You must have quite a few watching out for you."

"My grandmother." Addie let out a shallow breath before her teeth began to chatter. "She always told me I was her special girl."

"You are a special girl." I grabbed the blanket I kept in the back and tucked it around her. "Let's get you back to your family."

"Soup. Potato soup," she whispered.

God bless potatoes, I thought. And the angels that guided us.

Cymbeline

I woke disoriented. I'd fallen asleep in the chair by Addie's bed. My parents had been up for days, and I'd finally convinced them to go to bed. I'd promised them I'd look after Addie. Bleary-eyed, I sat up, heart racing. The bed was empty—nothing but wrinkled blankets tossed aside.

Heart racing, palms sweating, I sprinted out of the room and down the hallway to the bathroom. The door was open. No Addie.

I shouted her name. Doors up and down our hallway opened. Mama and Papa, in their dressing gowns, stumbled out of their room. Fiona, still dressed, did the same, with Delphia behind her.

"She's not in her bed," I said, breathless with fear.

There were no empty rooms upstairs, so we knew she wasn't anywhere on the second floor. I raced down the stairs, almost slipping in my stocking feet. Where could she have gone?

That's when I saw the front door ajar. She'd gone outside. Why? Snow fell heavily from the black sky, but I saw traces of her footprints. They were of boots, not bare feet. I shoved my feet into a spare pair of work boots in the closet and grabbed the first coat I could find and ran down the front steps. Light from the front porch only extended so far, and soon I was in the darkness. Behind me, I could hear Fiona's voice calling Addie's name, followed by Papa's deep baritone.

I heard a rumble of a car in the distance. Someone was coming down the driveway. Who would be visiting us at this hour? Theo? The sound didn't grow louder. Perhaps it was only someone on the road, not our driveway. I turned frantically in a circle, trying to find Addie in the dark. Snow fell in my eyes and stung my cheeks. She would not survive out here for long. What if she hadn't put on a coat? *Why, why, why, Addie? Why would you do this?*

I stumbled and fell in the thick drifts of snow. Wiping ice from my mouth, I clumsily rose to my feet. I ran one way, then the other as best I could in the drifts, disoriented and growing more lost by the minute. Where was I? *Keep going*, I told myself. I called out her name again and again as I tried to find the driveway.

Then a light flickered through the trees. A car. Headlights. I squinted into that light and ran toward it, falling several times. Finally I found the tire tracks in the driveway and ran as best I could in the skinny, icy trenches. I now knew where I was.

I rounded the corner. It was Viktor in the driver's seat. Was there someone beside him? Yes. The white face of my sister was barely visible, but it was her. Thank God. My knees weakened with relief.

I shouted to him. "Viktor."

He looked up at the sound of my voice. "She's here," he shouted back. "I've got her."

I sprinted toward them, slipping once before I arrived on shaky legs.

"Get in the back," Viktor said. "We need to get her inside to the warmth."

I did as he asked without question. How long had Addie been out here? She might have frostbite. The sooner we got her home, the better.

Addie had fallen asleep in the front, her head tilted at a sharp angle.

"I found her walking the driveway," Viktor said as he pressed on the gas pedal. "She told me she was a cat, looking for a place to die." His voice constricted. "But I persuaded her to come back home with me."

I started to sob. "Oh, Addie," I whispered.

"I think I've convinced her to eat," Viktor said. "I'll tell you about it when we get her inside."

I nodded, too bereft to speak.

The rest of the family were still looking for her when we arrived. Papa had turned on the light over the barn doors, making it possible for me to see their silhouettes.

Viktor brought the car to a halt. He went around to grab Addie from the front, lifting her as if she weighed nothing. I shouted that we had her. The rest of my family ran to us from all directions. Even Delphia had been out looking. It had only been minutes, I realized. Minutes that had felt like an hour.

Papa got to us first. "Goodness, Viktor, where did you find her?"

"She was coming down the driveway," Viktor said. "I just happened to be coming by to see how you were faring."

Papa lifted Addie out of the car.

"I'm sorry, Papa," Addie whispered.

"No, lamb. Nothing to be sorry for. Just rest." Papa headed toward the house. Mama, Fiona, and Delphia were all huddled together on the front porch.

We hurried into the house. Papa set Addie on the couch in the sitting room.

There were red embers remaining in the fireplace. I poked at them and added several logs. When they didn't immediately catch, I wanted to cry again. Instead, I knelt and blew as if my life depended on making the flames catch. When a bit of pitch caught and sizzled, I stood.

"Fiona, please go down and heat up some of Lizzie's chicken broth," Mama said as she perched next to Addie.

"Is there any of the potato soup left?" Viktor asked. "If so, give her that. It's bread that she can't eat."

Mama looked at him for a second as if she weren't sure he was real. "Yes, go ahead and do that, Fiona."

"Delphia, come with me," Fiona said. The two of them ran out of the room.

Viktor looked over at me before addressing my parents. Papa was pacing back and forth behind the couch.

Viktor hovered near the desk, seeming unsure of what to do.

"How did you find her?" Papa asked.

"Or even know she was missing?" Mama removed Addie's boots and began to rub her feet. I joined her, doing the same to my sister's cold hands. Addie's eyes fluttered open but only for a second. The poor little thing was exhausted from the cold and hunger.

"I've been with my parents," Viktor said. "My mother had a theory about Addie's illness that I wanted to share with you. When I turned the corner, I found her trudging down the middle of the driveway. She stopped when she saw my headlights. I ran and got her." His voice wavered. He took his hat off and held it limply against his thighs. "She said she was a cat, wanting a place to die by herself."

"No," Mama whispered.

Viktor wiped under his eyes. "But I told her my mother knew a girl like her back in Norway. She couldn't eat anything with flour in it either. I reminded her that the soup she'd eaten yesterday was fine, and she was only sick after the bread. I asked her to give it a try with another bowl of soup."

"And she agreed?" Mama asked.

"She did, yes." Viktor nodded. "We both felt angels around us. They led me to her. She said they whispered for her to go home but that she didn't want to be a burden any longer." A sob escaped from Viktor's massive chest. "But then when I reached her, Addie said her grandmother must have sent them."

"My mother?" Mama asked.

"That's right," Viktor said.

Papa wiped his eyes before grabbing Viktor in an embrace. "Thank you, young man."

"You're welcome," Viktor said.

"It seems you have a habit of saving my daughters," Papa said.

"It's my pleasure, sir."

Papa let him go and turned toward me. "Will you two go down and find something to go with the soup? Maybe a slice of ham? She needs real food."

"Yes, yes." I didn't stop to think any more about it, but charged out of the room and down to the kitchen. It wasn't until I reached the bottom of the stairs that I realized Viktor was right behind me.

My sisters had a pot of the potato soup on the stove. Both stared into it, as if willing the liquid to warm.

"Fiona, Papa wants us to bring ham too," I said.

The girls jumped at the sound of my voice. So absorbed in their task, they must not have heard us.

"Will she eat ham?" Delphia asked. "I want her to eat it." She stomped her foot. "I'm so very mad at her."

"She will," I said. "Viktor convinced her that it was the bread making her sick."

Fiona's eyes widened. "Do you really think it's true?"

Viktor told them what he'd already told me, twice now, although added a new piece of information. "Mother said it was rumored to be a Scandinavian trait."

"Mama said some of her people were from Denmark," I said.

Delphia took a running leap into Viktor's arms. "Thank you for saving my sister."

He held her tight against his chest. "Any time, little one."

"This is the second sister of mine you've saved," Fiona said to him. "Thank you."

"I'd do anything in my power for any one of the beautiful Barnes sisters." Viktor smiled over Addie's head at me. "It appears to be my life's work thus far."

"Yes, it does," I said, returning his smile.

"What about an apple too?" Fiona asked.

"Let's put them on the tray," I said.

"I'll do it," Delphia said. "I know exactly where the ham is in the icebox."

Viktor set Delphia down so she could do her part. I collected a tray from the pantry and put a napkin, fork, and spoon in one corner. Soon, we had a warm bowl of soup, a cold slice of ham, and one large apple for our Addie.

Addie was awake by the time we returned. She smiled weakly at the sight of all of us coming in with a tray. Viktor set it on the coffee table where we'd all shared tea so many times. Tea consisting of many items made from flour, I thought. All the while poisoning Addie without our knowing. *If* we were right, I reminded myself.

Papa brought an additional pillow to prop behind Addie's back. Mama picked up the warm bowl of soup and scooped up a spoonful. "Here you are, darling. Try a bite, please."

Addie opened her mouth obediently and Mama fed her, reminding me of a baby bird Flynn and I had once rescued. This was repeated a dozen times before Addie lay back against the pillows. "I might have a little ham."

"Yes, wonderful." Mama cut a corner and stuck the prongs of a fork into and brought it to Addie's mouth.

Addie closed her eyes. "It's so good, this ham."

"You should all go to bed," Mama said. "Papa and I will stay with Addie."

"I'm sorry I fell asleep," I said. "This is all my fault."

"Don't be ridiculous," Papa said. "We're all exhausted. You're not to blame."

"Anyway, all's well that ends well," Mama said. "Thanks to our Viktor."

He bowed his head at Mama. "Glad to be of service."

"I'll walk you out," I said. I had a plan to show Viktor just how much I appreciated him.

Addie's illness had made everything clearer. Family and friends were the most important thing. Bigger than my ego and pride. Pushing Viktor away served no purpose. It did not ensure that I would live a purposeful life. Not at all. In fact, it might be the opposite. Denying love was in direct opposition to adventure. Couldn't love be the biggest of them all? One that required courage and tenacity and generosity. All the qualities that summed up Viktor.

❧

WE STOOD UNDER THE AWNING HOLDING HANDS. SNOW continued to fall. "Will you get home all right in this?" I asked.

"Yes, I should be fine. But I should get going before all the tracks are covered."

I put my arms around his neck and kissed him. "Thank you from the bottom of my heart."

"It wasn't me. I told you—the angels led me here."

"Oh, Viktor, what would our family do without you?"

"You don't ever have to be without me," he said. "If you don't want to be."

"I don't want to be." I laid my cheek against his chest. "I hope your mother's theory is correct."

"Me too. It's strange how she thought of it. She said the memory came to her out of nowhere."

"Thank her for me," I said.

"I will. Although I'm starting to think it was the angels."

I looked up into his eyes. "I'd have thought you fanciful until tonight. It seems that you always know when we need you. How can that be explained except by the divine?"

"I agree," he said.

I looked out into the night. The snow falling made everything quiet. No scampering critters or owls hooting, everyone cuddled up in whatever shelter they called home. More and more, Viktor was becoming my shelter. "It's strange how everything changes when someone you love is sick. If it weren't for Addie, I'd be obsessed with the race and whether you were going to ask me to the fall party next week. Now none of it matters if Addie isn't better."

He lifted my chin, and I looked up into his eyes.

"We believe, we trust in the Lord," Viktor said. "Lean into your faith. Addie's going to get better. We shall go to the party. Even Addie will be there. Tonight proved it all to me, Cym."

"I believe, too. Right now, here with you, anyway."

He stroked his thumb inside the palm of my hand. "I'll come by tomorrow before work to see how she's doing." He kissed me. "Until then, try to get some sleep."

"All right."

"If she's better, would you like me to take you out to the underground club to dance?" Viktor asked. "You deserve a little fun."

"Yes. Unless the pond freezes over, of course." Every year a decision was made whether we would dance or skate. I sniffed the air. "It could get cold enough for the pond to freeze over."

"Either way. If you agree to hold my hand, then I shall not care," Viktor said. "Good night, fair Cymbeline."

"Go, before I drag you inside and make you stay forever."

He gave me one more quick peck and then darted down the steps and shuffled through the snow to his car. He waved before ducking into the driver's side. Headlights flickered on as the engine roared to life. And there, in the halos of light, I thought I saw the flutter of an angel's wing. I blinked and the image was gone, leaving only the snow falling gently in the night from a sky blanketed with stars.

Stars that were above the clouds, even if I could not see

them. How much else did the human eye miss? Not tonight. Tonight we had seen with our hearts that angels dwelled among us.

෨෪෩

I WENT UPSTAIRS AS QUIETLY AS I COULD. THE DOOR TO Addie's room was closed. Since Addie had been sick, Delphia had been in Fiona's double bed. I peeked through a crack in the door of Fiona's room. Wearing her flannel nightgown, she was in the rocking chair by the window looking out at the falling snow. Delphia was a sleeping lump in the middle of the bed.

The floorboards creaked as I entered. Fiona put her finger to her mouth, then pointed toward my bedroom. I nodded, and the two of us padded down the hall to my room.

I switched on the bedside lamp. Fiona yawned and shivered. "It's so cold tonight."

"Do you want me to light the fire?"

"Would you? And can I stay in here with you tonight?" Fiona asked. "Delphia kicks something terrible."

"Sure. Kind of like old times?" When we were young, Jo, Fiona, and I had all slept in twin beds in what was now the little girls' room.

I leaned down to light the fire laid out by our maid earlier in the night. Fiona went once again to the window and peered out as if she were looking for something.

"What's out there?" I pulled the grate close to the hearth to keep any stray pieces of burning wood from getting past the tile.

She slowly turned away to look at me. "Li's out there. He was supposed to come by earlier to see about Addie, but he never showed."

"Maybe something came up?"

"Yes, probably." She sighed and moved over to stand by the fire. "He's been getting threats."

"Threats? From whom?"

"We don't know. They leave messages on his porch or in his car."

"What do they say?"

"That they don't want him here," Fiona said. "To go back to China."

"Who would do such a thing?" My blood immediately went hot. "Have they threatened Mrs. Wu?" Fai was away at school, so she was safe. But Mrs. Wu was in her seventies and growing frail. Although she still lived here with us and helped Lizzie in the kitchen, she worked short days. Lizzie kept her tasks to a minimum but enough that Mrs. Wu wouldn't feel guilty about living in our staff quarters.

"I don't think so. Just Li," Fiona said.

"Do you know where he was earlier?"

"Playing for a party. I don't know who."

"Why weren't you playing too?" They usually were asked to play together.

"I had the feeling it was not a party for a young woman," Fiona said.

"Oh." I let that sink in for a moment. What kind of party would there be for men only? Or maybe there *were* women there —just not anyone like Fiona.

I went to the wardrobe to take off my dress and hang it up. Shivering in the chilly room, I quickly donned my flannel nightgown. "The party probably ran late and he didn't want to come by and disturb us."

"You're probably right. Still, I might drive out to his house first thing in the morning to make sure."

I went into the bathroom to wash my face and clean my teeth. By the time I returned, Fiona was in the double bed. She had her head on the pillow, but her eyes were wide open. They flickered my way as I dived into the bed.

"It feels good to get into bed." I yawned. "What a night. You want me to turn out the light?"

"Yes, please." She rolled onto her back and stared up at the ceiling. "I hope I can fall asleep. I feel quite unsettled about Li."

I leaned over to switch off the lamp. But first, I ran a finger over the pattern of pink roses on its base. The room went dark other than the glow from the fire. A log snapped and crackled, spitting out an ember.

Fiona reached for my feet with hers. Our wool socks scraped against each other. I closed my scratchy eyes but as tired as I was, I couldn't fall asleep. With everything with Addie and now this fear about Li, I might not sleep.

"You awake?" Fiona asked.

"Yes. Thinking about everything."

"I wish Li would never have moved out to his own house," Fiona said. "Then he'd be safe here with us."

"He's so proud to have his own house, though," I said.

"What's the use of a house if you can't fill it with family?"

I thought about that for a moment. Who would Li marry? Did he want to marry? Any white woman who married him here in America would have a hard time. "Does Li have his eyes on anyone?" I asked.

"I don't think so." Her voice wobbled slightly.

"It would be hard to be different from everyone around you," I said. "He's not different to us, obviously, but you know how people are."

"You know exactly how it is to be different," Fiona said.

"I guess I do."

"He's pure of heart. So good. He doesn't deserve to have to live in fear," Fiona said.

I paused before speaking, taking in the tone of her voice. Something was different. A quality I'd not heard before. A mixture of admiration and anger. Well, of course she admired him. What wasn't there to admire, after all? They were musical partners. She spent a lot of time with him. Any injustice in the world bothered Fiona, especially if it involved someone she cared about. That's all

I was hearing, I told myself. She couldn't possibly be in love with Li Wu. They'd practically grown up together. In addition, he was too old for her. She'd just turned eighteen, and he was twenty-five.

"Fiona, do you have your eye on anyone?"

She didn't answer. For a second I thought she was asleep, but then she moved her feet away from mine.

"Fiona?"

"No, I shan't ever marry. I want to live here with Mama and Papa forever. I can't leave my piano."

I breathed a sigh of relief. Thank goodness, I was only reading too much into the tonality of her voice.

"Go to sleep, dear sister," I said. "Everything's going to be better by morning light."

She sniffed. "I hope you're right."

Alarmed, I reached out for her hand. "Are you crying?"

"No. I might be getting a cold." Fiona's voice trembled again. She was most certainly crying.

"What's wrong, Fi? You can tell me."

"I might be a little in love with Li." She spoke so softly I almost thought I'd heard her wrong.

"Oh, Fi."

"I know." She sniffed again. "He's too old, for one."

"Which is not the main problem," I said. "As you know."

"What would people think? What would Papa and Mama think?"

I chose my words carefully. "They think of him as Li, a boy they've cared very much for. An American boy. Like us and everyone else in this town, his family came from somewhere across the seas."

"That's not how people see it," Fiona said. "There's hatred for Chinese."

"I wish it wasn't so, but I'm afraid you're right. Mama and Papa will be worried about how hard it would be for the two of you. However, I don't think they would forbid it if he's who you want."

"I don't think he cares for me anyway. He thinks of me like a little sister."

Was that true? I'd never watched him closely enough to have an opinion either way. He'd always been protective and polite with her. That was Li, though. He was the epitome of well-mannered and caring.

"Fi, you're still young. There's a lot of time to choose who you want."

"I won't want anyone else. You know how I am. I find something I love and that's it. Like music."

"But romantic love is different. You've not met that many men. There's probably someone out there for you that you don't even know exists."

"What about you and Viktor? You've known each other forever too."

"Yes, but it took me a long time to understand how right we are for each other."

"There's Theo and Louisa too."

They're roughly the same age, I thought. *And both of the same heritage.*

"Why do people have to be so awful?" Fiona asked.

"I don't know." I closed my eyes and tried to control my erratic breathing. The idea of anyone harming Fiona made me sick to my stomach.

"Why does where your ancestors come from have anything to do with love?" Fiona asked. "It shouldn't."

"It's ridiculous."

"Not ridiculous. Cruel and mean. Terrible. The worst kind of terrible."

"You're right, Fi. But the world's how it is."

"Yes, but it's up to people like us to try to change it for the better. You said so yourself."

"Actually, I think you're the one who said that to me." I smiled in the dark. "No one is as good-hearted as you. Not anywhere. I don't want anything to ever hurt you."

"Well, that's impossible. We're all going to have trials that hurt us. The most important thing is not to let them change us for the worse."

I hoped she could remain thus. However, if she and Li were to fall in love and marry, her life would be hard. *But it's love,* a voice seemed to whisper to me. Maybe the angels? *But this is a cruel world,* I thought.

"I'll be there for whatever it is," I said. "You can always count on me."

"Same goes for me."

"Snuggle closer. I'll keep you warm." We scooted into the middle of the bed and put our backs together and fell asleep breathing almost as one.

WE WOKE THE NEXT MORNING TO FIND THAT FIONA HAD worried for nothing. Li was fine. The party had run late, and he hadn't wanted to disturb us. He'd shown first thing the next day to assure us all that he was safe and to apologize for not calling.

That same day, Addie was much improved. Color had returned to her cheeks. Life had returned to her eyes. She was eating, small amounts so as to train her poor, shriveled stomach how to once again hold food. Had the crisis passed? We all hoped so.

Viktor

A ddie was much improved in the days that followed. She was well enough the week before Thanksgiving that Cymbeline felt ready for a night out at the underground club. I happily agreed, picking her and Fiona up at their house to take them to the resort. When we reached our destination, I parked and helped them both from my car. Flynn stood at the entrance talking to two gentlemen I didn't recognize. They were dressed in pin-striped suits and dark hats, but it was their multi-colored shoes that caught my attention. Men from the city? Perhaps Chicago? From the terse expression on Flynn's face and the way the shorter of the men leaned close to him, I suspected they were having a heated conversation.

"What's Flynn up to?" Cym asked under her breath. "Those men seem dangerous, don't they?"

"I've seen him with those two before," Fiona said. "They make the hairs on the back of my neck stand up."

"Mine too." Cym slipped her gloved hand into mine. "I think he's into something bad."

I'd heard rumors about a secret distillery somewhere outside of town. My brother had come right out and asked Flynn about it recently. Flynn had been adamant that talk was just that, talk with no truth to it. However, I'd known Flynn Barnes a long time. A hardness had come to his eyes when Isak pushed him further. He'd actually snapped at Isak, which surprised me. They had been at war together. Not much could break their bond or trust. Each time I'd seen Flynn of late, he'd seemed to have lost the playful zest for life. Seeing those men with him tonight made me wonder if the rumors were indeed true.

"I wish he'd talk to us," Fiona said.

"Fat chance of that," Cym said. "He seems to be drifting further and further away. Have you noticed it, Viktor?"

"Yes, somewhat." I didn't want to elaborate and ruin the evening. "But I'm sure everything's fine. He has a lot on his mind these days."

We started across the parking lot toward the door to the basement. A sudden thought struck me. "Fiona, when we're not here, you're careful, aren't you? If this is the type of man coming here, I'm not sure it's safe for a young woman."

"Like the night I came out for air." Cym shivered. "I don't like to think what might have happened had you and Theo not come to look for me."

"Li looks after me," Fiona said. "I *never* come out here alone. I'm much too afraid for that."

"Good, I'll rest easier knowing that." I didn't say it out loud, but I worried that Li Wu might be as much of a target as a young lady. Most folks in Emerson Pass were tolerant, but if there were men coming up from Louisville to enjoy the free-flowing booze of Flynn's club, they might not take favorably to someone of Li's origin.

The men in question, perhaps because of us, walked away from Flynn. We stopped to greet him.

"Good evening." Flynn tipped his hat. "Mr. Olofsson, what did you do to deserve such fine company as my sisters?"

"Lucky," I said.

"I'm working tonight," Fiona said. "These two are on a date."

"Addie's better," Cymbeline said. "So I felt all right about coming out."

"You've both been a great help to Mama," Flynn said.

"When did you see her?" Fiona asked, an edge to her voice. "I didn't think you'd been out to see Addie at all since she'd been sick."

An uncomfortable silence hung over us for a few seconds. I'd never heard Fiona use a sharp tone in my life until now.

"Mama was out to see us this morning." Flynn spoke lightly, as if he hadn't noticed the pointed question from his sister. "She gave us the good news about Addie. I'd have been out myself but I've been busy with work, and Shannon hasn't been feeling well."

"Or is it that you don't like sick people?" Fiona asked. "Anything unpleasant is too much for you and your pretend world."

Flynn blinked, clearly as surprised by his younger sister's bluntness as I. "Like I said, I've been busy. This business, which employs you and Li, I might add, doesn't run itself. Phillip's been busy making skis lately, so I'm on my own most of the time." He turned his attention toward Cymbeline. "Speaking of new skis, I'm surprised you're not too tired to be out tonight, given all your activity on the slopes." Flynn raised one eyebrow. "If I didn't know better, I'd think you were training."

"She simply wants to know without question that she can beat the boys," Fiona said. "Which she can. I've been measuring her distances."

"I hope that's all it is," Flynn said. "We don't need any trouble. I've heard from athletes all over the country. We're going to have quite the event."

"Speaking of trouble," Cym said. "Who were those men?"

"None of your concern." Flynn reached into his jacket pocket and pulled out a packet of cigarettes. He offered one to me, but I shook my head no.

"Since when do you smoke cigarettes?" Fiona asked.

"Now and again. Since the war," Flynn said.

"They cause cancer," Fiona said. "Did you know that?"

"That's propaganda." Flynn grinned and tapped his finger on the top of Fiona's head, as if she were a silly child. "Meant to keep us from doing as we please."

Fiona frowned and pulled her jacket tighter around her middle. "It's almost time for us to start our first set. I should get inside."

Flynn nodded as he twirled the cigarette between his fingers. "You should. We're opening in five minutes. Li's been here for at least thirty minutes. He believes in warming up."

Fiona glanced over at Cym and a kind of understanding passed between them. One I could not read.

Before either of the women could answer, Flynn said, "I'd like to talk to Viktor. Cym, would you mind going in with Fiona?"

Cym opened her mouth as if to argue but seemed to change her mind. She squeezed my hand before following Fiona through the door.

Flynn took a drag from his cigarette and blew the smoke away from me.

"What is it?" I couldn't keep the briskness from my voice. I'd not thought it possible to feel at odds with Flynn. He and Isak had been best friends since I could remember. However, the man before me was not the one I'd known.

"Nothing in particular. How are you? I haven't seen you much now that you and Cym are spending so much time together. I miss you."

My irritation softened. "I'm well. Busy with Cym and my work." I indicated with my chin the direction from which the men had disappeared into the black night. "You sure you're all right? Those guys looked like thugs."

"Yep. All good."

"You said Shannon's not been feeling well?" I wanted desperately to explain away Flynn's abrupt manner. Perhaps he was worried about his wife.

"She's fine. Uncomfortable mostly. This is going to be a large baby by the looks of things. I'm hoping for a boy this time."

"I wish you the best."

Flynn shoved my shoulder. "What's gotten into you? Have I done something to offend you?"

I studied the points of my wing-tip shoes. I'd shined them before I came out, and they reflected the light over the doorway. From the parking lot came the sound of men carousing. "Nothing's gotten into me."

"Is it Cym's obsession with the competition? Has she turned you against me?"

"Don't be ridiculous. She would never do such a thing." I turned toward the sound of the ruffians and could see they were passing a flask around their circle of six men. Was Theo right about Fiona working here? Had it become too rowdy for women?

"What is it then?" Flynn asked.

I looked back at Flynn. The tip of his cigarette glowed red. Like a dangerous snake, I thought. "Do you really want to know what I think?"

"I asked you."

"You seem to have forgotten you're a Barnes. Your father didn't build this town to have it run by thugs. Or for you to become one."

He flinched, then dropped the butt of his cigarette and stubbed it out with the heel of his shoe. "You're not a Barnes. You do know that, right? Never will be. Even if you marry my sister. My father seems to have forgotten that Phillip isn't his real son. Favors him over me these days. I suppose the same will happen when you marry Cym."

"That's neither here nor there. Don't toss aspersions to make excuses for your behavior. I know your family. I've watched how your father and mother have conducted themselves all my life. Lord Barnes wanted reputable businessmen here."

Flynn straightened his tie and attempted a jovial response that fell flat. "You've become high and mighty now that it's obvious how my sister feels about you."

"I'm not high and mighty. The opposite, in fact. Having a

woman like Cymbeline in my life has humbled me." I placed my hands in the pockets of my coat. They were itching to ball into a fist and punch Flynn in the chin. "She's taught me how far I have to grow before I'm a man worthy of her."

"How are you doing that exactly? Becoming as whipped as a man can be? I know what you've been doing out at your house and on the slopes. Training her as if she had a place to go with all this. What's left for you? Holding her handbag?"

"Your sister's perfectly capable of holding whatever she needs to."

"Obviously. But I'm talking about you. What kind of life does a man have married to a woman like Cym? Don't get me wrong. I respect her as much as you do, but I have to wonder what's in it for you?"

"We're talking about your sister." I shook my head, amazed and disgusted. "You should be defending her, looking after her, not besmirching her to the man who loves her." I pressed my fingertips into the lining of my coat pockets. *Keep calm*, I told myself. Fighting with Flynn would be mortifying to all of us, most especially Cym. "It's a great way to get the daylights beaten out of you."

"Whoa up." He stuck his hands in the air as if I were about to hit him. "I'm not saying anything bad about her. She's a force, that's all. I worry about you. Is attempting to tame her for the rest of your life what you really want?"

"That's just it. I have no intention of taming her." I looked up at the sky. A few stars twinkled down at me, as if to remind me of Cym's light. "She's just right as she is." I shook my head. "You know what's sad? She believed that of everyone in her life, you'd understand the best."

"About what? The competition?"

"About everything. Her desire to be an athlete and have a job. Wear pants, for heaven's sake. I want her to do whatever pleases her. I'm not interested in changing who she is."

"It was all fine when we were kids, but she's an adult now with the ability to embarrass the family."

"If anyone's doing that, it's you."

His cheeks reddened. He leaned in to speak with a quality to his voice as hard as cast-iron into my ear. "Listen here, Olofsson. You and I go way back, but you have no idea what it means to be a businessman. You're like a child playing banker in your well-made suit. Keep that in mind before criticizing me."

A staff member arrived to man the door. Flynn greeted him and told him the secret word patrons would need to get into the underground club.

Flynn drew back and once again straightened his tie. "And now I have to get home to my wife and child. Lest you forget I'm a respectable man in this town. A family man."

With that, he walked away, disappearing into the night. I blew out a long breath into the cold air. What had happened to my fun-loving friend? Of all of us, I'd never have predicted he would become so heavy with the burden of living. Were the girls right? Was he in trouble?

To my surprise, Mrs. Barnes sent an invitation to my family for the holiday feast. Mother was so excited by the request that she was making herself a new dress.

Heavy snowfalls made our daily practice sessions at the mountain possible. Because of work, I was unable to accompany Cymbeline to the jump most afternoons. However, Fiona was often able to attend, measuring each jump dutifully for her sister. Several evenings a week, Cymbeline would come by my house to report on the day's accomplishments. During the week, the slopes were mostly empty, giving Cym ample time to perfect her skills.

News of the competition spread. Flynn reported confirmations from skiers all over the country.

One night after work, I went over to my parents' for supper. We enjoyed a nice meal, but I was distracted enough that my mother noticed and asked me if everything was all right.

"Oh, yes. I'm sorry," I said. "I've something I want to ask you about."

"What it is?" Mother looked over at me with concern in her eyes. "Is all well with Cymbeline?"

"Yes, quite well. I'd like to ask for her hand in marriage but would like your blessing."

Father and Mother didn't even try to hide their wordless exchange. Given the smiles, I could see they were pleased.

"We expected as much," Father said. "Here's my question. Would you marry her without our approval?"

I was taken aback. Did this mean they *didn't* approve? I thought for a moment about the question. The answer, I'm ashamed to admit, was yes. Obedient son though I was, Cymbeline was the woman I wanted. Nothing would get in my way, not even duty. "I would."

"Then that gives us our answer," Father said.

"It does?" I asked.

"We would never forbid you from marrying whomever you wish," Mother said. "But it's important that you begin married life dedicated to the idea that no one will keep you from the other. Not even your family."

My parents gave each other another look. Had they gone against their parents' wishes? "Is that what happened to you?" I asked.

"We were from different backgrounds," Father said. "You mother was practically a queen."

"What?" I asked, stunned.

"Your father exaggerates," Mother said. "My family had money and stature. That is all. We were not kin to royalty, as your father likes to tease."

"As you know, son, my father was a tailor and his before him." Father drummed his fingers against the tabletop. "I was not good enough for your mother."

She patted his hand. "Only from the viewpoint of my family —who didn't have the best eyesight."

How had I never heard this story before? "Is that why you came to America?"

"Not the only reason, but partly, yes," Mother said. "My family shunned me. Living there became painful. Especially after you boys were born and they wouldn't see you. We decided to start a new life here in America. When we got to Boston, we saw an advertisement in the newspaper from Lord Barnes, asking for tailors to apply for an opportunity to open a shop here in town. We didn't hesitate."

"A very good decision," Father said. "We've had a good life here."

My mind couldn't quite grab hold of this new information. I'd always assumed Mother and Father had come from similar circumstances. "But how did you meet?"

"He was my father's tailor," Mother said.

Father nodded. "I'd go the estate for fittings and such. One day, I was upstairs waiting for her father to come in for a final fitting. I looked out the window to pass the time. And there she was, sitting in the garden."

"Father needed a new tuxedo for the annual dance hosted by my family," Mother said. "I've been fond of that dance ever since."

Father's gaze moved to the far wall, as if he'd fallen into the past. "The way the sun glinted off her golden hair caught my attention first." He made a twirling movement over his head. "It was all piled up in this twist of a thing, as complicated as a cross-stitch. She had a cat in her lap and a book in her hands."

"Dordi," Mother said softly. "My first baby. She wore a tuxedo for her fur. A sign from God, I realized later."

Father chuckled and rested his hands on the table. "I thought to myself, 'What a gift to be idle with enough time to read and stroke a cat.' I would have dismissed her from my mind completely if she had not taken that moment to look up."

"Startled to see anyone there, I simply stared at him." Mother smiled at the memory. "Such a large man. Big enough to fill in the entire frame of the window."

"She waved at me, and I waved back."

"Next time he came to see my father, I made sure to be inside."

"We started to see each other in secret, and then we eloped," Father said. "And that was that."

That was that. No couple could ever really explain what had happened in those moments when they fell in love. The deepness of their love and connection wasn't something to be summed up in a few words. To sustain that love over decades, too? What was the secret?

"I learned as much as I could so that I could help him run the shop," Mother said. "I'd always been clever at math. To my surprise, I was useful for something besides being pretty. I often wonder what would have become of me if I hadn't met your father. Women should have more than being like a vase of flowers for everyone to enjoy until they grow limp and wither."

"It's important to build something together," Father said. "Whether it's raising a family or running a business, working together keeps you close."

"Like this jumping competition," Mother said. "Even though it is her work to do, she couldn't have done it without you. You are a team."

Had there been something of my mother's that was hers alone? Or had she taken on Father's life without any sense of what she would have done otherwise? Was I like this with Cym, taking on her dreams as if they were my own? "I don't have anything that drives me like it does her. I'm content. Is that wrong?" I sighed, relieved to say my fears out loud.

"Her dreams have become yours," Father said. "There's

nothing wrong with this as long as you don't have to give up too much of yourself."

"But what about you, Mother? Did you ever feel like you gave up too much?" The words were out of my mouth before I concluded it might be a hurtful thing to ask in front of Father.

"Quite honestly, no," Mother said. "My life would have been one of leisure but without the fullness of living every day with the person I loved. We've been rich with love. Growing our business together has given me purpose and satisfaction."

"And you boys," Father said. "Our greatest pride and joy."

I choked back tears. "I hope I will always make you proud."

"Have you been worried?" Mother asked. "About you and Cymbeline?"

"No, not really. Just something Flynn said to me the other day had me thinking."

Mother made a tutting sound. "That boy."

I didn't ask what she meant—I already knew. Cym and Fiona weren't the only ones who'd noticed the changes in Flynn Barnes. "I'll have to ask Lord Barnes for permission, of course."

"We wish you the best of luck," Father said.

"Will you want to marry right away?" Mother asked.

"I wouldn't want to spoil anything for Nora," I said. "Depending on what date she and Isak pick, as soon as possible."

"That's thoughtful of you." Mother patted my shoulder. "Good boy."

"I couldn't care one way or the other as long as she marries me. Her mother and sisters will have some ideas, I'm sure."

"Knowing Cymbeline, she might like to have a ceremony on the side of the mountain," Mother said. "Hopefully not while in air."

I laughed. "You might be right."

Cymbeline

The next day, Fiona and I went out to the ski jump. I practiced for several hours with my dutiful sister recording the length. Despite my best efforts, I'd not yet beaten my own record of just over fifty meters.

"I don't know, Fi. This might be my best," I said as we were walking toward the car.

"It might be good enough to win."

The sky was a cobalt blue this afternoon. Sunlight made the snow almost blinding. I leaned against the side of the car as Fiona took my skis and put them in the back. "I want to win, obviously, but lately it seems more important to simply be able to compete."

"You say that now but wait until the day. You'll be ready to win." Fiona came to stand next to me. We watched the skiers on the mountain for a moment. Mostly locals still; I knew the weekend would bring people from Denver and Louisville.

We were distracted by the appearance of Li striding toward us, his head down as if he were deep in thought.

"Li, hello," Fiona called out to him.

He lifted his gaze and gave us one of his shy smiles, then

rushed over to us as best he could over the slick ground. "Hello there. What are you two doing out today? Skiing?"

"Practicing my jumps," I said.

His dark eyes shone with encouragement. "Good for you, Cym. I wish things were different, but you should never give up."

"Thanks," I said. "As Fi says, at least I'll know if I can beat them."

"What brings you out here?" Fiona asked.

"I had to pick up my pay from the party the other night. The one that kept me out so late."

"Why would you be picking it up here?" Fiona asked.

"Just because." Li shoved his hands in his pockets and looked away, but not before I saw a look of guilt cross his even features.

Given Fiona's next question, she sensed something too. "Was the party you played at hosted by Flynn?"

"I can't say." Li looked at the ground as if desperate to see a crack in which to disappear. "So please don't ask."

"Hosted by Flynn?" I asked out loud. "What kind of party would that be?"

Li continued to look at his feet. "You'd have to ask your brother."

"What's he doing?" Fiona asked me, as if I would know.

"Is it dangerous, Li? Can you at least tell us that?" I kept my voice steady even though my stomach clenched.

"I'm sworn to secrecy," Li said. "I can only tell you that I wasn't in any danger."

Perhaps feeling a presence, I happened to glance over at the club. Flynn stood in the window, watching us. Dread draped over me like a heavy cloak. Something was not right. Flynn was in with dangerous people. What they were doing, I couldn't imagine. My instincts told me it was something bad. Something that could get him hurt.

"Is it only me who senses something dark has come to our town?" Fiona asked. "Li, please tell us you're not a part of it."

Finally, he met our eyes. "I play music, Fi. That's all I've ever done and all I'll ever do. Which is why I'm poor and your brother's rich."

I sucked a breath through my teeth, fighting a wave of nausea that I was afraid would make my breakfast come up. "Li, don't get involved further," I said. "Whatever this is, stay away. My brother will bring you only trouble."

Li gazed at me for a long moment. "I can't understand why a man with everything would take such risks."

"Is he in danger?" Fiona asked. "Please, you have to tell us what you know."

Li turned slightly toward the lodge, then back to us. "He's standing there, watching us."

"I know," I said.

"Which should tell you that whatever this is he's involved in —it's better that you don't know."

Fiona's eyes filled. "I'm scared, Li."

His expression softened at the sight of Fi's tears. He touched the sleeve of her jacket and spoke kindly. "If I knew anything that would be helpful instead of worrying you more, I would tell you, but I don't."

"What kind of party was it?" I asked.

Li closed his eyes for a second. "I'll talk to your father. Will that appease you for now? What I know—it's not something I can share with either of you."

Talking to Papa seemed like a reasonable request. "Yes, that will be fine. Thank you," I said.

"Try not to fret," Li said. "Flynn's like a cat. He always lands on his feet."

But did he have nine lives? That I wasn't so sure about.

※

FIONA AND I TALKED ALL THE WAY HOME ABOUT WHAT WE could do to help the situation. By the time we pulled into the garage, we'd convinced ourselves to talk to Mama and Papa. "Just to warn them that Li will be coming to see them," Fiona said as if we needed a justification.

"We don't want him to surprise him, especially with Addie still recovering."

It was obvious neither of us was convinced this was a good tactic. By the time we'd arrived inside and taken off our coats, we'd changed our minds. Papa and Mama had enough troubles without us adding to their burden.

As it turned out, we didn't have to make the decision. We'd just hung our coats when Papa summoned us into the study. A fire roared in the fireplace, warming the small room. Tea was set out on the table between two armchairs. My stomach rumbled at the sight of Lizzie's biscuits and raspberry jam.

Mama and Papa were both there, sitting side by side in the armchairs in front of the fire. We were not often asked to come into the study. It was reserved for serious talks, like the one we'd had about my attending college, and their alone time.

"Hello, girls," Papa said. "Come in. Here, take my chair. Have some tea."

"Nothing for me, thank you." Fiona brushed her fingers over her throat, telling me that her stomach was too upset to eat.

"No tea, just a biscuit," I said. "But later, after we talk."

Mama lifted her cheek for us each to kiss. "Look at you both, so rosy." She looked so much better than she had over the last few weeks. Now that we could feel more than a little hope about Addie, Mama's sparkle had returned.

"You're looking pretty too, Mama," I said.

"Addie's much improved," Mama said. "She's upstairs with Delphia. Out of bed and playing checkers. She ate ham and cheese for tea."

"Enthusiastically ate," Papa said.

Fiona and I settled together in Papa's large chair. "Why are we in here?" Fiona slipped her forearm between the two us. I did the same, and we held hands under the folds of our dresses. "Instead of the sitting room?"

"We wanted to make sure we could talk to you in private." Papa went over to shut the door.

"So the little girls don't hear us," Mama said. "To be frank, we're worried about Flynn."

Fiona squeezed my hand harder. "What about?"

"We've heard rumors," Papa said. "About an establishment he's running outside of town. Do either of you know anything about this?"

"Not really," Fiona said in a trembling voice. "Other than..." She stopped, looking over at me. "You tell them, Cym."

"We saw Li just now at the mountain. He said he played a party for Flynn the other night."

"He refused to tell us where or who," Fiona burst out, seeming to have put aside her reticence for the moment. "But he's coming to talk to you, Papa."

I continued. "We had the feeling it was something proper young ladies shouldn't know about." *Like so many other topics*, I thought.

"But Li was there? At this place?" Mama asked.

"We assume so," I said. "Or somewhere."

"We want you both to stay out of the underground club," Papa said. "No more playing, Fiona. And no more dancing, Cym."

Our parents seemed to brace themselves for an argument, but we kept quiet. I didn't know about Fiona, but I understood exactly why they wanted us out of there. They suspected nefarious doings, perhaps by our own brother, and they didn't want one of us to stumble into a dangerous situation.

We both nodded our consent.

Despite my run-in with a couple of drunks last year, I'd thought of the underground club as fairly innocent. The local liquor, wherever Flynn got it, was tame enough when watered down that most patrons kept their senses. I'd heard around town that moonshine in other places was strong enough to knock out a large man. Phillip had insisted they add water to everything before they even mixed it into the drinks.

"We know you'll miss playing there," Mama said. "I'm sorry, Fiona."

"It's all right," Fiona said softly. "I wish you could forbid Li too."

"He's a grown man," Papa said. "But I'll suggest it to him when he comes to talk to me."

"We appreciate your cooperation," Mama said. "It seems Flynn has been worrying us all."

"The underground club was one thing," Papa said. "I figured the people should have a saloon and a place to hear music if they wanted. No harm there. The sheriff being one of the frequent visitors, I haven't been concerned about Flynn getting in trouble with the law. This is the West, after all. But this other thing—" He abruptly stopped talking. Most likely because of the pointed look Mama had given him. She didn't want us to know too much.

"Flynn's acting strangely. Surely you've seen it too?" My voice caught in the back of my throat.

"We've been preoccupied with Addie, but yes, we've noticed," Papa said.

"We're afraid he's in trouble," Fiona said. "With bad men."

I told them about the dangerous-looking fellows Flynn was with at the club the other night.

"They gave us a shivery feeling," Fiona said. "Flynn was acting jumpy, too."

"When does Li plan to come see me?" Papa asked.

"He didn't say." I rubbed my knuckles together, fidgeting.

"Thank you both," Mama said. "You may go now. But take a biscuit. You're both probably half starved from being out on the mountain."

The strain in her voice hurt me. As did my father's slumped shoulders as we filed out of the study. A flurry of angry thoughts tumbled through my mind. How could Flynn worry us all so much? How could he have gotten Li involved? Why couldn't he have been happy with everything he already had? What was this unrelenting ambition to make more and more money?

Fiona and I went upstairs to my room. As we sprawled out together on the window seat, the sun lowered and spread golden arms through the spaces between the trees. The fallen snow was a myriad of different colors ranging from white to yellow, delineated like puzzle pieces.

"I love the light this time of year," I said.

"Me too. Though it seems the last few weeks I've been too nervous to notice it much."

"Our family seems to be having problems one after another."

"They say bad things come in threes." Fiona set her biscuit on the plate and pushed it away.

"I hope you're wrong. Anyway, Addie's better. This is just the first bad thing."

"Addie's sickness counts as the first one," Fiona said.

A knock startled us. "Can we come in?" Delphia's high-pitched voice came from behind the door.

"Yes, yes, enter," I said.

Delphia, followed by Addie, came bursting into the room. Seeing them cheered me some. Addie's appearance, while still gaunt, was no longer gray and sallow. She looked more like Delphia for the first time in ages.

"What are you two rascals doing?" Fiona held out her arms, and Delphia ran over and sat on her lap. I moved over so Addie could sit between us.

"I've eaten gobs of cheese and ham," Addie said. "I don't feel sick at all."

"You look much better." I placed my hands on the sides of her face. "Beautiful."

"I'm sorry I scared everyone the night I walked outside," Addie said.

"Never mind that," Fiona said. "You're better now, and that's all we care about."

"You're not mad?" Addie asked.

"We could never be mad at you," Fiona said.

"That's right. We could never be mad at either one of you." I tousled Delphia's hair. "Even when you're naughty."

"What if I spilled something on your piano?" Delphia asked Fiona. "On purpose."

"You would never do that," I said. "Would you?"

"No, not on purpose." Delphia sounded slightly disappointed with herself.

"Then it's not a reasonable question," Fiona said, "if you know you would never do that."

"What if it was an accident?" Delphia asked.

"Wait a minute. You didn't spill something on Fiona's piano, did you?" If she had, Fi wouldn't be able to play here or at the club.

"No, I didn't really. This is pretend." Delphia's tone now suggested that I was slower than I should be to comprehend. "I'm trying to understand how deep this love goes with you two."

I laughed. "It's called unconditional love and it means just that. No matter what you did, we would still love you."

"What about Flynn?" Addie asked softly. "Will you still love him if we find out he's done something bad?"

"What do you mean?" I asked, alarmed. Had they heard our discussion downstairs?

"The question is, what did you hear?" Fiona asked.

"We could hear you all talking just now." Delphia raised her tone an octave. "Mama's voice got like this."

"That's because she was upset," Addie said.

"I know that." Delphia made a face at her sister. "Now that you're better, you can't start bossing me around again."

"I've never bossed you around," Addie said.

"We're getting off subject here," Fiona said. "Do either of you know anything about Flynn that you should tell us?"

"This morning, we heard Jasper and Papa talking," Delphia said. "We don't know exactly what it was, only that Jasper heard something bad about Flynn at the barbershop."

"Old men clucking like hens," I said as I took in this new information. "Did you get a feeling about what the bad thing was?"

"He has a secret business outside of town," Addie said. "Where he makes something bad."

"Which made me really want to go there," Delphia said.

"God forbid," Fiona said. "You're to stay right where you are, little missy."

"Trouble might still find her," Addie said.

"No, it won't," I said. "You're to be good and sweet like Fiona."

"What about you?" Delphia asked. "What are you?"

"I'm the problem child. Everyone knows that." I grinned to show them that it wasn't any concern to me. "But there's only room for one in every family, so you'll have to figure out something else."

"You're no longer the problem child," Fiona said. "I think someone's taken your place. And the problems he's causing are far greater than your sass and desire to trample most men in sports."

We locked eyes for a moment. Our shared history was there between us. All the memories from our childhood. We'd all gravitated toward Flynn. He was the most fun of all of us. He'd been able to make a game out of anything. No one had had a bigger heart under all his bluster and rambunctious antics. If I recalled correctly, he'd been the one to first suggest that the then Miss Cooper should be our new mother.

"Listen, little ones," I said. "Tonight, in your prayers, you make sure and say a big one for Flynn."

They both nodded with great solemnity.

"Nothing bad will happen to Flynn, will it?" Addie asked. "He sent Shannon with a quarter to give to me when I was sick. I put it under my pillow for safekeeping. All night I dreamt of money."

"You didn't," Fiona said.

"No, I'm just kidding." Addie giggled.

I stared at her, my heart full. "I can't remember the last time I heard you laugh, pet."

"I like laughing," Addie said.

"Me too," Delphia said. "It's like bubbles inside you that come out."

"How perfectly perfect," Fiona said. "I shall put it in a song."

"Will you dedicate it to me?" Delphia asked.

"Yes, I think I will." Fiona kissed the top of Delphia's head. "For my little sister who always makes me laugh."

Delphia sighed in a happy way and settled further into Fiona's arms. "Sing to us, Fi."

And so she did, a lullaby that Josephine had taught us long ago when we were innocent children without a mother. As her beautiful voice filled the room, I took it all in, knowing a moment as sweet as this should be savored.

Viktor

The day before the Thanksgiving weekend festivities were to begin, I was finishing up paperwork at my desk when my boss sank into the chair across from me. Mr. Owens was a short man but made up for what he lacked in height with the girth of his belly. He always wore a black suit no matter the weather. A silver mustache coaxed into a pigtail-like curl with some kind of sticky ointment made it seem as if he were always smiling. Indeed, he was a jolly man with a heart as large as his midsection. I admired him tremendously, especially knowing he'd been handpicked by Lord Barnes himself to run our bank around the same time my parents came to Emerson Pass.

"Viktor, old boy. You've been smiling to yourself all afternoon. I know that look, having had it myself forty years ago for Mrs. Owens. Should I take it you've finally won Cymbeline's affections?" Mr. Owens placed his arms over his stomach and peered at me from above his round spectacles that perched just above the bulge of his nose. His ruddy complexion, along with his suit, never changed with the weather. However, today a gray tinge made it seem as if he'd been dusted with ash.

"Sir, I do believe I've finally turned her head," I said. "I'd like to ask her to marry me, but I have to get Lord Barnes's permission first. Which, frankly, scares me more than a little. We both know I'm unworthy of her."

"Nonsense. You're a handsome feller with a fine head on your shoulders. A promising future, too, I might add."

"It's kind of you to say so. I hope Lord Barnes agrees."

"I don't think it'll take much." Mr. Owens tugged on one side of his mustache. The bags under his eyes had grown heavier over the last few months. "They've known you most of your life. Your family too. Good people. Lord Barnes knows that."

I glanced at the clock. It was nearly five, almost time to close up for the day. "Mr. Owens, go home. I can close up without you. Surprise Mrs. Owens."

"I'm dog-tired. Sadly, I don't mean just today. I reckon, in general. I'm not getting any younger. The missus wants me home more. She's afraid I'm going to keel over dead on her."

"What are you saying?" I set aside the pen in my hand to peer at him more closely.

"I'm retiring, young man, and leaving you in charge. Got the blessing from Lord Barnes yesterday. We both believe you're the one to take us into the future."

"Me? But I don't know what I'm doing."

"If that's so then you've got me fooled. And if I'm fooled then our customers sure will be too. You've got a way about you that instills trust. Keeping money in the bank makes a lot of folks real nervous, but you put their minds at ease. I've been watching you all these months, looking for some crack in you."

"Crack, sir?"

"A crack in your integrity or good humor. Gosh darnit, there isn't one. You're as unflappably decent as any man I've ever met. Except, perhaps, Lord Barnes."

"I'm flattered, Mr. Owens, but decency doesn't run a bank."

"That's where you're wrong. It's the very best quality to have."

A rising panic had me blinking in rapid succession. "You're not leaving right away, I hope? Please say you're not."

"No, we'll have a transition, which will give me the time to teach you any details you need to know."

I looked up when the front door opened, and Lord Barnes walked into the building. He wore a long black coat and top hat. Framed in the doorway, he seemed larger than life. "Good afternoon, gentlemen."

I stood. He strode over to greet us with handshakes.

Mr. Owens asked us to join him in his back office. "We'll keep an ear out for any visitors, but I expect we're mostly done for the day."

My stomach fluttered with nerves as I followed the two men into Mr. Owens's office. I sat in one of the customer chairs next to Lord Barnes, who had taken a moment to remove his coat and hang it next to Mr. Owens's on the hook attached to the wall.

The office was bare of any decoration, leaving only a desk and a notebook. Crude wood filing cabinets lined both sides of the room with details of loans and accounts. Our vault was downstairs. On my first day of employment, Mr. Owens had taken me down to show it to me, as well as teach me the combination for the lock. My heart had pounded and my palms sweated. I'd thought they were foolish to give a kid like me all this responsibility and trust until I'd remembered I was a grown man. I'd trained for a job just like this one. Still, I'd been as nervous as a cat in the presence of a coyote.

"Lord Barnes has come by to discuss our transition," Mr. Owens said as he settled behind his desk.

"Lord Barnes, respectfully," I said, "are you sure this is a good idea? I'm still green, as they say."

"We're quite sure," Lord Barnes said in his clipped English accent. "But there are a few things for which we need consensus. Succinctly speaking, we're dedicated to the idea that we run things our own way, without interference from the government."

"Yes, sir," I said. When I'd come to work here, I'd quickly

realized that all money in Emerson Pass led back to Lord Barnes. As the town grew, so did his wealth. By giving loans to businessmen and property buyers with low interest rates, his wealth may not have grown as quickly as other lenders, but he didn't seem to care.

"We don't want anyone telling us who we can or can't give loans to," Lord Barnes said. "Or making interest rates so high that regular chaps can't make their payments. That's not how one builds community."

I nodded in agreement but held back from another "yes sir." As much as I was in awe of Lord Barnes, I didn't want to sound like a boy instead of a man. If I were to be given this responsibility, I would have to act confident. Even if inside I was back to being that cat staring down a coyote.

"We don't want to get mixed up with all that Wall Street nonsense," Lord Barnes said. "The crashes earlier in the decade gave me great pause. I sold everything I had and reinvested it in land and other businesses. The stock market is too volatile for me. We like to keep things local here in Emerson Pass. What do you think, Viktor? Can you do business that way?"

"Yes, of course, sir."

"Good. Now that we've got that settled, let's talk about the future. Come out to the house for dinner tonight. We can go over a few things."

"I'd be happy to," I said. "Thank you. Thanks to both of you for believing in my abilities."

"We know you won't make us rue the day." Mr. Owens sat back in his chair and placed his hands over his stomach. "I'll be happily retired but also available if you ever need anything."

"Thank you, Mr. Owens."

We talked for another half hour about details and how much time I would have to absorb everything Mr. Owens knew before he handed it all over to me. By the end, my head felt as muddy as one of our country roads at springtime.

Finally, Lord Barnes clapped my shoulder. "Come out

tonight about seven. We can toast to your new position." I exchanged a glance with Mr. Owens. He gave me an encouraging nod. This was the sign from God I'd been looking for. The opportunity to formally ask Cymbeline's father for his blessing.

"I'll be there. I'd appreciate it if I could have a moment alone at some point in the evening. There's something I'd like to ask you." I cleared my throat. "Of a personal nature." I swallowed and folded my hands together to keep them from shaking.

Lord Barnes gave me a long, hard look. "I'll look forward to it."

DRESSED IN MY FINEST SUIT, I KNOCKED AT THE FRONT DOOR of the Barnes estate. Seconds later, Cymbeline opened it and ushered me into the foyer. "I'm so glad to see you." She looked around to make sure no one was watching and put her arms around my neck and give me a lingering kiss. "Papa told me the news about your promotion. I'm so very proud of you."

"I'm glad you are. I'm sure they've made a terrible mistake."

"I do hope you're kidding. You're the perfect one to take over. Papa said so."

"I appreciate his confidence in me. I'll do my best."

"You always do," Cym said.

I stood back to take her in. What a sight she was, wearing a light blue dress made from chiffon with a matching scarf that she'd wrapped around her curls. A touch of rouge and lipstick brightened her face. All in all, she reminded me of a perfect spring day. She smelled of the flowers that dotted the hillsides in the first warm months of the year. "You look and smell like a May afternoon. The prettiest day of the year."

"You look fine yourself, Mr. Olofsson." She tugged on the lapels of my black suit. "We're having roast beef for dinner. Papa said it would be a celebration for your new position."

"This is very kind of him," I said. "There's another reason I'm here."

"Besides seeing me?" Cym asked.

"I'm going to ask him for your hand tonight."

Her mouth dropped open, and for one terrifying second I thought she was going to tell me not to do it. However, a split second later her face lit up with obvious joy. She took both my hands and gave me a searching look as if I had a secret I hadn't told her. "Viktor, are you sure you really want to marry me?"

"Yes. It's all I want. I wanted his permission before I asked you."

Her eyes widened. "What if he says no? I'd never thought about it until just now."

"Do you think that's a possibility?" My heart sank. Why would she ask unless she was worried? No, it couldn't be. He'd offered me the bank job. If I was good enough for that, wasn't I good enough for Cym?

"Not because he won't want you in the family," she whispered. "Because of me. He knows how I am. He might think I'll ruin your life. That's what Flynn thinks, isn't it?"

"That's not what he said."

"I knew it. He said something about me the other night at the club, didn't he?"

I looked at the ceiling, avoiding her peering eyes for a moment to gather myself. "It doesn't matter what he thinks. I love you."

Tears sprang to her eyes. She stepped backward, staring at me. "Say it again."

"I love you, Cymbeline Barnes. You know I do."

"But it's the first time you said the words." She waved her hands in front of her eyes. "I didn't think it would sound quite so large." She elongated the word *large* and opened and closed her hands in a way that reminded me of butterfly wings.

"Large?" I asked, laughing. "What does that mean?"

She tapped her chest. "Large. Profound. I felt it in here. In my *actual* heart. The blood pumped a little harder. How is it that a man like you—Viktor Olofsson, town hero, handsome, talented, and smart—loves me? Me—Cymbeline Barnes—sassy, opinionated, troublemaking me. You. Actually. Love. Me."

I laughed and pulled her to me. "I didn't think that was an unknown."

"Say it again before we go inside to see the others."

"I love you," I whispered in her ear. "More than you could ever know."

"I love you," she whispered back, then pulled away slightly to look up at me with sparkling eyes. "It's love, isn't it?"

"Is what?" My entire body hummed with happiness. I was intoxicated with her. So much so, I could hardly follow her.

"My adventure. Everyone's adventure. It takes the most courage of all. The most strength."

"Not for me. Loving you is the easiest thing I've ever done."

"Well, that's just you now, isn't it?" She straightened my tie. "Come on. The family's waiting."

I deflated some, remembering the task at hand. "Would you tell him I'm here and ready for our talk?"

She kissed me. "Yes, silly. But you have nothing to worry about."

I leaned against the door, heart beating fast, as she scampered off to fetch her father. As many times as I'd been here, this time felt different. The light in the foyer was dim and cast shadows about the walls. From here, I could see the stairs that led up to the bedrooms. These were the spaces that had helped make Cymbeline. I could almost hear the echo of her little-girl voice between the walls. The same voice I'd heard on the very first day I'd gone to school. I'd been afraid to attend school and had begged Mother to let me stay and help at the shop. "Send Isak," I'd said. "He can learn how to be an American for all of us."

My mother had had none of that. She'd told me they needed both of us to read and write in English. To be American. Educated and ambitious. "To own businesses someday. Not back-bending ones like your father," she'd said in Norwegian.

I closed my eyes, remembering that first day. Pretty Miss Cooper had welcomed us as we were, no matter if we spoke English or how long we'd been in America. She promised us all that we'd learn to read and write and do numbers. I'd loved school from the first moment. Academics had come easily to me, as had making friends. I'd been blessed with some of the best ones.

And then there was Cymbeline Barnes. She'd always been just out of reach, either challenging me to a race or tossing her saucy curls at my attempts to become her friend. Now, though? She loved me. She'd finally caught up to me.

Please, God, let me be worthy of her. Please have Lord Barnes say yes.

I was about to ask him for such a huge gift. He would have to trust me to take one of the most precious aspects of his life and make sure she was well cared for and loved.

Lord Barnes appeared in the foyer. Wearing his formal dinner attire, he looked even more intimidating than he had at the bank earlier.

"Viktor, nice to see you, lad. Come sit with me in the study. You look like you could use a drink."

"Yes, sir."

He had me sit in one of the armchairs while he poured us both a whiskey. After handing me a glass, he sat next to me. "What brings you here?"

"You invited me to dinner. It was tonight?"

The corners of his eyes crinkled. "Yes, it was tonight. I mean, what brings you here to my study?"

"Oh, right." I cleared my throat and took a tentative sip of the drink. "I'd like your permission and blessing to ask Cymbeline to marry me. I'd like to ask her on Thanksgiving Day, as she's what I'm most thankful for this year and all the ones to come. That is, if you say yes and she says yes."

"I see." He looked into the fire and swirled the whiskey in his glass.

"I'd take good care of her, sir. She'd be everything to me, and I'd treat her thus. I know I can't provide what you have here, but I have a house and, as you know, a good job. She'll not want for anything."

He turned slowly to look at me. "I've no doubt of any of those things. You're a fine young man. But there's something even more important when it comes to Cymbeline. She's my special one, you know. The one most like me. All that curiosity and need for adventure comes from me. I gave up my whole way of life in England just so I could see America and become the maker of my own destiny. I traveled for years until I found this small part of the world. I fell in love immediately and knew this would be my home. She's like that too. There's an itch to her. A desire to see what's around the next corner."

What did he mean? Was he implying that Cymbeline would be bored with a small-town banker? "Do you think she'll be unhappy if she stays here with me? She told me you suggested university for her. Is that what you want?"

"Oh, goodness, no." He patted my knee. "She belongs with you. You're the only man I know who wouldn't want to break her —take all the Cymbeline out of her. I was simply telling you how precious she is to me, how much I understand her heart. I'm grateful. For the way you look at her. The way you see her. How gentle and understanding and good you are. I couldn't ask for anything more for her than you."

I breathed a sigh of relief. "All I want is to see her shine. I don't need anything but that."

"You have my blessing. Always have and always will." He smiled and raised his glass. "Welcome to my family, son."

I almost cried from relief and pure joy but kept myself from doing so by clinking his glass and taking a swig of the whiskey. Then I coughed.

Cymbeline

On Thanksgiving morning, we awoke to a fresh layer of snow. My stomach fluttered with excitement. As the first day of our Thanksgiving festivities, which began the holiday season in Emerson Pass, it would be filled with fun activities and end with a scrumptious meal. Viktor and his family were joining us for the feast, as were the Cassidys.

I went to rouse my sisters but found they were already up and most likely downstairs for breakfast.

After dressing quickly and fixing my hair, I bounded down the stairs. The entire family was at the table, talking excitedly about the day's plans. For a moment, I froze in the doorway, taking in the scene. All the breakfasts I'd eaten at this table with my siblings and parents seemed to flash before me all at once. Soon, I would no longer be here listening to the voices of my family. I'd be a married woman. As much as I loved Viktor, the idea of not being part of this every day saddened me. How often we take for granted the ordinary occurrences in our days. We're too busy living to notice how quickly it all passed. The milestones of childhood are only noticed by the generations above us until we look back to pull out the memories.

I couldn't imagine the day when this room held only Mama

and Papa. Everything in this house had revolved around us. Would they be lonesome in their later years? Or perhaps happy to have a little peace and quiet?

"Cym, did you hear? The pond's frozen," Addie said.

I took in her shining eyes and flushed skin. Even her hair seemed thicker and more luxurious than it had been only days ago. "I had a feeling," I said. "Joyous day."

"Will you go with us?" Delphia said. "Papa's going to hitch up the horses and sled and take us into town."

"Yes, of course I'll go with you." My mind sped ahead. Would Viktor be there? I went to the window. At least another foot of snow had fallen last night. "Is there too much snow to drive the cars?"

"I believe so," Papa said. "It'll take the snowplows all day to dig us all out. Your mother thought it was time to bring out the sleigh for the rest of the season."

"I love winter." I went to the buffet and helped myself to eggs, potatoes, and toast. "Can we pick up Viktor on the way?"

"If you wish," Papa said.

"But he won't know we're coming," Delphia said. "What if he's in his pajamas?"

I patted her head before taking the chair next to her. "He gets up early to take care of his chores. I don't think we need to worry that he's not dressed."

"Good. Because we don't want him to be embarrassed." Delphia scooped a bit of Lizzie's fluffy scrambled eggs into her mouth.

"Delphia, that's thoughtful of you," Mama said. "I like to see you thinking of others."

"Thank you, Mama. I'm growing up rather nicely, don't you think?" Delphia smiled, looking a bit like a kitten after eating an entire bowl of cream.

I bit the inside of my lip to keep from laughing.

Mama raised one eyebrow. "Yes, darling, rather well."

Fiona, who had been listening with obvious amusement,

pushed her plate aside. "I hope our whole crowd will be there today."

"If I were a betting man, I'd say the whole town will come out this morning," Papa said. "We all look forward to the beginning of our winter skating."

Talk turned to plans for our Thanksgiving meal. Since we were having company, we planned on entertaining in the formal parlor. Lizzie and the rest of the staff had been cooking for days. Downstairs in the kitchen, pies and cakes were piled up on the table. For dinner we would have a roasted turkey and all the trimmings.

Best of all, Viktor would be there with us. The first of what I hoped were many Thanksgivings together.

ॐ

As predicted, Viktor was not in his pajamas. He was outside shoveling his walkway when our merry group arrived. The horses wore bells around their necks, announcing our presence. Viktor looked up as we came to a halt near the house. Papa and Mama were in the front, and my sisters were tucked under blankets in the middle seat. I occupied the back seat, hoping that soon Viktor would slide in beside me.

Viktor leaned on his shovel as he called out a hearty greeting. "What have we here? The entire Barnes family come to see me?"

"We're taking you to town," Delphia shouted. "To skate. The pond's frozen."

Viktor grinned and made his way through the snow to us. He took off his hat and bowed his head toward Papa and Mama. "Lord Barnes. Mrs. Barnes."

"Sorry to come without an invitation," Mama said. "We were hoping you'd come in with us, as the roads are bad."

"Much obliged, thank you," Viktor said. "I'd be delighted to join you."

"If you're not too afraid I'll beat you in a race," I said.

He laughed. "That, my dear, is not something I fret over."

"We're glad you're not in your pajamas," Delphia said.

"Not at this hour, young lady. A man has work to do." Viktor turned to say hello to Addie. "You're looking very well."

"Hi ,Viktor," Addie said shyly. "I'm feeling quite well."

"I'd be delighted to join you," Viktor said. "If you can wait a second, I'll just go inside and grab my skates."

Delphia cheered and clapped her mittened hands together. "Hurry, Viktor. You can sit by me."

Viktor winked at her and then headed toward the house. I leaned forward. "Delphia, Viktor's going to sit by me. He's my beau."

Delphia's brow creased. "But I like him too."

"We all like him," Mama said. "However, he and Cym will sit together, as couples do."

"Will I ever have a beau?" Delphia asked.

"Someday, in the very far future," Papa said. "Far, far away."

"When I do, I want him to be just like Viktor," Delphia said.

"Me too," Addie said. "Someone strong, brave, and good."

He was all those things. I smiled with pride, as if I'd had anything to do with making him.

Soon, Viktor returned with his skates. Papa urged the horses onward. Fiona started singing "Jingle Bells" and encouraged us all to join her. Viktor and I held hands under a wool blanket. Although glad for gloves and our heavy coats, I still wished I was barehanded so I could feel his skin against mine. Regardless, I sighed with contentment and breathed in his woodsy scent.

Everything was covered in white except for a few trees that had managed to shake their limbs free of snow. Overhead, the sky was overcast. Snow might fall again by later today. I hoped not. I didn't want anything to ruin our Thanksgiving supper.

When we arrived in town, people had already gathered at the pond. Lights were strung in a crisscross over the ice. My uncle Clive's sausage cart was out, with one of their workers selling hot dogs to hungry skaters. Mrs. Johnson, as was tradition, was serving popcorn from her new machine. The moment I jumped from the sleigh the buttery, salty scent made me wish for a bag.

Li met us as we crossed over to where crowds of people mingled near the ice. He carried his violin case; Fiona had her guitar. They would play together under the gazebo while she sang. Fiona's face turned even more radiant at the sight of him. A pang of worry interrupted my happy mood. I'd put it aside for now. Today was a good day. No time to worry about her or Flynn.

"I'll see you all later," Fiona said. Without a backward glance, she and Li left together, chatting already about which songs they would start with. They did look right together, both so earnest and gifted and pure. Would it be possible to keep them apart? Would Papa want to, or would he grant them permission? That is, if Li felt the same way as Fiona.

Mama and Papa went off to meet up with Aunt Annabelle and Clive. Delphia ran ahead to gather with some of her friends from school, but Addie lingered behind with us.

"What do you think, Miss Addie?" Viktor asked. "Are you going to skate today?"

"My legs are weak," Addie said. "What if I can't even get around once? What if I fall and everyone laughs at me?"

"We'll go with you," I said. "Viktor will take a side, and I'll take the other. If you feel weak, you can lean on us."

"You don't mind?" Addie asked.

"I'd be honored to skate with not one but two of the lovely Barnes sisters," Viktor said.

A cloud passed over Addie's face, but she didn't say anything. Did she think she was the only Barnes daughter without beauty? If only she could see her future. Now that she was on the mend, she would bloom like a rose in the years to come.

We all attached our skates and went out to the ice. My legs were strong from all my training with Viktor and the subsequent jumps. I ached to take off at full speed but held back for Addie's sake. We each took one of her hands and we started out in the same direction as everyone else. I never knew why, but we always skated counterclockwise. We had since the very first time the pond became a community gathering place.

On the far end, a group of boys were racing one another.

"Do you see that?" I asked Viktor. "Not one girl."

"I think you're mistaken," Viktor said. "I see a little blue hat."

It was Delphia, smaller than anyone, about to race a much larger boy. Another of the children shouted, "Go," and the two broke out across the ice. Delphia didn't have a chance. Still, she was fast for being tiny. At least she was in the race.

"That's my girl," I said under my breath as we rounded the corner.

"She reminds me of someone." Viktor's eyes sparked at me over Addie's head.

"I can't think who," I said.

"Do you love me as much as Delphia?" Addie asked in a quiet voice.

"Me?" I asked, surprised.

"Yes, you." She glanced up at me.

"Of course I do, goose. I love all my sisters the same, which is as big as the Colorado sky. Why would you ask such a thing?"

"I don't know." Addie ducked her head and continued to glide over the ice with slow, deliberate movements.

She *did* know. Addie thought because Delphia and I shared a temperament and had common interests that I cared for her more.

A memory came to me. Before Mama had arrived into our lives, Papa had always seemed to dote on Fiona, carrying her around and kissing her chubby cheeks. I'd thought he didn't love me as much as her. I figured it was because of all my naughty ways. Thinking I was second best had made me feel helpless and horribly jealous. Looking back, I could see that Papa loved all of us, but Fiona had been an infant when our mother died. He'd been left alone to care for a small baby. He'd probably felt alone and frightened. "Just because she and I are more alike than you and me doesn't mean I love her more or less than you."

"You're always calling her your girl," Addie said. "I'd like to be your girl."

"You're both my girls," I said. "My baby sisters. Do you know how pleased Fiona and I were when you were born?"

"You weren't jealous of us?" Addie asked. "I would've been."

"Not me. I was almost eight when you arrived, so I was excited. Fiona was a tad envious though." I smiled at the memory. Fiona had been almost six when Addie had arrived. "She'd been the baby all her life, so when you came along it was a shock for her."

"I can't imagine Fiona being jealous," Viktor said. "She's serene all the time. I don't think I've ever seen her flustered."

"She was Papa's princess. That's what he always called her, so when suddenly he started paying attention to the new baby, poor Fiona had a hard time adjusting. Fortunately, she was able to go to school around then, which she loved. Mama suggested she start playing the piano. Cleverly, she thought Fiona needed something to do while she was with the new baby. She hired a piano teacher to come to the house a few times a week. Mrs. Fudd." I shuddered at the memory of the elderly piano teacher. She'd had a mole on her chin from which thick silver hair sprung. "She was scary. I was glad they didn't make me take lessons. Fiona took to it right away, though. Even back then she used to practice for hours."

"Fate," Viktor said.

"I guess so," I said.

"Was I cute?" Addie asked.

"You were such a tiny thing. I was afraid to hold you in case I broke you. But after you got a little bigger, you were my little pet."

"Is that why you call me pet or goose?" Addie asked.

"Yes, I suppose it is. When you started to walk, you used to follow me everywhere." Her hair had been so fair and fine back then that it was almost white. I could remember her playing with blocks in a spot of sun in the sitting room and thinking she looked like an angel. I'd imagined I saw a halo, but in hindsight it was probably just a play of the light.

We'd made it all around the pond. "Look at that," Viktor said. "You did very well, Addie. We're already back."

"My legs feel wobbly," Addie said.

"We'll take a break, but we should come here every day we can so you can build up more strength in your legs," I said.

"What about your training?" Addie asked. "I don't want to get in the way of that."

"I have time for that too." We skated over to a bench so that Addie could rest. She'd just sat when a girl about her age skated up to us. I didn't recognize her. Another newcomer to town, I guessed.

"Hi, Addie."

"Hi, Rose." Addie suddenly seemed very interested in her own knuckles.

"I've missed you at school." Rose had dark hair braided into pigtails. She wore a red coat and hat. Brown eyes peered at Addie from under the brim. I had a momentary memory of Poppy as a child.

Addie looked up, an expression of surprise on her face. "You have?"

"Sure I have. I haven't had anyone to study with. The other girls don't care about books like you and me."

"Oh, well, I do like books." Addie looked up at me, as if she wanted me to confirm this. "I didn't know you'd miss me at all. It seemed like you decided to be friends with Mary and Gertie instead of me. You were with them that one day."

"What day?"

"The day I was sick and they told everyone."

Rose's mouth formed a circle before she sucked in a breath. "How could you think such a thing? They're terrible. I would never be friends with them. In fact, they both were sent home for a whole week after you left. Miss Swallow said she'd had enough of their behavior. I think she even called their mothers in to talk to them too."

"That must have been awful for them." Addie smiled.

"I think it was."

Viktor nudged me. "Let's skate and leave them be," he whispered in my ear.

As much as I'd have liked to stay and make sure this Rose was telling the truth, I knew he was right. It was better for Addie to navigate through her own childhood. If there were battles to fight, she would have to do them herself. If there were friendships to forge, she must do those alone as well.

"We'll see you later, Addie," I said.

"All right." She gave me a quick wave, already focused on her friend rather than us.

Viktor offered his hand, and I took it. We sped away, skating in perfect harmony. Li and Fiona started to play a rollicking tune on the other end of the pond.

"That Rose better have good intentions," I said. "I'm not sure if she's telling the truth."

"Addie's smart. She'll discern for herself."

I glanced up at him. A muscle near his eye twitched. Now that I thought about it, he'd been quiet. Was it because he couldn't get a word in between Addie and me? Or was something bothering him? "Is everything all right?" I asked.

"With me? Yes, yes. Fine."

"Have I done anything to upset you?" I asked.

"What? You? Never. No, I've been preoccupied. I want this moment to be perfect."

"What moment?" We turned the corner, still holding hands. Delphia was no longer at the racing section and instead was twirling in the middle of the ice with a friend.

"The moment we tell our children about." Viktor veered to the right, pulling me into the middle of the ice. We came to a stop. He took my other hand and drew me around to face him. "I'm going to pull a ring from my pocket and offer it to you."

Startled by this sudden turn of events, I was speechless. The music from Li and Fiona had changed to the unmistakable melody of "When My Baby Smiles at Me." One of my favorites from the underground club.

Viktor reached into his pocket and came out with a ring. He held it between his thumb and index finger. A simple design with a small sapphire and a few tiny diamonds, it shone under the lights. "Do you like it?"

"It's pretty," I said. "But I didn't need a ring. You're enough."

"I wanted to get you the best ring in the world, but this is all I could afford."

"I like it very much." My vision blurred with tears.

"I picked it because it goes with your eyes—both the blue sapphire and the way the diamonds shine."

I drew in a shaky breath. Had he asked me already? Was I supposed to say something now? "Is this the part where you ask me or did you already?"

"I haven't yet, but I'm about to. Should I get down on one knee?" Viktor asked.

"No, then everyone will look." I wiped my eyes to rid them of the tears that gathered in my lashes before they froze.

"Too late," he said.

Glancing about, I realized everyone had stopped skating and were gathering in a circle around us. Papa and Mama were standing with Viktor's parents. The twins and their wives were with Phillip and Jo. The whole town appeared to be here, and they were all focused on us.

"I didn't think anyone would notice what I was doing. " From the flushed look on Viktor's face, it was clear he hadn't antici-pated this.

"Look in my eyes. This is still just us. Pretend no one else is here."

His eyes seemed to come into focus. For a second, we

centered ourselves in the other's gaze. "Cymbeline Barnes, will you be my wife?"

I was overcome with emotion and also embarrassment because of all the onlookers. My legs were shaking so hard I thought I might fall over, but I managed to whisper, "Yes."

From the crowd, a voice shouted, "What did she say?"

Another voice, a woman this time said, "I can't tell."

"She said no, I think."

That rippled through the crowd. There were a lot of sighs and "poor boy." A myriad of opinions were uttered about me, ranging from dying an old maid to wild child and dancing fool.

"What a shame," an elderly lady behind us said.

"I told you she'd never marry."

"Too stubborn, that one, to see what's right in front of her face."

"Such a nice boy."

"A looker too, ain't he?"

Viktor leaned close. "I'm sorry. This was a mistake. I wanted to do it somewhere meaningful to us."

"No, it's fine. I don't care about them." I held out my hand. "Put the ring on, please."

He blinked and then looked down to his finger and thumb, which still clutched the ring. "Yes, right. But you have to take off your glove."

I giggled and tugged my glove from my hand. "We're doing this all wrong."

"This is a disaster. I don't like them saying all those things about you."

"I couldn't care less. In fact, I love it."

Despite everyone thinking I'd said no, not one moved away. I'd have thought they'd have skated off by now, disappointed in wild Cymbeline Barnes, but they must have sensed the moment wasn't yet done. I held my hand out to him. He slid the ring onto my finger, but it stuck at the knuckle.

"Oh dear. I didn't realize how wide it is there," Viktor said.

"It's fine. If I have to cut off my knuckle, this ring is going on my finger." I had to take off my other glove and stick both of them in my pocket so that I could push the cold ring over my knobby knuckle. "I don't suppose I'll ever get it off again."

"Good."

"Let's give them what they want," I said in his ear. "Maybe they'll forgive us later when they learn I pretended to be a boy in the race."

"Good idea."

I raised my arm high in the air and called out, "I said yes." A happy roar went through the crowd before arguments broke out around us about who had been right and who wrong. Regardless and perhaps satisfied, people skated away, leaving us to stare into each other's eyes in peace.

"I hope our wedding itself goes better than that," Viktor said.

"I hope our marriage goes better." I tilted my head so he could kiss me.

After a quick peck, Viktor motioned toward my family, who were now congregated over by the bench where I'd left Addie. "I think we have some folks to see."

We skated over together. Mama grabbed me first, pulling me to her slender frame. "You did it, my girl."

"What did I do?"

"You opened yourself to love." She placed her hands on my face. "I know it wasn't easy, and I'm very proud of you."

"Thank you, Mama, but it's all Viktor. He's the only one it could be."

"That, my dear, is love." Mama let me go so that Papa could embrace me.

"You're always my baby girl," Papa said. "Don't forget that."

"Oh, Papa."

He withdrew to shake Viktor's hand.

Delphia threw herself around my waist. "I'll miss you when you move away."

I knelt down to her level. "I won't be very far, and I'll come see you all the time."

"You won't forget about me?"

"Never." I pulled Delphia into a hug, breathing in the sweet scent of her. "You would be unforgettable even if you weren't my sister."

When I straightened, Fiona was there. We embraced, holding on to each other as if we were parting forever. Thinking of not waking in the same house as her was impossible.

"I'm happy for you," Fiona whispered. "But I'm going to miss you more than you know."

"I do know, because I'll miss you just as much."

The rest of the afternoon was a blur. Viktor and I skated many times around the rink we were so familiar with, basking in the day and each other. We didn't talk much, but there seemed to be nothing to say that hadn't been said that day already.

Viktor

My mother's hands shook as we all gathered around the long table in the Barneses' dining room. She'd been to the house for parties many times before but never as a guest at the table of Lord Barnes and his wife. The ladies were all dressed in finery, including my mother, who wore her new frock made from fine blue silk. I couldn't remember her ever looking as pretty as she did that evening.

Thankfully, Mother had been seated next to Mrs. Cassidy, whom she knew well and would be comfortable with. On the other side of her was my father, who also seemed nervous even though he and Cymbeline's father were good friends. Lord Barnes had been one of his best customers for years.

Covered with a white cloth and decorated with candles that ran down the middle, the table had been elongated to accommodate all the guests. Copious forks, including a small one placed at the top of the plate, confused me, but I would follow Cym's lead.

Mrs. Barnes said the prayer, thanking the Lord for the food, for one another, and for the good health of all around the table. After a chorus of amens, Lord Barnes stood. He'd asked Jasper to bring up bottles of champagne from the cellar so that he might toast my engagement to Cym as well as Isak and Nora's. Once everyone had a glass, he raised his.

"Might I propose a toast to the happy couples and congratulate them on their engagements. It seems the Olofsson, Cassidy, and Barnes families will be more united than ever. If I may be so bold, I'd like to think of us all as one big, extended family for which I'm very thankful. Welcome, all, to our home. May God bless us all."

I clinked my glass with Cym's and my mother's and then leaned across the table to toast Fiona and Addie, who were seated directly across from us. The dinner was delicious, and conversations flowed. Before I knew it, the meal was over and we went on to the next part of the evening. I'd rather have stayed with Cymbeline, but the party divided into men and women. The ladies went back to the formal parlor whereas the men retired to the library.

Lord Barnes gave all the men cigars and whiskeys. My father looked uncomfortable as Flynn leaned over to light his. I wasn't sure my father had ever had a cigar. Sitting close to him on the couch, I leaned over and advised him not to inhale. Isak had told me this the first time I'd had a cigar with him and the twins, which had saved me from coughing and embarrassing myself.

There were seven us altogether gathered in the library. My father and Lord Barnes sat together by the fire. The twins and Isak were in a corner talking about old times. I'd wandered over to the window seat and sat with Phillip. Soon, we would be brothers-in-law, and I wanted to get to know him better.

He clinked my glass. "To you and me. I have to say, it's nice to have another man around who isn't a blood-born Barnes. Welcome to the family."

"Thank you. I appreciate it." I lowered my voice. "Any advice for me?"

He chuckled and played with the cuff link on his left wrist. "Don't underestimate a Barnes woman. They might be pretty on the outside, but inside they're made of iron."

"Even Josephine? I mean, I know all about Cym, but your wife always seems gentle and cerebral."

"She is for the most part. But when it comes to our kids, no one better mess with them, or expect the wrath of Jo."

What would Cym be like as a mother? If the Lord blessed us, I reminded myself. There were no assurances that would happen. Theo and Louisa hadn't had any yet. Maybe we wouldn't either.

"But you can't be in a better family than this one," Phillip said. "They look out for one another and when you marry in, they consider you one of them. They're the family I always wished for."

"Dreams come true, don't they?"

He smiled and nodded. "We weren't sure you'd ever break her down. She's a tough one."

"Yes, she is. But worth all the trouble."

"Cymbeline's special to me. When I first came here, she was only fifteen. Full of sass and vinegar, but she made me feel very welcome."

"I remember." I smiled thinking about Cym at fifteen. She'd still challenged me to races back then.

"Her nemesis," Phillip said.

"I didn't know it was possible to be someone's nemesis without knowing you were," I said, chuckling.

"She's always loved you, even if she didn't recognize it. I'm happy for you two. More than I could possibly express with words. You're both lucky."

"I'd say the same for you and Josephine," I said.

He reached over to clap me on the shoulder. "I'll never be able to repay you for saving my Josephine. I hope I've thanked you enough over the years."

"You have." Every time he saw me, he thanked me in one way or the other. "No need to thank me again. It was my honor."

Isak and Flynn had started reminiscing about the war. Theo had left them to sit with Lord Barnes and my father. He was an old soul, our Theo, who seemed to belong more to the previous generation than the one he'd been born into.

"I've never heard you talk about the war," I said to Phillip. He'd served at the same time as Isak and the twins, but they'd not known one another until Phillip came to Emerson Pass.

"I'd rather leave it in the past where it belongs." He sipped from his glass before continuing. "I've no interest in visiting those memories. Not when I have all this." He swept his hand through the air to indicate the room and all it symbolized.

"I was only a kid when they all left. They were too, for that matter. But I remember hearing my mother cry at night. I hope we never have a war like that again."

"Agreed." He looked down at his lap, seeming to drift away.

"How's business?" I asked, hoping to distract him with whatever dark thoughts had come to him.

His gaze drifted toward Flynn. A muscle in his cheek flexed. "Business is fine. Good."

"Phillip? Is there something worrying you?" I kept my voice low.

He kept his eyes on Flynn and spoke so quietly I had to lean closer to hear. "He flies too close to the sun."

"What does that mean?"

He turned back to me, speaking at the same low volume as before. "There are aspects of the business I don't know about. He keeps it that way so that I don't have to lie about anything to Jo."

"What's he doing?"

"I have some ideas, but I don't want to know. Jo and I keep no secrets from each other. We vowed to each other that no matter what else happened, we would always tell each other the truth. Flynn knows that, which is why he keeps me in the dark about a lot."

"Cym thinks he was with some bad men the other night. Thugs."

Phillip closed his eyes as if he had a sudden pain. "Whatever he's into, I think he's in over his head."

"You should tell Lord Barnes."

He looked at me for a long moment. "Would that be best? I don't know."

"Lord Barnes built this town. If anything is threatening it, he should know what it is so he can fix it."

"Have you ever known anyone closely who seemed to make trouble for themselves? A man who has everything and yet seems to want to sabotage himself?"

"I certainly have."

We went quiet, both in our own thoughts. My ears perked up when I heard the others talking about the ski competition.

"We've got men from all over the country coming," Flynn said. "This is going to be one of the ski events of the year before you know it."

"Any Europeans?" Theo asked.

"None thus far." Phillip got up from the window seat to stand closer to the fire. "And the response from American skiers hasn't been as robust as we'd hoped. But if all goes well this year, maybe we can attract more next time."

"We will," Flynn said. "Once they realize what they missed out on."

"It's a long way to come for a ski race," Lord Barnes said.

"Especially given how hard it is to get here," Flynn said. "If it weren't for the road up from Louisville, we would never have been able to do this." His eyes flashed. "I told you all building that road was necessary."

"I didn't want it. Still don't," Lord Barnes said. "But if you think it's bringing you more business then I suppose I should. There was something so nice about thinking of Emerson Pass as a community without strangers."

"People came on the train, Papa. Same thing," Flynn said.

"Yes, but motorcars make everything different," Lord Barnes said. "I wonder how long we'll be a small town?"

A commotion from the foyer interrupted our conversation. Jasper's voice came to us first. "Sir, they're enjoying a family holiday. You'll have to come back."

Whoever was there with him said something I couldn't hear. A second later, the double doors to the library burst open and two men in blue suits walked in as if they'd been invited.

We all stood. The hairs on the back of my neck did too. My stomach dropped. They were the same men we'd seen outside the club the other night.

Jasper moved around them. "I'm sorry, m'lord. I couldn't stop them."

"Quite all right, Jasper." Lord Barnes strode across the room and introduced himself. "I'm Alexander Barnes. What can we do for you?"

"Name's Roland Fossi. This here's my business associate, Marco Chetta."

Lord Barnes shook each of their hands. "What brings you to my home on Thanksgiving?"

"We're here to see Flynn."

In the light of the room, I could see them better than I had the other night. One was of average height and slightly rotund with doughy cheeks and hard eyes. The other was tall and wide, larger even than Isak or me. A bulge in his jacket told me he carried a pistol. Not unusual for these parts, but it made the palms of my hands sweat. These were dangerous men. Violent men. What did they want with Flynn? I swallowed as bile moved into my throat. Something was very, very wrong.

Flynn came to meet them. His eyes shone with anger, not fear. Was that wise?

"You've got nerve coming to my family's home," Flynn said.

"We told you loud and clear what we wanted," Rossi said. "You give it to us and we go away."

"And I told you my business isn't for sale." Flynn's voice brought the image of an icicle breaking off from the side of a house and falling to the ground.

Instinctually I moved to Lord Barnes's side. Despite his height and good health, he suddenly appeared older to me. The tension in his face alone was enough to have aged him ten years.

Rossi stepped closer. The scents of cigarette smoke, gin, and the bottom of a cast-iron pot emanated from him. The smell of violence.

Isak and Phillip came to stand on either side of Flynn. Theo, as he always did, kept his head and went to stand near the cabinet where I knew Lord Barnes kept his rifle. We might appear civilized, but the lot of us had grown up in these woods and knew how to shoot a gun.

"Our mountain's not for sale," Phillip said.

"We're not talking about your slopes," Rossi said.

Chetta grunted.

"Flynn, what is this?" Phillip asked, fear making his voice sound higher than usual. "What are they talking about?"

Flynn ran a hand through his glossy brown hair. "This has nothing to do with you, Phillip. This is my business." He pointed at Rossi. "Let's take this outside. My family's enjoying the holiday."

Rossi didn't move for a several seconds. I wasn't sure he would, but in the end he nodded at Chetta. "Don't keep us waiting." Their shoes clicked on the hardwood floors before they disappeared into the foyer.

"Flynn?" Lord Barnes asked. "What are you doing?"

The front door slammed shut.

"It's nothing to worry about." Flynn shrugged as if there were nothing that particularly concerned him.

Lord Barnes raised his voice. "Two thugs just walked into my home. I'd say that's something to worry about."

"Papa, I'm a grown man. This is my business, and I'll take care of it. I'll be right back." Flynn crossed the room and disappeared into the foyer. The door slammed a second time.

"What do we do?" Theo asked. "Should I go out there?"

"If you go, I should go too," Isak said.

"And I." My gun was under the seat of my car. I'd never have thought I needed it at Thanksgiving dinner.

"What is this?" Lord Barnes asked Theo. "Do you know?"

"Papa, I've no idea."

"Nor do I." Phillip scratched the back of his neck. "But Flynn's been secretive and elusive lately. He obviously has another business that I don't know about."

Isak made a noise at the back of his throat. "I have a guess."

We all turned to him. "What is it?" Lord Barnes asked.

"Flynn hasn't told me, but I think he's running a distillery," Isak said.

"What? No, that's impossible," Phillip said. "We buy the booze from some moonshiner who lives in the woods."

"I think he's making it," Isak said. "I've seen him drive out to the old mine area a couple times."

"He's set up out there?" Phillip asked.

"It would be a good spot. Out of town and deserted," Isak said. "My guess is he's using the old office building."

"If he does run a distillery, what would those men want from him?" I asked.

"He said something about not selling," Lord Barnes said. "Maybe they want to buy it."

Theo had paled. "This isn't an offer to buy. It's informing him that they're going to take it one way or the other. That's the way these mobsters work."

"They don't want anyone distributing booze other than them," Isak said. "Since Prohibition, criminals have taken over the making and distribution."

"Why would they care about a small distillery out here?" I asked. "One that probably makes just enough to sell locally?"

"I don't know about that," Isak said. "This is Flynn we're talking about. He sees a business opportunity, he's going to take it. Maybe that's why he wanted the road from Louisville opened."

That should have been obvious to me but had not been. Hearing it out loud, the theory made perfect sense.

Theo sat down hard on one of the chairs and let out a long, despairing sigh.

"Here to take what he built for their own," Isak said. "They probably work for someone who wants Flynn to stop interfering with their business."

"Do you mean he's getting in the way of their distribution?" Lord Barnes asked.

"Isak's right," Theo said. "They don't want any of the smaller distilleries in their territory selling to speakeasies or individuals."

"Emerson Pass is no one's territory," Lord Barnes said. "We run this town, not mobsters."

"He opened us up to it when he started making gin," Theo said, then cursed under his breath. "If he doesn't give it over to them, they could kill him or his wife or one of us. That's how they do."

"My God, Flynn, what have you done?" Lord Barnes sank into a chair and put his head in hands.

It was then we heard the gunshot.

Cymbeline

We'd all heard the gunshot just as Fiona was about to sit down at the piano. For a moment, no one had moved. By then, Mr. and Mrs. Olofsson had already departed since they had to open the shop early but the rest of the women in our merry group were still gathered enjoying the evening. Mama had asked Jasper to pour a glass of sherry for whomever wanted one. Except for Shannon, the younger generation had all accepted one, including even Jo and Louisa, who usually refrained. I suppose we were all in a festive mood. We'd played cards and become giggly as though we were back in school. I didn't even mind that Nora had continued to win. Mama, Mrs. Cassidy, and Shannon had sat in one corner chatting. Only Jo was missing having gone upstairs to check on the kids, who were with the nanny.

We'd sat in stunned silence for a moment. Mama asked if it were a gunshot she'd heard. I'd nodded and thought—had the boys gone outside for fresh air and seen a creature? A bear? Why else would a gunshot ring out on Thanksgiving evening?

Fiona had caught my eye and mouthed the word *Flynn*.

Flynn? Why had she said that?

Now, as if waking from a dream, Fiona went to the French doors that led out to our covered porch and turned the lock.

Fear struck me dumb. I shivered, remembering the men from the club the other night. Was it possible the unsavory men had come here to our home? What was it that they wanted? What did they want with Flynn?

Was it possible that Flynn was involved in something illegal? The way he'd been acting lately, anything was possible. *Don't lie to yourself*, I thought. *You know what this is about.* I knew in my gut this had something to do with illegal gin. I'd suspected the booze he so readily had his staff pour at the club was too easy to get. His vague explanation about moonshiners had not satisfied me.

"I'll go find out what it is," I said.

"No, let's wait for your father to come back and tell us everything's all right," Mama said.

"Yes, stay put," Mrs. Cassidy said.

We waited for at least five minutes until finally I couldn't stand it any longer. "I'm going to see what's happening. This is stupid."

"No, Cym, please," Mama said. "If it's something dangerous, I don't want you out there."

Footsteps running down the hall drew our attention. Seconds later, Viktor appeared. He had not an iota of color in his face. His eyes were wild and frantic. I stood, limbs tingling with fright.

"Viktor, what is it?" Mama clutched the collar of her dress.

Viktor's voice shook. "Some men came by and wanted to talk to Flynn. He's gone outside with them."

"What? Was it Flynn? Is he hurt?" Shannon rose from the rocking chair where she'd been working on a needlepoint.

Viktor held on to the back of a chair as if his legs were about to crumble. "Yes, they shot Flynn."

Shannon cried out and ran toward the door. Viktor stopped her. "He's being looked after by Theo. You don't want to go in there."

"Is he dead?" Shannon asked, trembling.

"No, but the bullet is in his...actually I don't know where it was. There was so much blood. But it was somewhere on his upper torso."

Mama, who had been staring at Viktor stupefied, started for the door.

"Mrs. Barnes, please, I'm begging you. Stay here." Viktor went to her. "Theo asked specifically for you and Shannon to remain here. They're going to take him to the surgery room at the office."

"Lord have mercy," Shannon said. "Who would do this? Why would they shoot Flynn?"

Mrs. Cassidy got up and put her arms around her daughter, then led her back to sit on the sofa. However, Shannon didn't stay put for long. She got to her feet as fast as she could, which wasn't very because of her large pregnant belly. "I should get the baby from upstairs." She waved her hands as if she were trying to dry them.

"What good will that do?" Mrs. Cassidy asked. "She's asleep by now. The governess is looking after all of the children."

For the first time, I looked over at my baby sisters. They were sitting together on a love seat clutching each other. I'd forgotten they were even in the room. Good Lord, they must be scared out of their minds.

I went to sit next to them, pulling a trembling Delphia onto my lap.

"Were they the men from the other night?" I asked Viktor.

He nodded. "Yeah. They barged in and insisted that Flynn come outside with him."

"Shannon, do you know anything about these men?" Mama's voice remained sharp as a razor's edge. "Who are they?"

"I have no idea what anyone's talking about. What men? I have no idea why anyone would want to hurt Flynn." Shannon started to cry. "Everyone loves him."

Not everyone, I thought.

"Viktor, what do you know?" Mama asked.

Viktor looked a bit like a trapped animal. "Isak thinks Flynn's been running a distillery and these are criminals who want to take it from him. He's said no and they didn't like that answer."

"But why?" Shannon asked. "Why would anyone but the police care about an illegal distillery?"

"Because they're mobsters." Mama's voice had gone eerily calm. "They've shot him because he wouldn't cooperate. Is that it?"

"We believe so," Viktor said.

"Mobsters?" Shannon asked. "How would he get involved with gangsters?"

"He didn't get involved with them," Viktor said. "They came to him. They want control of all the illegal liquor market. That's how it works now. I've read about it in the Chicago papers. The entire city is run by mobsters now. Apparently they're widening their territory."

"Why would they care about our little town?" Mama asked.

"They don't," I said, as everything started to make sense. "They care about the gin. They want Flynn and Phillip and whoever to have to buy from them, not make their own."

"And whoever Flynn's been selling it to," Viktor said.

"My God, why would he do such a thing?" Mama asked. "He's put his family in danger."

"How could I not know?" Shannon asked. "He's never said a word about a distillery."

"Where is it?" Mama asked.

"We're not sure," Viktor said. "No one knew, Shannon. Not Theo or Isak. Or Phillip."

As if hearing her husband's name conjured her, Josephine appeared in the doorway. Tears stained her rouged cheeks. Her dress was covered with blood.

Mama rushed to her. "Jo, are you hurt?"

"No, it's not my blood. I saw it happen. I saw Flynn get shot."

"No, Jo," I whispered. "Not that." I balled my fists at my side.

"I was up in your room, Cym," Jo said. "Looking at the stars for a moment and enjoying just a few minutes of silence. I saw the car pull up, and these two awful-looking men got out and went to the front door. I waited, expecting they had the wrong house. A few minutes later they came out, followed by Flynn. They pushed him against their car and waved the gun in his face. Flynn lunged at them and the gun went off." She cried as she spoke, the words coming out jumbled and slurred. "Flynn fell to the ground, and the men got in the car and drove off. I ran downstairs and out the front door to him. The rest of them arrived seconds later. But I knew to press the wound to help stop the bleeding. Theo taught me that."

Her knees buckled, and she fell to the floor. Viktor picked her up and carried her over to the couch.

Tears dampened my cheeks. In my lap, Delphia shook like an aspen leaf in the wind and cried into my neck. I looked at Viktor, hoping he would come to sit with us. He understood and rushed over, plopping next to us on the floor.

"It's all right," I whispered in Delphia's ear, and then kissed the top of her head.

Shannon had stopped crying. Anger had replaced shock and dismay. "Why would he do it? Why would he fight that way when he knows I'm in the house with our unborn child and our baby? Just give them what they want. What kind of man does that?"

"A proud one," I said. "He built something for your family. A business that would make money for you and the kids." Why was I defending him? I felt the same as Shannon did, but I was empathetic to Flynn's point of view. He'd have thought he was doing the right thing.

"We didn't need more money," Shannon said. "What more could we need? And now I may have to go on without him and raise these two kids by myself."

"That's not going to happen," Fiona said. "Theo will fix him."

"Flynn's too tough to die," I said.

Mama went to sit next to Shannon. She took her hand. "We must have faith. But I understand your anger. I'm angry too."

"Why would he ruin our perfect life?" Shannon asked.

No one could answer that question. As much insight as I had into Flynn's character, being so close to mine, I could not comprehend why he didn't simply agree to give them the distillery before it led to violence. He'd risked everything. His wife and children and the rest of us, too. They'd come to my father's house on Thanksgiving. Now he was lying in a pool of blood. No ambition or money was worth risking the safety of your family or yourself. Shannon and these children needed him. He'd made a selfish decision. As he often had. Convincing Theo to go to war with him, for one. There were others too. Not that I could remember right now.

You better live, I thought. *So that I can throttle you.*

Jasper came into the room and cleared his throat. His hands shook, but his expression remained stoic. That English butler training had conditioned him for whatever our family tossed his way.

"Jasper, what's happening?" Mama asked, rushing to him.

"They've taken him to the doctor's office. Dr. Neal will meet them there to assist with the surgery. Theo was able to stop the bleeding. The wound's in his chest but appears to have missed his heart."

"How do you know?" Shannon asked.

"Theo says he wouldn't still be breathing," Jasper said.

We were all stunned into silence. The only sounds in the room were of Shannon weeping and the attempts at comforting her by Nora.

Mama seemed to gather herself by sheer will. "Jasper, please go home to Lizzie. We're going to need you both tomorrow, and you should get some rest."

Jasper nodded his head in agreement and ducked out of the room.

Papa and Phillip appeared. Both had blood on their suits and looked as though they'd been punched numerous times in the gut. Papa put his arm around Mama. Phillip rushed to his wife and took her by the hand. "Isak and Theo have taken him into surgery. I'm going to follow them and wait while they perform the operation."

"I'd like to go too," Shannon said.

"Wouldn't you be more comfortable here?" Mama asked. "You should get rest. For the baby."

"No, I want to be there," Shannon said.

"Nora and my mother will stay." She shifted her gaze from one to the other. "For when Pearl wakes?"

"Yes, we'll take care of her. We can take her back to the farm with us," Nora said. "She can stay all day with us, depending."

I couldn't help but ask myself, depending on what? Squeezing Delphia tighter, I buried my face in her soft hair and prayed silently. *Please God, take care of him. Don't take him from us. We all need him.*

Nora had mentioned earlier that the new owners of the farm were to take possession at the first of the new year. After Nora and Isak wed and she and her mother had moved into Isak's home, would Flynn still be with us?

With help from her mother and sister, Shannon lumbered to her feet. This baby would come any day. What had Flynn been thinking? Would we ever have the chance to ask him?

"I'm going too," Mama said. "I can't sit here all night and wait."

"You'll be waiting either way," Papa said gently.

"I want to be with you," Mama said. "And for Flynn when he wakes up."

Papa looked over at me and my sisters. "You all look after one another."

As a unit we all moved over to hug Papa and Mama. Delphia had started to cry again. Mama knelt to take her into her arms. "Be brave for me, won't you? Flynn needs you to be strong."

"I'll try." Delphia sniffed.

Mama stood and brushed off her skirt. "We'll go then."

Delphia moved back to stand by me. Addie had already retreated to sit over with Josephine.

Nora had been pacing by the window. "Please let us know if you need anything."

"Absolutely," Papa said. Worry creased his brow, and his shoulders slumped slightly. I'd never seen him that way. Nothing terrified me as much.

Mama took one of Shannon's arms and Papa the other. We all watched in silence as they walked out of the room. Their footsteps seemed uncommonly loud as they headed down the hallway.

After a few seconds of silence, we all seemed to wake from a dream to deal with the practical matters.

Nora would drive herself, Mrs. Cassidy home and the baby in Flynn's car. Josephine and Phillip had already planned on staying overnight with us. Fiona had given them her room, and she would sleep with me.

I was comforted knowing that Jo and Phillip would be here with us, especially with everything that had happened tonight. Would the men return? The thought sent a shiver up my spine.

There were only a handful of times Papa had not been in the house when I was sleeping. His presence was something I took for granted.

"I'll go up and get Pearl," Fiona said.

"I can help," Nora said. "Shannon had a bag for her."

Fiona and Nora headed upstairs to collect Pearl while I helped Mrs. Cassidy into her coat.

Phillip and my little sisters were standing at the foot of the stairs when Fiona and Nora came down with baby Pearl. By a small miracle, she hadn't woken and was resting peacefully in Nora's arms. Fiona carried a bag with diapers and pins. I sneaked a peek at her. At nearly a year and a half old, she was one of the prettiest babies I'd ever seen. With dark curls and a round cherubic face, she'd inherited her mother's beauty and sweet personality. Again, I wondered how Flynn could risk this for money.

After they were gone, I peered out the small window by the front door. The skies were clear, thankfully. All we needed was a blizzard.

Addie came to stand beside me. "I was hoping you would all have a break from being frightened," she said.

"What do you mean?" I asked.

"I'm getting well, and now Flynn's hurt."

"He's going to be fine. Theo and Dr. Neal will fix him."

She leaned her head against my shoulder.

I wrapped my arm around her thin frame. Behind us, I heard Phillip and Jo talking softly to each other. Addie and I turned in their direction.

"Cym, we're going to try to get some sleep," Jo said at the bottom of the stairs. "The children will be up at the first light, and we'll need to look after them properly."

"I'll be up and let you know if any news comes," I said. We embraced before she went up the stairs with Phillip.

I turned to see Viktor, carrying an exhausted Delphia on his shoulders. The four of us headed up to the second floor. I'd lost Fiona somewhere but assumed she couldn't be far behind. When we in their bedroom, Viktor took Delphia from his shoulders and laid her on her bed. "I'll wait downstairs for you," he whispered to me.

"I'll get them tucked in and be right down," I said. Would he stay all night with Fiona and me?

I sent the girls off to brush their teeth and put their night-gowns on and perched on the side of the bed. My stomach was in knots, and I felt slightly dizzy. Those men could be out there right now. Waiting to shoot another one of us.

Fiona rushed into the room.

"There you are," I said.

"Sorry for the delay. I was locking up," Fiona said. "I went down to make sure Jasper was heading off to his cottage."

"Was he?"

"No, but he went upon my urging. I locked the kitchen door behind him."

"I'm glad Viktor and Phillip are here," I said.

"Me too."

Addie and Delphia came out of the bathroom, scrubbed clean and wearing their flannel nightgowns. I grabbed two pairs of socks from the drawer. "Put these on your feet. I believe it's going to be extra cold tonight." Frost had already made a frame of the windows.

Like two meek lambs, they did as I asked and climbed into their twin beds. Delphia yawned so wide I was afraid her head might split in half. I tucked the blankets around her and kissed her forehead. "You be a good girl and go right to sleep."

"I'm scared," Delphia said.

"I am too," Addie said. "What if the men come back?"

"They won't," Fiona said, sounding surprisingly sure. I guessed it was probably an act for the girls. "It was Flynn they wanted. They don't care anything about the rest of us. Anyway, Viktor and Phillip are here. They won't let anyone come into our house."

They both nodded, ready to believe anything we said that was reassuring. I went to the other bed and kissed Addie. She turned over on her side and closed her eyes. As much as she'd improved, blue veins were still visible on her forehead. She was on the mend, I reminded myself. Lizzie had done a terrific job of making sure we knew what had flour and what didn't. She'd made a flourless chocolate cake for one of the desserts.

We said good night, and I reached to turn out the bedside lamps.

"Can we keep one on?" Delphia asked.

"Yes, and I'll leave the door open," I said. "Fiona and I are going downstairs to wait, so if you wake and we're not in my room, you may come downstairs."

Seeing the fatigue on both their faces, I doubted they would open their eyes until morning.

Viktor

When I entered the library, Daisy, one of the maids, was on her knees scrubbing at the blood left behind on the couch from Flynn's wounds. A bucket of bloodied water was beside her. From what I could tell, she was managing only to soak the cushions and make more of a mess. Blood, my father often told me, was nearly impossible to get out of certain fabrics. The light blue velvet couch was apparently one of them. Blood would have seeped into the fibers, determined to settle there for the rest of the sofa's existence.

She startled at the sound of my footsteps. "I'm sorry, Daisy. I didn't mean to scare you."

She ducked her head and fixed her gaze on the bucket. "It's all right. I'm shaken up with all this. Poor Master Flynn. Will they be able to save him?"

"God willing," I said. "Theo and Dr. Neal are skilled doctors."

"But a bullet wound?" She sat back on her heels, the folds of her dress damp from the cloth she didn't seem to remember she held in her hands.

"We must have faith," I said.

"Indeed." She returned to her work, scrubbing with more

vigor than even before, as if her hard work could alter the outcome.

While I waited for Cym and Fiona to come downstairs, I sat by the fire, overcome by the events of the evening. Despite the idyllic setting of our town, an undercurrent of darkness occasionally wove its way into our lives. Tonight, like the one in which Josephine almost lost her life, was one of them. Only this time I couldn't save anyone.

Flynn had brought that darkness to the surface. Running a distillery out of your own basement for your own purposes, or even for the underground club here in Emerson Pass, would have stayed under anyone's notice. What Flynn had done was to bring attention to himself. With that came the interest of folks who didn't have Emerson Pass's best interests in mind.

Now that I thought about it, neither did Flynn. His father had built this town under a set of guiding principles: God, family, and community. A distillery that distributed illegal gin to multiple cities, towns, and counties was not within those principles. Not at all. Did Flynn think only of himself and lining his own pockets with gold? Not the boy I'd known. Or even the young man who had come back from the war five years ago. What had happened to him that had changed him so?

I was thankfully drawn away from my thoughts when Cym arrived. She approached poor Daisy scrubbing away. "Oh, Daisy, you've done your best. There's not much more you can do with this anyway. We may have to throw the entire thing out. You may go. Get some rest."

Daisy stood and dropped the rag in the bucket. "Thank you. I'll take my leave then. Miss Cymbeline, you'll let the staff know, won't you? If anything happens one way or the other?"

"Yes, we'll be sure to tell Jasper the moment we know anything. Or Lizzie. Whomever I see first in the morning. But the staff is to get their rest tonight. We'll need you tomorrow more than we do tonight."

"Yes, Miss Cymbeline." Daisy bobbed her head in our direction and scampered out of the room, spilling drops of water from her bucket as she went.

Cymbeline sank onto the other couch. "What a horrid night after such a wonderful day."

This afternoon seemed like a lifetime ago. I looked at Cym's hand. Yes, the sparkling ring was still there to prove that it had truly happened.

Fiona arrived, breathless. She'd changed into a plain dress and had a knit shawl wrapped around her shoulders. "I can't seem to get warm."

"Would you like tea?" I asked her.

"Something else, perhaps?" Fiona asked.

Cym absently shook her head. She was far away from me, lost in her thoughts. I knew better than to pry. She would talk when she was ready.

Fiona sat next to Cymbeline and tilted her head back to stare up at the ceiling. "It all feels like a bad dream." She lowered her gaze to the bloodstained couch, as if she were seeing it for the first time. "But that's real, isn't it? Flynn's blood."

I blinked away the image of Theo and Isak carrying Flynn inside to this very room. Each had lifted one side, practically dragging him into the library and easing him onto the couch. In the dim light and with his dark suit, the blood hadn't at first been apparent. The way the bullet hole had torn through his jacket, though? That had been visible.

Cym nodded, answering Fiona's rhetorical question. "When I heard the gunshot, I thought someone had dropped something heavy. My mind took a moment to understand that wasn't the case."

"I didn't at first comprehend what the men wanted," I said. "Or even that they were the men we saw the other night."

"Did Flynn seem afraid to go with them?" Fiona asked.

I shook my head. "That was the strange thing. Not at all. He was defiant. I remember thinking so at the time."

"Perhaps that's what got him shot." Cym's pretty mouth twisted as if it couldn't decide between a smile or a frown.

"It caught my attention," I said. "Flynn's lack of fear. Just like when we were kids."

We all sat for a moment in silence. As I stared into the flames I thought about Flynn and the nature of his character. He had a lack of any sense of danger. A recklessness that had taken him down to the enrollment office at sixteen to fight a war across the seas. A sureness that defied logic.

What he didn't seem to recognize? Choices had consequences. Every action had a reaction. Tonight had proved that.

"Who are these men? Where do they come from? Who do they work for?" Cym's questions tumbled from her mouth.

"We know their names but not much else," I said. "Rossi and Chetta. Chetta, the big one, never said a word, other than a grunt. He seemed like the one who—" I cut myself off, alarmed at what I almost said.

"We know what you were about to say." Cymbeline got up from the sofa to sit on the arm of my chair. She rested her hand on my shoulder. "You don't have to treat us as delicate flowers."

"I know, but a man feels that way anyway," I said softly. "It's your brother. Shot in your very own front yard." My eyes stung. The image of Flynn's gray skin and fluttering eyelids played before me. Thinking of it, I felt sure he would not live. He'd looked bad.

"Rossi and Chetta," Fiona said. "Possible mobsters. In our house." She said it without a hint of wonder, only fear. "Viktor, thank you for staying with us."

"I wouldn't have it any other way. I'm glad to be here." I placed my hand over Cym's where it still rested on my shoulder, spreading warmth through my cold body.

"Did they say anything else?" Cym asked. "Anything that would give us a clue as to who they are?"

"Even if they did, it would mean nothing to us," I said. "We're not privy to the details of organized crime. We know all we need to know. They want Flynn's distillery and don't intend to go quietly."

"What a mess he's made," Fiona said.

We settled into a quiet abyss of our own thoughts. Cymbeline moved from my chair back to sit with her sister. The night wore on. Soon, the clock struck midnight. I continued to put logs on the fire. The ladies had started to fade. Twice I'd caught Fiona twitching in her sleep. I encouraged them to rest. "Sleep here on the sofa if you must. I'll stay up."

I found two blankets and covered them, one on each end of the sofa so that they looked like fetching bookends. When they were settled, I returned to my chair and this time faced the window, watching the darkness like an eagle waits for a fish.

I drifted off, dreaming of skating around and around the ice with Cymbeline. When I jerked awake, I didn't know where I was at first. In a flash, it all came back to me.

The clock said it was after three. Cym and Fiona were both asleep with their hands tucked under one cheek. I wandered over to the bookcase and chose a book at random, an Agatha Christie mystery called *The Man in the Brown Suit*.

I stretched my feet out toward the fire and opened to the first page. Soon, I was engrossed in the story. Another hour went by as I turned pages. Thank goodness for novels that helped a person escape, I thought. Otherwise, waiting would be unbearable.

Around four, lights flooded the windows. I leapt to my feet and went to look out, barely making out the figures of Lord Barnes and his wife in their car. What did this mean? They were home instead of calling on the telephone. My legs wobbled at the thought of what that meant. They'd have called if it was good news. If it were bad, they would want to tell the girls in person.

I drew in a deep breath to prepare for the worst. But that was impossible. The human heart could not prepare for the unthinkable.

M<small>Y STOMACH TURNED OVER AS</small> I <small>WALKED TO THE FOYER AND</small> opened the door for my future in-laws. Their faces were drawn and eyes dull. They looked as if they had aged ten years since last I saw them.

"Viktor, how good of you to stay," Mrs. Barnes said.

"Here, let me help you with your coat," I said.

She turned so that I might slip it from her shoulders. Lord Barnes opened the closet and seemed to freeze there, as if he were not sure why he'd opened it and for what purpose it served.

"Allow me, sir." I turned to hang both coats.

"Mama? Papa?" Fiona asked from the doorway. She and Cym clutched each other as if bracing for a storm. "How is he?"

"They got the bullet out of him," Lord Barnes said. "Theo's war experience as a medic was very helpful. He's lost a lot of blood."

"But Theo is optimistic. They patched him up and stopped the bleeding. The bullet missed his heart by quite a bit." Mrs. Barnes tapped her upper chest. "It lodged itself there near the shoulder area but by a miracle didn't hit a bone either." Mrs. Barnes leaned heavily against her husband and wrung her hands. "There's nothing else we could do there. We took Shannon back to their house. She wanted to be there in the morning for Pearl."

"How is Shannon?" Cym asked.

Mrs. Barnes eyes filled. "Devastated. Heartbroken."

"About all of it." Lord Barnes seemed to remember he still wore his hat and took it off, then handed it to me. "Thank you, Viktor. I can't seem to think what to do next or where my hat goes."

"Not a problem, sir," I said.

"Please, go up to bed," Fiona said. "We'll stay up and answer the phone if anyone calls."

"We will, thank you, girls. And you too, Viktor." Mama took Papa's hand and led him up the stairs.

The three of stared at one another for a good three seconds. "What now?" Fiona asked.

"We wait," I said.

"Viktor, you should go home," Cym said. "Sleep in your own bed. Come back in the morning."

"It's practically morning now," I said. The thought of my bed was enticing. However, what if they needed me? What if the men came back? An awful thought occurred to me. What if they'd meant to kill Flynn and when they hadn't succeeded, would they come back here and try for another family member? What lengths would these people go to to control the liquor distribution? "I'm staying. You two go upstairs to bed. I'll keep watch. If the phone rings, I'll answer it."

They yawned in unison.

I pointed to the stairway. "Up, now, please."

"Viktor," Cym said through another yawn. "I never knew you were so bossy."

"Me either," Fiona said.

Cym kissed my cheek. "Thank you for being here. We couldn't have gotten through this night without you."

"It's true." Fiona touched the sleeve of my jacket. "Thank you."

"You *could* have gotten through it without me," I said. "You're both strong and sensible. However, I'm glad to have been of service."

Cym kissed my cheek again and then the two of them walked up the stairs together, brown curls shining under the light as if to remind me that beauty existed in the world despite the tragedy we'd all witnessed.

⚜

AS IT TURNED OUT, THE PHONE DIDN'T RING IN THE EARLY hours of that dreadful morning. Around dawn, I fell asleep on the couch with the Agatha Christie novel on my chest. What seemed like minutes later, the scent of coffee woke me. I opened one eye to see Delphia's big blue eyes staring at me.

"Viktor, wake up. I've exciting news. Theo was here. He says Flynn's better."

I sat up and swept a hand over my face. My teeth felt woolly, and a terrible taste in my mouth had me yearning for a toothbrush. "Better? How much better?"

"He's awake and he talked." Delphia smiled and clasped her hands together. "We're all very happy. Mama stopped sniffling."

I sighed with relief. "Thank the good Lord."

"Mama said to ask you if you'd like breakfast. We're all in there having some. Not Cym and Fi, though. They're still sleeping."

"We were up late last night," I said.

"I'm aware of your bravery. Papa said you're very courageous and loyal to stay up all night. I want a steady beau like you when I get bigger. Do you think you could find me one?"

"When the time comes, I'll do my very best."

Delphia hurled herself at me for a spontaneous hug. "Thank you. He's to be handsome, wise, and good, too." Her brows knit together. "Should you write those down so you don't forget?"

"I'll remember. Especially if I'm to choose the man for you. He must be all that and more."

"I knew I picked the right person to ask." She tugged at the sleeve of my jacket. "Come on. Lizzie made waffles."

"Waffles?" My stomach growled. "I love waffles."

"Doesn't everyone? Well, if there's syrup. Do you like syrup?"

"Who doesn't?"

She slipped her small and surprisingly warm hand into mine, and we headed into the dining room. Lord Barnes and Mrs. Barnes looked much improved from the night before. Addie was at the table eating eggs and ham. There was no sign of Josephine and Phillip. Had they left already?

"Good morning, Viktor," Mrs. Barnes said.

"Good morning, all. I apologize for my untidy appearance."

Despite our shared harrowing night, I seemed to be the only one showing any signs of it. The rest were clean, shiny, and bright-eyed.

"Not to worry," Lord Barnes said. "You weren't in your own home last night, and we're grateful to you for keeping watch over the house and our girls."

"It was my pleasure, sir," I said.

"You've just missed Theo," Mrs. Barnes said. "Flynn's awake."

"Delphia told me. I'm relieved, as I'm sure you all are."

"Help yourself to some breakfast, son," Lord Barnes said. "You're probably half-starved after being up most of the night."

"I could eat," I said before heading over to the buffet to scoop up eggs, ham, and toast.

"Sit next to me," Delphia said.

I did as commanded. Daisy came by with a pot of coffee and poured me a cup. Nothing had ever smelled better. I ate with gusto while they told me more of what Theo had said.

"Around seven this morning, Flynn opened his eyes and asked for a sandwich," Lord Barnes said.

"A sandwich?" I chuckled under my breath. "He must not have known what time of day it was."

"He really likes sandwiches," Addie said.

"Theo said his color was back and there's no fever. Thank God," Mrs. Barnes said.

"Which means there are no infections in his body," Addie said, sounding grown up.

"I'm glad," I said. "He gave us a fright, didn't he?"

We talked for a few more minutes about the status of the rest of the family. Jo and Phillip had indeed taken their little girls home. "They wanted to get the children back to their routines," Mrs. Barnes said. "Jo doesn't like them to be out of sorts for long."

"And Phillip needed to go to the lodge," Lord Barnes said. "To take care of things."

That hung in the air for a moment.

"Addie and Delphia, you may be excused now," Mrs. Barnes said.

"Can we feed the animals?" Delphia asked. "Even though it's not Saturday, there's no school."

Lord Barnes made eye contact with his wife. The weight of that exchange seemed to suck the air from the room. He didn't know if it was safe for the girls to roam their own property. As fond as I was of Flynn, I couldn't help but think disparagingly of his decision to unleash darkness into our community.

"If you wait for a few minutes, your papa will take you out to the barn," Mrs. Barnes said. "First, we need to talk to Viktor alone. Go upstairs and read for a bit."

"Yes, Mama." A slight frown turned down the corners of Delphia's mouth, but she knew better than to contradict.

After the girls left, I finished my piece of toast but it tasted suddenly of wood chips. The reality of our conundrum was still with us, even though Flynn had made it through the night. Usually, if I thought about a problem long enough, I could figure a way out, but not this one. None of us were equipped to do anything about ruthless criminals. Not even our Sheriff Lancaster, who as far as I could tell was worthless.

"The sheriff's been informed of what happened," Lord Barnes said, as if he knew my thoughts. "He said he'd look into this, but we all know that's not true."

"Parents cannot be afraid to let their children play outside or in their very own barns," Mrs. Barnes said.

"What do we do?" I asked.

"We could burn the distillery down," Lord Barnes said. "Without it, the problems go away." He didn't sound at all sure that was true.

I wasn't either. "What about the inventory that would burn with it?" I asked. "Would that anger them further?"

"I've no idea." Lord Barnes pushed away his breakfast plate. "This is why we don't let mobsters into our town."

"Couldn't we ask them to take whatever they want and leave us be?" Mrs. Barnes asked.

"They want to be the distributors," Lord Barnes said. "That might be more important to them than the stock already made. However, it would be logical to assume they would take whatever inventory was available."

"The equipment too," I said. "I'm assuming there's equipment?"

"I know nothing of making gin, but one would assume so." Lord Barnes looked toward the windows that lined one wall of the dining room. "The distillery has to be shut down. That's all there is to it. If I could get past my anger at Flynn, I might be able to think straight."

"If we burn it down, we know it's gone forever," Mrs. Barnes said. "They'll not care to come back to ashes."

"What about Flynn's wishes?" I asked. "Will he fight you on this?"

"His wife will make sure he understands exactly where we all stand on this issue," Lord Barnes said. "She's madder than a hornet."

"Between you and me, Viktor, she was scary." Mrs. Barnes lips twitched in a momentary show of her usual good sense of humor. "Who knew little Shannon Cassidy would grow up to be so fierce?"

"That's what love does to a person," I said.

"True enough," Lord Barnes said.

"After breakfast, we're going to see Flynn," Mrs. Barnes said. "We're going to tell him exactly what's going to happen."

"Who will meet with Rossi and Chetta?" I asked. "For that matter, how do we get in touch with them?"

"I'll take care of that," Lord Barnes said.

Fear thumped my chest. Lord Barnes, as respectable and impressive as he was, might not be a match for thugs. What if they didn't want to take our offer? What then?

Cymbeline

That afternoon after Flynn was shot, we all wanted to visit him at the hospital, but Mama told us he was too weak for visitors. She suggested I take all my sisters out to check on Shannon instead. Lizzie packed us up a wooden fruit box of food to take, and we headed out to their house.

The skies were clear, but the temperatures had dropped into the teens, making the roads icy. I took it slow and made sure to stay in the tracks made by others. Soon, we arrived. Wrung out from the tension in my body and hands during the drive, I took a second to gather myself before following my sisters to the front door.

Their maid, Gilda, opened the door. Greeting us with a smile, she beckoned us inside the house. We were greeted by the scent of cinnamon and apple.

"It smells good in here," Delphia said.

"I'm making an apple pie for the missus," Gilda said in her Irish lilt. "It's Mrs. Barnes's favorite. I hoped it would cheer her."

It would take more than apple pie, I thought.

"Mama sent some food over." Fiona set the heavy box on a the hallway table.

"How kind of her." Gilda lowered her voice. "Perhaps it'll

tempt the missus to eat a little something. She won't eat anything I put in front of her."

"If anything can tempt her, it's Lizzie's chicken stew," I said. "She needs to eat for the baby." I shrugged out of my coat and hung it on the rack by the door, as did my sisters.

Gilda, who couldn't have been much older than Addie, nodded and lowered her voice. "I'm worried sick over her. She won't rest or let me take the wee one." Her freckles and red hair in contrast to her fair skin seemed to reflect the cinnamon and apples in the pie. "Would you talk to her, Miss Cymbeline? She'll listen to you."

I doubted that but nodded in agreement. "Thank you for your help, Gilda. There are some fresh scones in the box. Should we serve those with some tea?"

"I'll take care of it right away," Gilda said.

"Girls, why don't you help Gilda while Fi and I talk to Shannon?" I asked.

Addie and Delphia agreed, seeming relieved at the idea. The thought of Shannon being sad or upset had obviously frightened them.

"The baby's napping. Mrs. Barnes is in the sitting room," Gilda said.

"We can find the way," I said.

The little girls went down the hallway with Gilda. I looked at Fiona, who was fidgeting with the cuff of her sleeve. "Fi?"

She looked up at me and whispered, "I'm nervous. What do we say to her?"

"We'll be like Mama," I said, "and simply ask her if she needs anything."

Fiona reached out to me with fingers so cold I could feel them under the fabric of her gloves. "I'm mad at him. I've never been angry at any of you, really. Irritated, maybe, but never angry. I am now. So much so I can't see straight."

"I know, Fi. But right now, anger has no place. No good will come from it. We're to be good sisters to Shannon. That's what's required of us right now. We're not to judge."

She stared at me, obviously dumbfounded.

I laughed softly. "I sound like you. What's become of me?"

"Love has made you a stranger to me," Fiona said, teasing, before hugging me tightly. "I love you so."

"I love you." Tears stung my eyes. "We can do this. Have courage." I took her arm, and we walked toward the sitting room. We found Shannon by the window in a rocking chair. She had one hand draped over her stomach. The other grasped a handkerchief while dangling over the side of the chair. Although dressed, her hair wasn't combed, and as she turned to greet us, it was obvious by the dark smudges under her puffy eyes that she'd not slept.

"Hello. I didn't hear you come in." Shannon moved as if to stand, but I stopped her.

"No need to get up. We've come to see if there's anything you need."

"Please, have a seat," she said.

"Mama and Lizzie sent over several meals," Fiona said. "Including some fresh scones."

"That was kind of them. Thank them for me."

"Gilda said she'd bring out tea with the scones," I said. "You should eat."

She nodded, vaguely. "Have you been to see Flynn?"

Fiona shook her head. "No, Mama thought we shouldn't all be there at once. The Barnes family can be overwhelming. As you may know." She smiled.

"The Barnes family has been nothing but good to me," Shannon said. "I love you all very much."

Why had she said it as if she were saying goodbye to us? I darted a glance at Fiona. From the stupefied look on her face, she must have thought the same.

"Have you ever wished you could go away? Start a new life?"

Shannon turned back to the window. The frost on the glass had made a pattern like delicate lace.

"Everyone thinks that way sometimes," Fiona said.

"Sure," I said. Did they? Shannon had seemed happy and content with her life. She and Flynn had been so in love.

"What he's done—I don't know if I can forgive him." Shannon pulled a handkerchief from the sleeve of her dress and dabbed under her eyes. "When my father died, I thought I'd never cry as much again. I was wrong."

I swallowed, unsure what to do or say. Her talk of starting a new life had made my limbs heavy with dread and worry.

She continued, almost as if she'd forgotten we were there and was talking to herself. "Our marriage was supposed to be built in trust. He's been lying to me. And now he's put us all in danger. I've read about these kinds of people. They kill men's families when they don't get what they want."

I looked around the tastefully decorated sitting room. The soft colors and simple furniture reflected Shannon. Beautiful but understated. Uncomplicated. She'd always been that way, satisfied being a wife and a mother. Faithful to God, her husband, family. Made for motherhood. More than that, she'd glowed from the union between her and Flynn. She'd told me once that she never in a thousand years would have thought he'd choose her out of all the girls in the world who would have been happy to have Flynn Barnes's attention. Or that he would settle down to family life. He'd proved her wrong, she'd said. Now, though? Had her fears become a reality?

"He's reckless sometimes, but he'd never want to hurt you," I said.

"But you see? He has. Flynn's ripped out my heart. And for what? More money? We already have more than my father could ever have dreamt of. I've been grateful that Flynn wouldn't have to work himself to death on a ranch as my father did. And here he's managed to put his life in danger anyway." Her voice shook with anger. She crumpled her handkerchief into a ball. "I've been sitting here thinking I never knew him. Not really. I was naive and stupid. He's the boy I knew when we were children, not the man I thought he was." A tear slid down her cheek. She dabbed at her face with the back her hand, obviously forgetting she still held her handkerchief.

"He's made a terrible mistake," I said. "People do. That doesn't mean he's not the man you think he is."

"Thought he was. Past tense," Shannon said. "And now your father's going to have to figure out how to save us. Your father, who is the best man I've ever known, other than my own, will be in danger because of it. This whole town—everything your father worked for—is ruined. My husband brought evil to us."

I opened my mouth, then shut it again. I'd had an identical thought last night. Flynn had brought bad people to us. "There's always been vile men here, lurking in the shadows. Look at what happened to Louisa. Or Josephine and that awful man she thought she loved."

"That was two bad men," Shannon said. "This is a group of people. Men who run Chicago and terrorize innocent people. Do you think any of us will be free now? They'll make every businessman in town bend to their will. Pretty soon everyone will be paying these mobsters just for the right to run their shops."

"How do you know this?" Fiona whispered.

"I read the papers." Shannon gestured to a stack of newspapers on the table where Flynn usually sat. "He reads them too. Voraciously. Now I know why. He was keeping up with the competition."

My chest had tightened. I felt as if I couldn't breathe. Dots danced before my eyes. Was she right? Had Flynn changed everything?

"Papa won't let that happen," Fiona said. "He'll discover a way to drive them away."

I clung to her words as if my life depended on it. Perhaps it did. Or, at the very least, our way of life.

Shannon grimaced and made a sound somewhere between a groan and as if someone had socked her in the belly.

"Shannon, what's the matter?" Fiona asked.

Shannon's face twisted in pain. "I've been having contractions on and off all morning. I think the baby's coming. Get Louisa."

※

LOUISA ARRIVED THIRTY MINUTES LATER. WE'D REACHED HER at home and she'd promised to come out straightaway. Theo, however, was doing rounds so she left a message at the hospital for him to come out to the house when he was able.

We helped Louisa out of her coat while we answered her questions. How long had she been in labor? How far apart were the contractions?

"If by that you mean the agonizing pain," I said, "then it's about five minutes."

"We still have time then. Where is she?" Louisa asked.

"We helped her upstairs to her bedroom," Fiona said. "Is that all right?"

"It's as good a place as any." Louisa was different in this capacity. Instead of quiet and shy, she was firm and self-confident. Soon, she had us fetching this and that, including clean towels and hot water.

"How long do you think this will take?" I asked Louisa at one point. She'd come out to the hallway to drink a cup of hot tea.

"One never knows," Louisa said. "But I'd say it'll take us into the night hours."

"I'm going to take the girls home, then," I said. "But I'll leave Fiona with you."

"Good, yes. Theo hasn't yet called, so he may be a while. He had quite a few folks to visit this afternoon." She explained that he'd collapsed into bed when he returned from taking care of Flynn. "He couldn't keep his eyes open, so I let him sleep."

"Can you do this without him?" I asked.

"Yes. These days I do most everything without him. He checks to make sure the babies are all right, but I look after the mother. Unless she needs stitches, which Theo has to do."

My eyes widened in horror. Stitches. For where? I put that out of my mind, or I might faint right here in the hallway.

I gathered my sisters up and herded them out to the car. Once they were in the back seat, I told them why we were going home in such a rush. "Shannon's going to have her baby."

They nodded, solemnly. I glanced at them before backing out of the driveway. "Why the long faces?" I asked.

"Shannon will be all alone without Flynn," Addie said. "Won't she be scared?"

"Women have been giving birth for centuries." I put the car in gear and headed down the rocky, slick driveway. "They don't need a man to do it. Especially not someone as tough as Shannon."

That seemed to satisfy them. Which was good because the jitters had taken over my faculties. What if Flynn didn't make it? What would we all do then? If he did make it, what would happen to his marriage? I couldn't fathom a divorce, but it wasn't completely out of the question. There were women who divorced if there was justification, such as adultery or abuse. What about for a lie such as the one he'd told his wife through omission?

We arrived to the house a few minutes later. I walked the girls in, hoping to see Mama and Papa to tell them that Shannon was in labor. However, I found only Jasper at the desk in the sitting room writing down figures in a notebook.

He looked up as we walked in and stood. "What's happened now?"

"We've come from Shannon's. She's going to have the baby. Louisa's with her, and I'm going back but wanted to bring the girls home."

"We miss all the fun," Delphia said.

"You'll have a more enjoyable afternoon here," Jasper said. "It's time for your dinners. Go on down to the kitchen. Lizzie has chicken and dumplings and a stew for Addie. Florence is there as well."

They gave me a wave before heading out of the room. Their footsteps clattered on the stairway down to the kitchen.

The clock read a little after noon. "Where are Mama and Papa?" I asked Jasper.

"They're in town with Flynn." Jasper adjusted his already perfectly arranged tie.

"I'm going back to be with Shannon. Will you give them my message when they return?"

"Yes, of course." Jasper winced and touched his forehead.

"Are you ill?" I asked, alarmed.

"No, not ill unless you count heartsick." Jasper sat back in the chair at the desk. He didn't seem like himself. I'd never seen him sit in front of me unless we were downstairs.

"Jasper, what is it?" I came around the desk to stand next to him.

"Flynn." He closed his eyes for a split second before opening them to peer out into the yard. "When I think of him as a little boy—how full of life he was—mischievous and playful with all that energy. He used to wear your father and I out before Quinn came. I can't imagine him at death's door. Or hurt at all. He survived the war without a scratch, for goodness' sake. This is all so hard to understand." He let out a sigh. "And now his poor wife, facing all this alone."

My eyes pricked at his show of emotion. "Jasper, he's going to be fine. He has nine lives like a cat. At least that many." I paused, and the next thing came out of my mouth before I thought too much about what I was saying. "I'm more worried if he has a place to go home to after he's well."

"Is it that bad?"

"Yes. We talked to her this morning. I'm not sure what to

think. She's angry. I wouldn't be surprised if she doesn't let him back in the house."

"Surely not. Couples go through hardships and get through them, Cymbie."

Cymbie. My childhood nickname. Jasper was truly shaken.

"I hope you're right," I said. "What about the rest of it, though?" I shared with him my thoughts about how vulnerable we were. "This has opened us up to the outside world, one we don't want in Emerson Pass. How will we manage to rid ourselves of these men?"

"We need some pitchforks and a mob," Jasper said.

I felt fairly certain he was joking. Not that I'd ever known him to make a joke. This entire incident had turned everything upside down. Regardless, perhaps he was right? What if we got the whole town together and ran these men out of town? "We do have a lot of pitchforks in Emerson Pass."

Jasper rose to his feet. A sense of purpose came back to his eyes. "We do. Guns too."

"What if we take back our town? We might be able to do it if we get everyone together. Pitchforks, rifles, knives. Whatever it takes."

"You should call a family meeting. If your father agrees, we could have a town hall and see how much support we can get."

"I'll see what I can do."

"That a girl," Jasper said. "You always were a smart little thing. Even that time you got stuck in the dumbwaiter."

I groaned. "Don't mention that. I still have nightmares."

"It was one of many times I had to stifle my laughter," Jasper said.

I blew him a kiss. "Tell the staff our plan, and I'll get back to you later if I'm able to get Mama and Papa to agree."

Jasper nodded, and off I went.

Viktor

I'd just finished my lunch of leftovers Lizzie had sent home with me when I heard the rumble of a car. Hoping it was Cym, I rushed to the front door. It was her. I watched as she parked and jumped out of the car as if someone chased her. The determined set of her jaw and spring in her step told me she had an idea.

I greeted her and scooped her into my arms and kissed her.

"Hi. Aren't you a sight for sore eyes. I feel as though I haven't seen you for a week, and it was only last night."

"Did you get any rest?" I asked. She hadn't yet woken when I'd left that morning to go home.

"Yes, plenty. You?"

I nodded as we walked into the house. "Slept like the dead for most of the morning."

"I can only stay a minute. Shannon's having her baby."

A wave of dismay came over me. Shannon would be without Flynn for who knew how long, and now a new baby? "With Flynn sick?"

"Yes. As if she didn't have enough to face without Flynn. She has us, though. We'll all be there to help."

"Her mother and sister too," I said.

She took my hand and brought it to her cheek for a moment. "I needed to see you. Take in your smell before I return to Shannon and Fiona."

"I'm glad you did." I pulled her tightly against me. "I wish I could help."

"You help by just being you." She rested her head against my chest before withdrawing to look up at me. "I have an idea about how to get rid of our unwanted guests."

"If it involves you doing something dangerous, then I would humbly request you not do it."

"It wouldn't. Not just for me alone, anyway."

"Go on." I was afraid to hear and braced myself for whatever would come next.

"Here it is." She proceeded to tell me her idea about getting the town together, all carrying weapons of one sort of the other, and running the thugs out of town. "Or metaphorically anyway. Basically, we would let them know to leave us alone or face the consequences of an entire town hunting them down."

"Won't that just make more of them invade?" Invasion. That's what this felt like to me. Was this our own war?

"Not if we do it right. Scare them properly," Cym said. "I'm going to call a town meeting at the schoolhouse. We need to tell everyone exactly what we're up against. This threatens our whole way of life. We'll need every man physically able to participate."

"And then burn the place down," I said. "That's what your father suggested."

She cocked her head to the right, observing me. "So they have nothing to come back for?"

"We could offer them the gin, and if they don't take it with the promise to leave us alone, then we would take the next steps."

"It's a good idea," she said. "Will you go into town and spread the word that everyone's to pretend there's a dance at the schoolhouse that starts at seven? Tell them to pass it on to whomever they see."

I agreed, already planning on who to tell first. Mrs. Johnson. She saw the most people in one day and would pass it along. I'd drop by the butcher shop as well.

"I'll do my best," I said. "If you promise to be careful."

"I will." She kissed me, and then she was gone, as quick as the wind.

Cymbeline

W hen I arrived in town, an unfamiliar car was parked in the lot behind the doctor's office. My heart skipped a beat when I saw the inhabitants. Rossi and Chetta lounged in the front seat as if they were on a Sunday drive and had stopped to eat a sandwich.

With shaking legs, I got out of my own car, determined to confront them. It was the perfect opportunity to set their trap. I came to a halt beside the car. My heart beat as fast as a hummingbird's wings. I prayed for my angels. *Protect me and give me courage.*

Rossi turned his head. When he saw it was me, one eyebrow shot up over his button-like eye. He stepped out of the car and leaned his backside against the door. "Well, if it isn't the enchanting sister."

I shivered under my coat and felt the immediate need to wash my hands. "Good afternoon, Mr. Rossi."

Chetta had lumbered out of the other side and come around to stand next to Rossi. The man was like a tree. Not many men were wider or taller than the Olofsson boys, but this Chetta had them beat.

"You here to see your brother?" Rossi said. "We hear he got shot. Almost didn't make it."

"You know very well he was shot since it was you who did it." My voice was remarkably calm. Fortunately, he couldn't see how my legs trembled under my dress.

Rossi put a hand over his chest, as if I'd hurt his feelings. "Whatever makes you think it was us?"

"What do you want?" I asked.

"We made it clear to your brother how this was going to work. It's simple." Rossi smiled, revealing remarkably straight white teeth for a mobster. Not that I'd seen a mobster before now. Maybe they all had white teeth? His smile didn't change the glittery danger that emanated from his dark eyes.

"My brother may not have wanted to do business with you," I said, thinking fast. "But our family disagrees. We have a proposition for you."

"We make the propositions. Not your family." Chetta spoke for the first time. His voice was so low he could have been cousins with a grizzly.

Stay polite, I told myself. "*Proposition* may have been the wrong word." Never in my life had a I used my womanly charms to get what I wanted. I was starting to regret that decision because right now I could use a little charm, and I had nothing from which to conjure anything close. "We're prepared to give you all the inventory and our word we'll not make or distribute more. In exchange, we'd like you to take it and leave us be. This town doesn't want any trouble with you or whomever you work for."

Chetta spat out a wad of tobacco onto a snowdrift. I pushed back a wave of nausea. The scent of their hair tonic mixed with stale cigarette smoke made me feel even sicker.

"That won't work for us, I'm afraid," Rossi said.

"You can take the equipment too," I said. "Whatever you want is yours."

"Who are *you* to be making these offers?" Rossi said. "You're nothing but a girl. What if your brother won't abide by our agreement?"

"He will," I said. "Almost dying has a way of changing a man's mind."

"Boss won't like it," Chetta said. "He wants it all."

Rossi nodded. "Yeah, here's the thing, miss. We don't make the decisions. There's someone we answer to, and he wants the factory."

"But why? We're between mountains. It's impossible to get here."

"Not anymore," Rossi said.

"This is a family community," I said. "Can't you just take what you want and go?"

"What we want is your brother's operation. We ain't seen nothing like it anywhere," Chetta said.

"But think about how hard it'll be to get all of it out of here in the dead of winter. The roads are terrible."

The men exchanged a glance. That told me something. They agreed with me. It was whomever they worked for that did not.

"What's so special about Flynn's way of doing it?" I asked.

"His brew's better than any we've found. It passes for the good stuff we had before Prohibition," Rossi said. "The man we work for wants it for himself."

All right, I told myself. *He's made himself clear.* That made the decision. We would have to do this with our guns and pitchforks.

"I'll give your message to my father," I said. "There's a dance tonight at the schoolhouse. Meet him around eight tonight and he'll give you the keys. We don't want further trouble."

"Who made you in charge of your family's business?" Rossi glared at me with a mixture of irritation and admiration.

"I'm not in charge, but I can assure you we all want the same thing, and that's for you to not hurt any of the rest of us." I glared back at him, hoping to God I appeared a lot braver than my shaking legs indicated. "Please, gentlemen, we're God-fearing people. Family people. Flynn's wife's having a baby as we speak."

"All he had to do was hand over the keys in the first place," Rossi said in a tone that implied this was actually our fault.

"You tell your dandy of a pop to meet us there at eight and no one else gets hurt." Rossi reached into the inside of his coat and came out with a pack of cigarettes. He took one out and dangled it in front of him. Chetta scrambled for his lighter.

The end of the cigarette flamed red. After taking a drag and letting it out slowly, Rossi pointed at me with his chin. "You ever thought about a job? A way out of here?"

"I don't want out of here." What was he talking about?

"A brave girl like you—we could use you in our line of work," Rossi said.

"A pretty girl gets what she wants," Chetta said. "Sometimes, anyway."

"What exactly is this work you do?" I asked. "Terrorize decent people? Kill a man in front of his family?"

"He's not dead," Chetta said.

"Not for want of trying," I said.

"We had to send a message." Rossi lifted one shoulder in a shrug. "Nothing personal."

"Will you bring people with you to work at the distillery?" I asked.

"Depends," Rossi said.

"What about the trucks? Will they destroy our roads and our forests?" I asked.

"I never met more people concerned about trees in all my life," Rossi said. "We're interested in gin, not wood."

"Preserving the beauty of our land is important to us," I said.

"You're too pretty to have such a big mouth, but I could overlook it if you married me. What do you say? Come work with us and live like a queen?"

"I already live like a queen," I said. How much gin had this man had this morning? Marry him?

"But not my queen." He reached for me, but I was too quick for him. I darted away before his hands could snatch me and ran toward the front door of the hospital. The sounds of their laughter told me they hadn't followed me.

It wasn't until I was inside that I took in a breath. These two had to go.

The waiting room was empty. Any other time I was here, Dr. Neal and Theo's nurse had sat behind the desk. I knew from earlier that she'd been here assisting the doctors all through the harrowing night. They'd sent her home in the morning. Just as well. I needed to talk to my parents.

Dr. Neal and Theo's offices, which we sometimes called the hospital and other times simply "the doctor's office," consisted of a waiting area, two exam rooms, and a surgery at the back. Today, the surgery room was also a recovery room.

It was already two. I'd been gone for several hours by now. As much as I yearned to get back to Shannon's, I knew she had whom she needed to help her. My gifts were better served here.

Papa and Mama were reading when I came into the room. Flynn was asleep on the bed. I greeted my parents with a wave of my hand. Papa motioned for us all to go out to the waiting room.

I took a deep breath to steady my nerves. There was much to cover and not much time to do it. "Darling, are you all right?" Mama asked. "You're as jittery as a cat."

"Yes, I'm fine." I smiled to reassure her. "Shannon's in labor. Louisa's with her. When Theo returns here, will you send him out?"

Mama's hand fluttered to her hair. "She's having the baby today? How can this be?"

"Louisa assured me all was well," I said. "Fiona's with her."

"Poor Shannon," Papa said. "Now this on top of everything else."

"Perhaps it'll give her something happy to focus on," Mama said.

"Yes, quite right." Papa wrapped his arm around me. "Thank you for being our rock, Cym. I'm very proud of you."

"There's something else. Rossi and Chetta are waiting outside in the parking lot."

"Lord have mercy," Mama said.

"Did they do anything to you?" Papa's fists clenched at his sides.

"No, but I talked to them. I told them we would give them the booze and equipment. But it's not enough. The man they work for wants the factory too. Apparently, the quality is better than anything else they have. We'll never get rid of them unless we do something drastic."

"I want to burn the place down," Papa said. "Then there's nothing to come back for."

"I agree. But we need to drive them away for good. Using force if we have to," I added. "So that they don't retaliate."

Papa, who had been listening with a furrowed brow, nodded. I couldn't be sure what that meant.

I slid my gaze to Mama. She had turned to a painting of a rooster that hung on the wall, peering at it with a faraway look in her eyes.

"Mama?"

She slowly turned to look at me. "An angry mob? Is that what you're suggesting?"

"I guess you could call it that," I said. "But this is Emerson Pass, Mama. We have to protect what you and Papa built."

She didn't look convinced, so I turned back to Papa. "I told Rossi we had a dance at the schoolhouse tonight and that you'd meet him there to hand over the keys."

"And the whole town will be there?" Papa asked. "To chase them out of town."

"Something like that." Now that he said it out loud, the idea seemed flimsy.

"I don't know if this will work," Papa said. "It could make them angrier. They could bring back more people."

"All we want is for them to leave us alone," I said.

"It's the only idea that's given me any hope," Papa said. "We have to try."

⊙⚜☙

I went in to see Flynn before I left to return to Shannon. For a moment, I stood by the side of the bed watching him sleep. Except for the bandages around his chest, he looked like the same brother I'd loved and admired all my life. Same dark lashes, high cheekbones, and full mouth. All the girls in town had been in love with him. There had been more than a few tears shed for Flynn Barnes.

I brushed a lock of his hair away from his forehead. A lump developed in the back of my throat. The last time we really talked, words had been harsh between us. What if he hadn't made it? Those would have been the last we spoke to each other.

His eyes fluttered open. They were leaden, as if the violence had stolen part of his soul. "Cym?"

"How are you feeling?" I hastily wiped under my eyes.

"I hurt. Everything hurts."

Mama and Papa entered the room. I glanced over at them. "Is there anything for the pain? He's hurting."

Mama rushed over to a table where she mixed a white powder into a glass of water. "Theo said to give this to him sparingly."

Papa helped him sit up slightly to drink. Mama sat next to Flynn on the bed and lifted the glass to his mouth. Flynn took several sips before lying back on his pillows.

I hovered on the other side of the bed, unsure what to do. Seeing him this way had flustered me even more than the dangerous men waiting outside.

Flynn tugged on my sleeve. "Shannon?"

"She's fine." I looked over at Mama. *Should I tell him?* She shook her head.

"Mad at me," Flynn whispered.

"Yes, but you'll make it up to her," I said.

Papa was at the foot of the bed. "We're giving the inventory over to them and then burning the place down."

"I should have. Pride." Flynn closed his eyes. The pinched look around his mouth from the pain softened as the medicine took hold. "Burn it down, Papa. Burn it all down. Tell Shannon I said so. And that I'm sorry."

"Don't worry," I said. "Just rest and get better. Everything's going to be all right."

His breathing steadied. He was asleep. I relaxed, realizing I'd been holding my muscles tight, unable to tolerate seeing him in pain.

"I should go to Shannon," I said.

"I'll go with you," Mama said. "If your papa will stay here?"

"Yes, go. I'll keep watch and send Theo out the minute he's back from doing his rounds." Papa kissed the top of my head. "You're a good girl. You always have been the one I'd want by my side in a crisis."

"Really, Papa? I always thought I was just the problem child?"

Mama placed her hands on my cheeks. "You're strong and opinionated, yes. But we love you that way. It's people like you, Cym, who change the world. We've always known that to be true."

For the second time that hour, I teared up. "Thank you, Mama."

"Cym, I beg you though. Be careful," Papa said.

"You as well."

※

MAMA WAS QUIET AS WE HEADED OUT OF TOWN TOWARD Flynn and Shannon's house. I didn't want to disturb her with unnecessary chatter.

So I kept mum as we drove out to the icy dirt road. In the years since Mama had come to us, I'd not known her to have dark moods or fits of temper. She was as steady as they came. However, when she was worried about one of us, she seemed to draw deep within herself. I wondered what she pondered during moments such as this.

"Have I ever told you much about my father?"

I took my eyes from the road for a brief second to look at her in surprise. Of everything I thought she'd say, this was not one of them. "Not really. Grandmother talked about him sometimes. She told me they met at a dance. He spotted her across the room and decided he had to have her. Isn't that right?"

"Yes, I believe so." She went back to staring out the window.

"Why do you ask?" My natural curiosity made it impossible for me not to want to know more.

"I've been thinking about him a lot the last few days. There was a time when I was young that he was gone for a while."

"For how long?"

"A month or so, I think. Mother told us he'd gone off for a job, but later I wondered if that were true."

"Where else would he have gone?"

"I don't know. For some reason, I think he and Mother had had a fight and he'd left so that they might recover from it."

"Recover? From a fight? Is that what people do back in Boston?"

She laughed somewhat mirthlessly. "No, not just there. Sometimes marriages have troubles and people separate for a time."

I thought about that for a moment. Was she worried about Shannon and Flynn? "Mama, surely Shannon will forgive him?"

"I hope she will, but..."

"But what?"

"Your brother has made a great error. A decision he made out of greed and a hunger for power and prestige. One in which his wife and little daughter were not considered. Your father would never have done that. From the moment I met him, he was concerned only with the five of you and then with me, of course. Later, with the little girls." She wiped her cheeks. "I've never been ashamed of any of you. There were times when you all needed a scolding, mostly when you were small."

"Especially me."

She smiled and wiped her cheeks with her handkerchief. "You and Flynn the most, yes. But it was never mean-spirited. Neither of you had a mean bone in you. You were always curious and adventurous. Two qualities sure to lead to trouble when you're a little girl. Still, I was never ashamed. Not even when Flynn ran off to enlist. I was terrified but not angry or ashamed. This, however? I'm not sure what I'm to do with my anger toward him. He's my child. My beloved boy who I watched grow into a man. But to do this to your father...possibly destroying the town he spent his lifetime building into a true community from a pile of burned boards. I don't know, Cym. I'm at a loss."

I turned the car into Flynn's driveway. A string of smoke from their chimney rose up and out of the surrounding trees like a ribbon. Wild turkeys, looking affronted by the cold, pecked at the snow under a pine.

"Mama, it's all right to be angry with people you love. You told me that."

"I did?"

"Yes, recently in fact. When I was so angry at Flynn for not allowing women into the competition."

"Ah, yes, I suppose I did."

"It helped me," I said. "Like most things you tell me."

"I'm glad, darling." Mama returned to looking out the window.

"Mama, he made it through a terrible injury. We should focus on that."

She turned back to me, her hat shifting slightly when the car slid in the icy channels. "I agree that we should be grateful he was spared. However, the mess that he's made is now being left for the rest of us to clean up. When I think about you outside talking to those men. Making a deal with them. Criminals. I see red. That's all I can see."

"He's changed, though. You heard him say so himself. He realizes his errors in judgment."

She nodded and adjusted her hat. "You're a good sister."

I parked in the same spot I'd been in earlier and turned off the engine. "Mama, wait. I'll help you out. It's slippery."

She put a hand out to stop me. "Cym, I know what you and Viktor have planned for the jump."

I gulped. "You do?"

"The knickers gave you away."

"Does Papa know?"

"Of course. There are no secrets between us."

"Are you mad?"

She shook her head. "You give them all you've got, my girl. Show them how it's done. Don't ever let them tell you no. Even when it's your own brother."

"Viktor said yes instead of no, Mama," I said softly. "To everything I've ever asked of him. He said he's perfectly happy seeing me shine. And he loves me just as I am. He doesn't want to change me."

Mama's brown eyes glistened. "Darling, that's the sweetness of true love. I felt the same way when I met your father. Please, don't ever risk what you have by keeping anything from him. Secrets are like a sickness in the marriage. Eventually, they will come out and make you both ill."

"I promise, Mama. Anyway, there's nothing I would want to do unless Viktor gave me his blessing. The same goes for him too."

"You can't imagine how happy it makes me to see how well you're loved," Mama said. "I'm glad you finally opened your eyes to the possibility."

"I did, Mama. And he was right there. He's been there all along."

THE HOUSE WAS QUIET WHEN WE WALKED THROUGH THE front door. For a moment, I froze, fearing the worst. Then I heard a faint cry, hardly louder than a kitten's mew, coming from the back bedroom. Fiona, perhaps hearing us come in, popped out into the hallway and ran to greet us. "The baby came already. It was the most perfectly perfect thing I ever witnessed. Shannon hardly even perspired. She was outstanding."

"Is she all right? The baby?" Mama asked.

"They're perfectly perfect too," Fiona said. "You only barely missed the excitement. She arrived about fifteen minutes ago."

"What a blessing," Mama said. "A short birth is the best you can hope for."

"Mrs. Cassidy and Nora are in with her now," Fiona said. "Helping Louisa get Shannon and the baby cleaned up. They sent me out to make tea, but I think it was because I was in the way." She shook her head. "It was like witnessing a miracle. One second, there was no baby and the next there she was. She's beautiful, too, with a shock of black hair."

The teakettle whistled, and Fiona dashed away to help Gilda put everything together. Mama and I hung up our coats and went to wait in the sitting room. A minute later, Sally appeared with little Pearl on her hip. She squealed when she saw Mama. Sally let her down, and the baby wobbled on chubby legs to climb into Mama's lap.

Mama kissed the top of Pearl's head and closed her eyes. What should have been a happy occasion had only made Mama's burdens heavier. I knew without her saying so that she was thinking about this dear little family and whether Shannon and Flynn could come through the hurt and betrayal intact.

Viktor

The word about our town meeting had spread fast throughout our small community. I imagined the words roaming along the board sidewalks and into each of the businesses. It would have started as a cluster at the Johnsons' store and out the country roads to farms and ranches until, at last, the final message had been delivered.

Now it was a little before seven. As I looked up and down Barnes Avenue for any last stragglers, a shiver ran through me. We were a community of peaceful people. We'd arrived in sleighs, cars, and trucks and by ski to meet in the hub of our town, the school. A schoolhouse that Lord Barnes had insisted upon all those years before when he'd hired Quinn Cooper to be the first teacher in what had then been one room and a little over a dozen children.

How much simpler things had been then. In only fifteen years, crime had come to our community. Not the kind that grew from within but the insidious variety that came from greed. Men who had not earned their riches as so many of the immigrants who populated this town had. Not by hard work and an undying belief in the American dream but by crime and violence.

Could we rid ourselves of these men easily, or would some of us die trying only to succumb to the invisible man who gave orders from his throne in Chicago?

It was standing room only. Women had taken the available chairs while the men stood along the walls. Children too young to stay alone were playing in the upstairs classroom, supervised by Addie and Florence.

Lord Barnes wore one of his fine suits, made by my father's own hands. His hair, peppered with silver, had been slicked back from his forehead. His tall, slim frame and squared shoulders gave him an elegant presence. He'd given many rousing speeches through the years, mostly at celebrations. A few times he'd been called upon to give us hope during the war and then when the Spanish flu had swept the world. He'd had to rally the good citizens to band together to keep the flu out, and he'd succeeded. Now he must do it once again. I couldn't help but feel this time would matter more than ever.

"Thank you all for coming." Lord Barnes gazed out over the expectant faces, all counting on him for leadership. By now everyone knew of the distillery hidden in the old mine building. Earlier that day Isak, Lord Barnes, and I had gone out to see it for ourselves. As angry as I was with Flynn, I had to admit the location was clever. It was no wonder none of us had caught on to the fact of its existence. No one went out that direction these days.

"My apologies for dragging you all out of your warm homes tonight," Lord Barnes said. "I've gathered you all here because of a threat to our very way of life. When I dreamt of what we could become as a community, I never imagined we would build something as great as we have. Together. We've worked hard, each of us with our own talents and expertise to contribute to the whole. This is a peaceful place where we can raise children and build businesses and grow old with the comfort of those we love. Today, I have learned of something that threatens all of that. As I'm sure you've read in the papers, with Prohibition has come men who profit from the making and distribution of illegal alcohol. There are rumors about how these men operate, as well as the accounts of their violence in the papers. For months they were watching my son's distillery and his distribution of liquor to Louisville and to our own underground club."

His voice broke, and for a moment I wasn't sure he would be able to continue. He peeked at his wife, who sat in the front row between Fiona and Cymbeline, and seemed to gather strength from her.

"When he began the business, Flynn did not anticipate the interference of mobsters who want the distillery for their own use. They came here and threatened him. He would not give in to their demands. Because of this, they shot him, intending to kill him, to send a message to all of us. The message is loud and clear. Do as we say, including allowing us to take over your town and businesses, or there will be more violence. Perhaps even to another member of my family."

He choked up and hung his head for a moment. His knuckles whitened as he gripped the side of the lectern. "I'm sorry to have to ask you to save my family when we've done this to ourselves."

Not "we," I thought. *Flynn.*

One could have heard a pin drop in the room. No one moved. A crackle from the woodstove in the corner seemed to bring Lord Barnes out of his stupor. He peered back at the crowd with feverish eyes.

"I'm humbly asking you to join us this evening. The men will be here in an hour to meet with me. They want the factory, not just the goods. This would mean we'd be bound to them. At their mercy. We'll be paying a criminal organization for the right to operate our businesses. Everything will change. We will no longer be in the land of the free. To save our community, we're going to have to uprise together. We will tell them, as a group, that we do not want them here. If they don't go, we will hunt them down."

A few men shouted back answers to his request.

"Men, please go home and get your weapons as quickly as you

can. Be here to meet these thugs and tell them who controls this community. Ladies, I ask you all to join together to pray at the church. Pastor Morris has opened it for us tonight. We must take back our town, but we must remember we answer to God. If we can avoid violence, I know we will do so."

Someone called out from the crowd. "What about the sheriff?"

I looked around the crowd, searching for Sheriff Lancaster yet knowing he wouldn't be there. The man could and would be easily convinced to take money in exchange for protection. He would not protect our town. I'd not even given it a thought until now. Lancaster had been worthless for as many years as I could remember. I thought back to that day long ago when Louisa's father had come to our classroom and tried to choke our beloved teacher. Lancaster could have done something about Kellam before it had gotten to that point, but he'd turned the other way. Lancaster might look clean on the outside, but he was as dirty as any of the criminals in our jail, and especially the mobsters who threatened us today. Perhaps we should run him out of town next?

"I cannot answer for Sheriff Lancaster," Lord Barnes said. "But I do not see him here this evening."

"So we're without him," someone shouted.

"As usual," someone else said.

Mumbles of dissatisfaction rumbled throughout the room. Clive Higgins, who stood two men away from me, said something under his breath about getting rid of Lancaster.

"I stand before you tonight as honest as a man can be," Lord Barnes said. "You know as well as I that we have not had law enforcement in this town for as long as he's been sheriff. We're blessed to have been a law-abiding community of God-fearing people, so it's not been necessary. After we're through this crisis and have taken back what belongs to us—our freedom—we can have another town meeting. It's time we elect a mayor and a sheriff and ask Lancaster to politely leave."

"Heck yeah," a man said.

The crowd broke into cheers.

Lord Barnes put up his hand to silence the room. "Does anyone have any questions?"

A man in the back asked, "What's he need more money for? Why'd he have to do this to us?"

Lord Barnes shook his head. "I cannot speak for my son, but I think you should feel free to ask him that when he's well enough to answer."

Someone else said, "He's paid for his mistake, now hasn't he? God says to forgive our neighbor."

"There's women and children to consider," another said. "What happens to them if we're killed because Flynn Barnes had to have another car?"

Lord Barnes once again looked at his wife. Mrs. Barnes stood and went up to the lectern. She paused before speaking, then looked out to the crowd. "Who amongst us hasn't made a mistake or misjudgment in our youth? Are there any mothers out there who haven't wrung their hands in despair over the misguided mistakes of their child at least one time or another?"

A murmur went through the women.

Mrs. Barnes continued. "We understand your concern. We feel them ourselves. Why should we have to risk our lives for the mistake of another? If it were one of your sons, I would like to believe that those same thoughts wouldn't go through my own mind, but I know they would. I can ask you only this: if there are any of you who have not made a mistake or had a child do something you wish they wouldn't have, then you may leave. You may consider yourselves exempt from participating in what is a necessary act as part of a community."

The room once more went quiet. I could almost feel the reckoning people were doing with themselves.

"When I first started as a teacher here in 1910," Mrs. Barnes said, "I told the children there were three rules in my classroom."

Without thinking, I blurted out, "Be curious. Be kind. Protect one another."

Then the rest of us in the room who were in that first class repeated the same words, in unison, as we'd done back in the day.

Mrs. Barnes beamed at us before going to the chalkboard. She wrote those same words on the board, as she'd done that very first day of school.

I traveled back in time, seeing before me the wisp of the young woman she'd been as well as the shocked faces of my classmates. I hadn't known what to think.

At dinner that night, my brother and I had told our parents about what she'd said. Isak had imitated her scrawling the words across the board with her precise handwriting. My mother had said in her thick accent, "She must be a remarkable woman. How lucky you are to have her as your teacher."

As I stood watching her tonight, I couldn't agree more.

Nora Cassidy stood and began to speak. "None of us are perfect. No one in this room can say that, now can we? We all do our best with what we're given. I know Flynn Barnes. I've known him since we were children." She made a gesture with her hand to indicate a small stature. "What he did may not make sense to us. We may condemn him for it, but he had his reasons. He's a good man. One who may have made a decision that in the end was the wrong one. But I can guarantee you he did not make it solely from a place of greed. His father taught him that community was more important than the individual. When he is well enough, he will explain himself, and we will have a better understanding of why. Whatever it was, he almost paid for it with his life. Our work as Christians is to forgive, not judge. Please, I'm begging you, join us. Do not be afraid. In numbers, there is power." She sat, a flush to her cheeks.

To my surprise, my father stood. I'd never seen him say a word in public. He barely spoke to his clients, let alone in a public forum such as this.

"Lord Barnes, I think I speak for many of us when I say my family would not have the life we have if it weren't for you. You've not asked anything from us, and I have no intention of turning my back on you when you need me. My sons and I will be there."

"Thank you, Anders." Lord Barnes scanned the room for further questions.

Isak, up at the front, turned to the audience. "What about the rest of you? Do I have to toss some sweet rolls your way, or are you with us? Raise your hands if you're ready to protect our town?"

One by one, the men raised their hands.

"May God be with us tonight," Lord Barnes said.

Pastor Morris called out, "May I pray for us?"

"Yes, please," Lord Barnes said.

The pastor prayed over us without any mention of fire, brimstone, and damnation. Perhaps he was coming over to our ways after all?

Mrs. Barnes, still at the lectern, smiled out at the room. "Be here a quarter before the hour. Ladies, anyone who would like to wait with me at the church is welcome to do so."

The crowd moved out of the building and into the night air as if they were the flow of the river. Soon, it was empty save for only me and the Barnes family. Cymbeline came to stand beside me. I took her hand in mine. She trembled against me. Fiona and her mother and father remained at the front of the room, wearing the same tight, fearful expression.

Lord Barnes and his wife came to stand next to us. "Viktor, Theo, Phillip, and I will be at the front of the line. We'd like you to stand with us but understand if you'd rather not."

"No, sir. If I'm to be a part of this family, then I stand with you."

Fiona's bottom lip trembled. "I'm afraid."

"Don't be." A voice near the door drew our attention. Li Wu stood there, carrying a rifle. It was such an odd thing to see him with a weapon instead of an instrument that I could scarcely believe my eyes.

"There is power in numbers." Li strode across the room to stand with us.

"Li, you have a gun?" Fiona asked.

"I owe my life to your father," Li said to Fiona. "Now I will stand with him. Anyway, I will not sit back and let these pigs hurt the people I love. Your brother has made a mistake, but haven't we all benefited from his businesses? Working at the club has allowed me enough to build my own house. Nothing is as black and white as piano keys, Fi. If anyone knows that, it is I.

"It is my pleasure, Lord Barnes."

Fiona ducked her head but not before I saw the tears that gathered at the corners of her eyes. *She's in love with him,* I thought. It was as plain to see as the freckles that spotted Cymbeline's pert nose.

"I should like to be here too," Cym said. "I'll fight with the men."

"Cym, no." Lord Barnes shook his head. "Not this. Please. If anything were to happen to you, I couldn't bear it."

"But the boys are doing it. What's the difference?"

Lord Barnes seemed to crumple like a piece of tissue, as if it were too much to hold up his head. "Oh, Cym." That's all he said. Then he turned away and headed for the door.

"Papa?" Fiona asked, turning as if to follow him.

"Let him go," Mrs. Barnes said. "His heart is broken today. He needs time to think."

"I won't do it then," Cym said. "If it upsets him."

"Thank you, darling," Mrs. Barnes said. "Girls, shall we head off to the church?

Cym gave my hand one last squeeze before leaning close to my ear. "Please come back to me."

"I will."

"Li, be careful," Fiona said. "I can't be a duet without you."

"And protect your hands," Cym said. "God knows we're going to need some music after this."

"I'll do my best," Li said.

The women left, leaving me with Li. "I've got to drive home and get my gun. Would you care to accompany me?"

"If you'd like company," Li said, "then I shall provide it."

We walked outside. The air had dropped to below freezing. Above us, the stars shone with a confidence I did not feel myself. A new worry had come to me. What if someone in the crowd lost their temper or panicked? If one or both of the men were killed, the man they worked for would bring his wrath down upon us.

I said a silent prayer before Li and I walked across the quiet street to Lord Barnes's lot behind his office building.

We didn't speak as we got into the car and drove out of town. I didn't know him well, other than our interactions when we were boys. He'd always been quiet and reserved, preferring to communicate, at least it seemed to me, though his music.

The road was clear this evening. It had been several days since the last snow, and the plows had cleared the main roads. Albeit frozen, the ground was not slick.

Soon, we arrived at my house. I pulled my watch from my pocket. We had another half hour before we had to be back in town. "Do you want to come in? Get warmed up before we have to head back?" I asked Li.

"Please. That would be most appreciated."

We went into the house. Embers in the fire were resurrected easily with a few small dry logs.

"I could make us some coffee," I said.

"I wouldn't turn it down."

I told him to make himself comfortable and went back to the kitchen to brew a pot of coffee. My stomach growled. When had I last eaten?

I stuck my head out from behind the kitchen door. "Are you hungry? I've not had dinner."

"Famished," Li said.

I quickly put together butter-and-ham sandwiches using some of my brother's bread. By the time I had those ready, the coffee had percolated. Li joined me at the kitchen table. We ate in silence for a few minutes before Li looked over at me. "I don't suppose you're scared at all?"

"Me? Sure I am."

His dark eyebrows shot up in surprise. "I'd have not thought that possible."

"Why would you say that?"

He shrugged. "I don't know. You're so big."

I chuckled and picked up my sandwich for the last few bites. "I don't think size has anything to do with it. In fact, the more you love someone, the more scared you are. I'm more scared tonight than I would have been just a year ago. I have so much to live for. Cymbeline. Our life I hope to build together. The more love we feel, the more it makes us want to live."

"Yes, I suppose that's true." He looked down at his plate. A crease between his eyebrows told me something troubled him.

"It's all right to be scared," I said. "Doesn't mean you're a coward. That's only if you ran away."

"It's not that." He lifted his gaze. "I love someone too. A woman I shall never be allowed to have."

Taken aback, I pushed aside my plate to gather my thoughts. Who did he love? Why couldn't he have her? "Does she not love you?"

"I'm unsure. I've no experience with women. We have deep respect for each other and are great friends."

"Well, then, all is not lost. I won Cym over, and she didn't even like me."

He narrowed his eyes, seeming to take me in for a moment before speaking. "It's not because of that. I cannot have her because of this." He pointed to his eyes and then brushed a finger over his hand.

I stared at him, blank for a moment, unable to understand his meaning.

"I am Chinese," Li said.

"You're American. As American as I. Our parents came here to give us that privilege."

"You look like everyone else here," Li said. "I do not."

The hairs on my arms stood up as I realized what he meant. I did not think about our differences because I looked like most everyone else in town and could afford blissful ignorance. Other than the Coles, who had moved away just a few months ago, Li and his family were the only ones in Emerson Pass who were not of European descent. "I see." Perhaps the Coles had moved away so that they would feel less alone?

"When I was in Chicago, I wanted to play in the symphony, but it was impossible. I came back to Emerson Pass because I'm accepted here, even if my differences make me unable to live as I'd like to. You're not the only one, Viktor, who loves a woman. The difference between you and I? You are free to spend years wooing Cymbeline Barnes and winning her heart. I cannot."

"Who is it you love?" Even as I asked the question, I knew. He and Fiona were surely as close as two people could be, making music together the way they did. Was it more than friendship? Two souls who were connected by music might be connected in other ways as well.

"You do not know how she feels?" I asked.

"I know only how she looks at me. The way her eyes—" He stopped for a moment, seeming to search for the right word. "They turn soft, almost dreamy, when she looks at me and thinks I don't see her."

"That should tell you what you need to know."

"If only it were that simple," Li said.

I drank the last of my coffee before I spoke. "The affliction of the Barnes sisters. Not for the faint of heart."

"Yes." The corners of his mouth twitched into a sad smile.

"Fiona doesn't care about convention. As different as she and Cym are, they share that quality."

His eyes flickered with something akin to hope before dulling once more. "Her father rescued us from starvation. Did you know that?"

I shook my head. "No, I thought your grandmother had always worked for them." I'd never thought much about it either way. Li and Fai had been part of our group since their first days at school. For better or worse, it had never occurred to me that they might feel different from the rest of us.

"Do you think Lord Barnes would forbid Fiona to marry you?"

"What else could he do? He's from a bloodline of English noblemen. Fiona could not marry a man from China."

"Again, you're an American. Perhaps Lord Barnes won't think that at all. You won't know unless you ask him."

"Fiona would have to love me first," Li said. "What if I'm reading her eyes all wrong?"

"She's only just turned eighteen. Perhaps time will tell?"

"Yes, perhaps." He got up, scooping both our plates from the table and putting them in the sink.

"We should go," I said. "I'll take care of the dishes later."

He turned away from the sink to look at me. "Please, keep this between us. I regret telling you."

"Your secret's safe with me."

"Especially don't tell Cymbeline," Li said. "She frightens me."

I laughed. "She's not as scary as she seems, but I understand. You want to tell Fiona yourself first."

"That's correct. Thank you."

"You're welcome. I'm always here if you want to talk."

He thanked me again before we went back to my sitting room to put our coats and hats back on. My stomach churned with nerves. Comforted only by the thought that Cymbeline would not be there, I held the door open for Li before heading out to the car.

Cymbeline

If anyone thought I was staying at the church to cluck about with the other hens, they had another think coming. While Mama and Fiona were helping Lizzie put together tins of cookies and muffins to take with them to the church, I slipped upstairs to put on my boy clothes. Daisy had washed them for me and hung them in my closet. *Bless her for not asking questions*, I thought.

Lizzie had promised to stay at home with Addie and Delphia while Mama and I went to the church. Once I had Mama safely inside with the others, I would slip away to the schoolhouse and wait with the men.

I dressed in my knickers and men's sweater, then disguised them with my long coat. The hat Mrs. Olofsson had knitted for the competition, a combination of a neck scarf and cap, had a hole for my mouth and eyes. Essentially, my entire face was covered. For now, I pinned my hair up and put on one of my girl hats. The one I'd use for tonight, I stuck in my pocket. Once I was in town, I'd ditch Mama and head over to where the action would take place. I'd fight right along with the men. After all, it was my family and my community too. Not to mention I was in better condition than most of those men. A better shot, too. All those years target practicing out in the woods with the twins gave me confidence.

I took my men's coat from the hook and opened my underwear drawer. I reached to the back until I felt the cold metal of my pistol. I grabbed it and headed for the door.

MAMA FIDGETED THE ENTIRE RIDE INTO TOWN. EVERY SO often she would bring up one of her concerns, to which I would mumble something I hoped was comforting.

We drove through town and parked in Papa's lot. The schoolhouse was all lit up as if there would be a dance that evening. Mama, Fiona, and I linked arms as we passed by, turning right to head to the church.

The lights were on there too, but again, this wouldn't be out of the ordinary for a dance night. Older ladies would rather knit or embroider than attend a dance. Rossi wouldn't think twice if he happened to see a bunch of women gossiping and eating cookies.

Many of the women were already there, including Aunt Annabelle, Jo, Louisa, Poppy, Emma, Mrs. Johnson, and her daughters. Only Shannon was missing from our usual group. She and the baby were resting at home with Sally to look after them.

Fiona and I placed the boxes of cookies and muffins on one of the tables. When my sister took off her coat, I realized a flaw in my plan.

I fake-shivered. "I'm going to keep mine on for a while. Just until it warms up in here."

Poppy and Jo came over to greet us. They'd both missed the meeting earlier but had been filled in on the details.

"Are we really going to stay here?" Poppy asked. "While they defend our town?"

"What would you suggest?" Jo asked before her face contorted in horror. "No, not that. Neither of you have any business going with the men. You're to stay put here. This is not a joke."

Poppy caught my eye. "Are you implying that our work is a joke, Jo?"

"Don't be ridiculous. This isn't the same thing at all," Jo said. "These men are dangerous. They almost killed our brother."

Poppy sobered. "I can't think of that, or I'll either be sick or start to cry."

"Don't even think about it. No crying. Not tonight," I said.

Jo scrutinized me. "Why is your hair up like that?"

"Don't you like it?" I asked, hoping to deflect her away from thinking about it too carefully.

"It looks nice with the hat," Jo said. "But different."

"Don't look like that," I said. "Don't you trust me?"

"As a matter of fact, I don't," Jo said. "What do you have on under that coat?"

"It's none of your concern," I said.

"You better not be planning on joining the men. She stepped closer and peeked under the collar of my coat. "Cymbeline Barnes, you're wearing your boy sweater." She said all of this quietly so only Poppy and I could hear her. Thank goodness. If Mama and Fiona discovered my ruse, they'd tie me up in the back room until the whole thing was over.

"Boy sweater? Why do you have on a boy sweater?" Poppy looked from me to Jo. "Is there something happening that I don't know about?"

"Not tonight," I said. "Jo's reading too much into my choice of a very warm sweater."

"Do you two think you can keep a secret from me?" Poppy asked. "I'm hurt."

"It's nothing really," I said. "But we'll tell you about it later."

Poppy's hands flew to her face. "I know what it is. You're planning on dressing like a boy to jump in that competition, aren't you?" She turned to Jo. "Did you know about this?"

"We had to keep it quiet or the whole town would know," Jo said.

"From me? I'm hurt." Poppy's usually mischievous eyes had darkened. She truly was hurt.

"I would've told you, but we've been distracted with all this." I gestured about the room. "With Flynn's terrible decision."

Mama came over with Fiona and saved me from further discussion. "Can you girls help pass out the cookies?"

"Don't think this is over," Poppy whispered in my ear. "You'll tell me everything or I'll fire you."

I smirked. "You can't fire me. Who else will mess about in the mud and put her arm up a cow's bottom?"

"I could find a replacement for you. I could."

"Well, you can fire me later. We've got cookie duty now."

For the next few minutes, we passed around cookies. Mrs. Johnson had brought a punch bowl and was serving refreshments to anyone who wanted a glass. In all the chaos, I slipped out unnoticed.

Or so I thought. I was about to round the corner of the church when someone hissed at me from a bush.

"Hold up there, Cym." It was Nora, dressed in her overalls and her father's old jacket.

"What're you doing?" I asked.

"Same as you, apparently."

I lifted my hat and scarf combination from my pocket. "Look what Mrs. Olofsson made me."

"What is that?" Her eyes narrowed, trying to see in the dim light.

"It goes over my face, so no one will know it's me." I took off my cloche hat and coat and laid them on top of a bush to gather up later.

"I only have this." Nora put a man's hat over her head. A rather small head, now that I looked at her more carefully.

"That thing covers most of you." I tugged the hat over my

head and pulled the scarf portion up over my mouth and nose, then buttoned them together.

"You look like a monster," she said.

"Good. Maybe we'll scare the thugs away."

"Come on. It's almost eight."

We strode down Barnes Avenue and then jumped into one of the alleys to take the back way to school.

"Thanks for what you said about Flynn today," I said.

"You're welcome."

I caught a glimpse of the front of the schoolhouse as we crossed behind some bushes toward the playground. The steps were empty. If our resident thugs knew anything about what our dances were really like, they would know this was suspicious. Usually, people spilled out onto the steps laughing and chatting in clusters. Nora and I ran across the playground to the back door. I put my finger to my mouth, and we entered as quietly as we could. What seemed to be the entire male population of Emerson Pass waited together in the room we'd occupied earlier. They were quiet, the tension thick as the air before a storm.

We slinked into one of the corners, hoping neither of the Olofsson brothers would notice two slight figures in the back of the room. The stifling scent of men filled the room.

I looked at the clock on the wall—two minutes until eight. Papa made his way to the front of the crowd, gave everyone a wave, and stepped into the hallway.

Viktor, Phillip, Theo, and Isak went to the front windows to look out. From what I could tell, Theo was supposed to give the signal for when the masses were to descend on Rossi and Chetta.

A stir of energy traveled the room. I felt for my pistol in my pocket.

"Do you have a weapon?" I whispered to Nora.

"Nothing but a pair of pruning shears."

"What are those supposed to do?"

"I don't know. It was all I could think of."

"You better stay close to me then," I said.

Theo's hand went up, motioning that it was time to go. With only the sound of boots shuffling across the floor, the men exited the room until most everyone was in the hallway in front of the double doors. Nora and I were at the very end of the line. We kept our heads down, hoping no one would notice us.

"Now," Theo called out from the front of the crowd. Phillip and Theo each flung open one of the doors. Viktor and Isak led the throng of men out of the building. I could see only a wall of bodies. We followed blindly. I had my pistol cocked and ready and held it high above my head. We moved fast, splitting off into two groups, one to the left and the other to the right.

Nora and I went with the batch that veered to the left. I caught a glimpse through the crowd of Papa standing with Rossi and Chetta as the men surrounded them. Guns, knives, and a few pitchforks, plus Nora's gardening shears, were raised. Strangely, the crowd was eerily quiet, other than heavy breathing.

"What's this?" Rossi asked.

"We want you to leave our town." Usually I couldn't hear Papa's British accent, but tonight I did. "And we're prepared to fight you for it."

I ducked between two men to get to the front. Rossi and Chetta had cocked their rifles and waved them around as if trying to decide who to shoot first.

"Put down your guns," Theo shouted to them. "And no one gets hurt."

Rossi shouted an expletive. A recklessness in his eyes reminded me of a rabid squirrel I'd once seen in our yard. Beyond caring if he lived or died, he would take out as many as he could before he went. He lifted his gun, aiming it at Theo. Without thinking, my hand having a mind of its own, I pulled the trigger of my pistol, aiming at Rossi's thigh. I got it just right. The bullet ripped through his flesh. He dropped his gun and fell to the ground, writhing with pain.

"Good Lord," Nora muttered. "Where did you learn to shoot like that?"

I started shaking. I'd never shot anything living in my life. Only the target the boys had set up in the woods. I couldn't bear to kill an animal. "My brothers taught me."

Chetta tossed his gun away and put up his sausage-fingered hands. "Don't shoot. I surrender."

Viktor and Isak moved in, shoving Chetta down and tying his hands behind his back with a piece of rope. Theo returned to being a physician, fulfilling his vow to heal the sick, no matter who they were or who wounded them. In this case, his sister dressed as a boy.

He and Dr. Neal knelt over Rossi. The snow had turned scarlet around the injured man. Would he bleed to death? From my wound? He'd tried to shoot Theo, I reminded myself. I turned away, unable to look.

Viktor ran to my side. Everything had happened so quickly, I'd completely forgotten my disguise. But as he drew closer I could see he knew it was me. Of course he would. He'd seen me all fall in these knickers.

He didn't grab me or acknowledge who I was, simply leaned close and said, "Heck of a shot."

"Thank you," I whispered.

Papa gathered the discarded guns before turning toward me. For a second, I could see he didn't realize it was me. Soon, though, the look of recognition crossed his face. He said something under his breath. I couldn't be sure, but I think it was a bad word. Not a good sign. He gave Isak the guns.

I'm sorry, Papa, I thought.

He sprinted over and took me by the arms. I braced myself, ready for a tongue-lashing. Instead, he pulled me against him in a rough hug. "My sweetheart," he whispered. "My baby girl. What am I going to do with you?"

Meanwhile, the men had all turned to see who had shot Rossi. Given Papa's reaction and subsequent embrace, they all figured out it was me with no trouble. Whispers went through the crowd. *Cymbeline Barnes. Dressed as a boy. Shoots like a soldier.*

"So much for your disguise," Nora said.

Papa turned to her. "Nora Cassidy, what are you doing here?"

"Same as Cym. Standing up for my town."

Isak ran over to us. "Nora, I had no idea that was you."

"You should have. You've seen me wear these same clothes every day I've worked my father's farm." She grinned at him cheekily.

"I'd scold you, but I know it won't do any good," Isak said.

"I'd scold you, but I know it won't do any good," Nora echoed back.

Viktor put his arm around my shoulders. "So much for keeping your disguise a secret."

NORA AND ISAK OFFERED TO GO TO THE CHURCH AND TELL the women what had transpired. I cringed thinking about Mama and Jo's reaction when they learned I'd shot a man.

Papa thanked the men for their contribution and told them to go home and warm up. The crowd began to slowly disperse, as if they were reluctant to let go of the excitement. At least a dozen men came up to congratulate me on my good shot. I'd imagined I'd like the attention for my sportsmanship, but shooting a man wasn't how I'd thought I'd get it. Now that they all knew it was me I figured my chances of competing in the ski jump unlikely. Somehow, at this moment, it didn't seem as important as it once had been.

Theo and Dr. Neal carried Rossi into the schoolhouse and laid him on the floor. Mama would cringe at the sight of all the blood spilling onto the boards. I'd scrub it out, I promised myself. Already, the idea of what I'd done was sinking in and making me feel sick. Once again, I turned away as Theo used a knife to cut Rossi's pant leg.

Viktor and Phillip shoved Chetta into one of the chairs and tied him to it.

"Bullet went straight through," Dr. Neal said.

"Probably won't find it until spring," Theo said.

Regardless, this was good news because it would be easier to clean the wound and sew him up without having to dig a bullet out as he'd had to do with Flynn.

Rossi groaned. "Give me something for the pain."

"You think we're interested in that?" Theo asked. "You shot my brother. I'm happy for you to suffer."

"We could give him something in exchange for a promise," Papa said.

"What do you want?" Rossi asked, sounding weak.

"Here's how it's going to be," Papa said. "We gave you the opportunity to take the product and be on your way. Since you wouldn't take it, we've decided to burn the factory down. The minute the doctors here patch you up, you and your friend here are going to get in your car and leave us for good. If you come back, the entire town will hunt you down and this time the bullet will go through your heart, not your leg."

"My boss won't like it," Rossi said.

"Too bad," Theo said.

Rossi screamed as Theo cleaned the wound with alcohol.

For the first time, it occurred to me that perhaps there wasn't a boss. Had he made that up to make himself seem more powerful than he really was? Without a crime boss as a threat, he and Chetta were just small-time bandits. Once they were gone, we wouldn't have to worry about someone more powerful coming to take revenge. If my hunch was right, that is.

I stood over him, determined to get an answer. "There isn't anyone in Chicago, is there? You're two small-time crooks playing dress-up. You don't work for anyone but the devil."

Rossi stared at me. "What is it with you? Are you a witch? They should burn you at the stake and be done with it."

I resisted the shiver that went up my spine. "You're leaving here and not coming back. It's not just me that's a good shot here in Emerson Pass."

"What you saw tonight, you'll see anytime you set foot in this town," Phillip said.

"We can sneak back here and kill your whole family," Rossi muttered without much conviction.

"But you won't," Viktor said. "Because you're cowards."

"There won't be any reason to come back here," I said. "We're burning down the distillery."

"Hand me the needle, would you, Doc?" Theo asked Dr. Neal. "The long one."

"Idiots. All of you," Rossi said right before he fainted.

Viktor

Two days after we sent the men packing, Lord Barnes asked Phillip and me to accompany him out to the old mine where Flynn had cleverly built his distillery. The actual operation was in the old office. Inventory had been stored in one of the mine shafts.

"Years ago, this is where I found Li and his grandmother and little sister," Lord Barnes said. "It wasn't fit to live in. They'd almost starved and frozen to death out here. I'd never have imagined it would someday be a place to make moonshine."

"How did they ever find this place?" I asked. We'd driven for a while down a dirt road. One seldom used, other than for Flynn's purposes.

"Flynn said he thinks they followed him out here one day," Phillip said. "One day he heard rustling in the bushes and looked around but figured it was a deer or some other critter."

"A critter all right," Lord Barnes said. "Two of them."

The day before, Phillip and I had come out to pack up the inventory and take it to the club. Lord Barnes had reluctantly agreed after Phillip had explained how it would hurt business to go suddenly dry. Where they would get more was a mystery still, but no one wanted to talk about that at the moment.

Mrs. Barnes had asked that they stop serving altogether, but I had a feeling Flynn wasn't that reformed. All I cared about for now was that he'd been well enough to go home that morning to his new baby and his wife. I hoped for the children's sake that Shannon could forgive him. Having parents at war would be terrible for the them. What other choice did they have, anyway?

Lord Barnes took a pile of rags out of the back of his car. We wrapped them around several sticks and soaked them in kerosene. The area around the old building was dirt and rock, all covered with snow. We figured this was enough insurance that the fire wouldn't spread, but it still unsettled me.

"The place will go up fast," Phillip said.

"Good riddance," Lord Barnes said.

"Should the car be a little farther away?" I asked. Who knew how far the flames would reach?

Lord Barnes nodded before driving his car a ways down the road and coming back to us on foot. "Ready?"

"Now or never," Phillip said.

We each lit our rag and tossed it into the building, then sprinted away to avoid the blast and the heat. From some distance, we watched the old place light up and burn. Thirty minutes later, it was nothing but a pile of charred wood.

Lizzie had packed us a lunch. We sat in the car and ate to make sure the fire was out.

"Only Lizzie would think to send a meal with us," I said.

"Everyone has their own way of showing love," Phillip said.

"Thanks for coming out here with me, boys. This has been a rough time for me." Lord Barnes opened the picnic basket to pull out an apple. "I won't be sorry to see all this end."

"Christmas is coming," Phillip said. "The best time of year."

"Before that, the ski competition," I said.

Phillip sighed. "I won't be sorry when it's over. Without Flynn, my workload has increased dramatically."

"He'll return shortly," I said. "Theo said he should be able to go back to work in a few weeks."

"Just in time for the event," Phillip said with a touch of bitterness in his voice.

I looked at him closely. Had his partnership with Flynn soured? I couldn't blame him. Flynn had kept a lot from him.

Lord Barnes took off his hat and ran a hand through his hair before putting it back on. "Phillip, I've been thinking. If you're unhappy working with Flynn, you have my permission to do something else."

"How could I do that? He gave me such an opportunity. One that supports my family."

"You make an impressive ski," Lord Barnes said. "Maybe you'd be more content working with your hands. When you came out, you wanted to build furniture. Perhaps you've gotten too far away from your calling. You could run your own shop. Do things your own way."

"Sounds fine. Very fine." Phillips eyes sparkled as he looked out over the terrain. "I've been thinking about it a lot. Perfecting my techniques. Like you said, I could have my own shop. Sell them to tourists and townspeople."

"I'd like to help Flynn run things out at the mountain," Lord Barnes said. "Just for a while. Until he gets back on his feet."

I wondered how much of it was helping Flynn versus keeping track of him. Either way, it seemed to be a good solution for all.

"You wouldn't think less of me?" Phillip asked Lord Barnes. "If I'm only a humble woodworker who makes skis?"

"Son, you've proven yourself to me time and again to be a fine husband, father, and friend as well as a son to me. It would take a lot more than a wish to follow your interests to dissuade me from my respect and love for you."

"Thank you, sir." Phillip cleared his throat and looked away. "I appreciate it."

"What about you, young Viktor?" Lord Barnes asked. "Are you content?"

"Yes, sir. All I've ever wanted was to have Cymbeline by my side. I'll work every day just to get home to her."

Lord Barnes smiled at each of us in turn. "My girls have excellent taste."

Cymbeline

The morning of the race, I woke before sunrise. I lay in the dark for a few minutes, hoping to fall back to sleep, but it was not to be. Finally, I gave up and tossed back the quilt to face the cold dawn. The moment I got out of my warm bed, I began to shiver. I put on my robe and lit the fire.

I wandered restlessly about the room as my nerves threaten to take hold. No, I wouldn't allow my anxiousness to ruin my chances of success. This was my day. The time I'd waited for. Still, the athletes that had been there at dinner the night before swam before my eyes. They were impressive. Male specimens of power, speed, and agility. However, there were only three others here for the ski jump. Phillip had told me in confidence that Flynn was very disappointed at the turnout.

Frankly, I was too. I wanted to beat as many of them as I could.

I paced for a few more minutes and then decided to bathe and get ready. My heart beat faster than usual, and my hands were clammy. I bathed and dressed as if I were going to the races as a spectator. Fiona and I had hidden my racing attire in the piano seat at the club.

I'd just put on a wool dress and stockings when Fiona entered the room, flushed.

"I'm a wreck," Fiona said. "It's as if I'm racing myself. I couldn't sleep last night."

"I slept but woke too early."

She patted my shoulder. "I know you're going to do your very best. We must remember that winning is not what we're after. Yes, it would be nice for you to score for your own sake. But this is for all women."

"All of us?" I flopped onto the bed with my legs dangling over the edge and looked up at the ceiling. "That makes me more terrified than ever."

Fiona laughed, a near-hysterical giggle that reminded me of when we were kids and pretending to be asleep after the lights had been turned out for the night.

"Why are you laughing?" I asked.

She rearranged her face into her usual placid expression. "I'm sorry. I didn't mean to make you more nervous. No matter what happens later, you have done the thing no one else has been brave enough to do." She fell back onto the bed next to me. Her fingers, as they had when we were small and she was afraid in the night, found mine. We stared up at the crack in the ceiling. Years ago, we'd agreed it looked like the face and ears of a jackrabbit.

Fiona bounced from the bed first, dragging me up by the hand.

We embraced, holding on to each other for a little longer than we normally would. I drew strength from that embrace. The love of my sister as strong as anything the world could bring.

For the rest of my days I would be loved. That was all that truly mattered. I knew that now. When this entire ruse started, I'd been desperate to prove that I could compete in a sport I loved so much. However, what it had brought me was so much more. A man who loved me. One to whom I'd given my entire heart without reservation. The support of my family was worth more than any medal could ever be.

Still, I would like to win and aimed to do so.

"I couldn't have done this without you, Fi."

"I wouldn't have missed it for anything in the world." Fiona gifted me with one of her dazzling smiles and squeezed my hands. "Let's go make history."

We walked hand in hand down the stairs. Our dining room was aflutter with activity. The little girls were eating and chattering away about the races of the day. Mama and Papa had finished their breakfast and were passing sections of the newspaper back and forth.

"They're covering the competition in the Chicago and Denver papers," Papa said. "Flynn and Phillip have pulled off a true feat."

Mama beamed at me and then at Fiona. "What a day it will be."

"Fi and I are thinking of getting an early start," I said. "We want a good spot on the spectator platforms."

"We can save seats for the rest of you," Fiona said.

"Don't forget," Delphia said.

"We won't," Fiona said.

As I walked out to the foyer to gather up my coat and hat, Addie followed me. She whispered in my ear, "Good luck," then pressed something into my hand. It was a purple rock. "I found it last summer at the creek. It's good luck. Just in case you need it."

"Thank you, pet. I'll see you afterward."

"I can't wait to see their faces," Addie said.

"Me too."

We walked out to the car in silence. Fiona had offered to drive, but I thought it would be better to have something to do so had taken the wheel instead.

"The sky's so bright today," Fiona said. "Will it hurt your eyes? The glare from the snow, I mean."

"No, the goggles take care of that. And keep my face hidden."

"Jo said she'd just have to see us afterward," Fiona said. "She's going to sit with the family and pretend she doesn't know anything. I hid your clothes and goggles in the piano seat at the bar as planned. Viktor's to meet us up at the ramp."

We'd been over this dozens of times. "Right. I know," I said. "Anyway, you'll be with me in case I forget anything."

"I don't know which I'm more agitated over. The actual race or the reveal later."

"I'll be lucky if I'm not called out right away." Since the night I shot Rossi, it had spread through town that I'd dressed up as a boy. "I'm pretty sure they'll know it's me."

"As long as you get to jump, we don't care," Fiona said.

෴

VIKTOR WAS WAITING FOR US IN THE PARKING LOT AT THE mountain. I'd never seen it as packed with cars and people as it was today. My stomach turned over at the idea of jumping in front of all these people.

"You're going to do great." Viktor kissed me. "Now, I'm going to leave you and go up to the spectator section and pretend like I don't know who you are."

I thanked him and promised to do my best.

"Now off you go," he said. "Fiona, good luck to you too."

"What do I need luck for?" Fiona wrinkled her nose.

"You're her manager," Viktor said.

"I thought that was your job," Fiona said, laughing.

"Don't fight over me," I said. "There's plenty of me for both of you."

We were all laughing as Fiona and I headed off to find my disguise.

I changed into my ski clothes and the head cover Mrs. Olofsson had made for me. When I'd told her I wore the first one the other night, she'd made a new one of a different color. I told her she should sell them, because they really did a good job of protecting one's face.

When we went outside, Fiona walked ahead of me, as if she didn't know me. I went over to the registration table to get my number. Flynn was on the other side of the table talking to several of the men here from the Denver and Louisville newspapers. He looked well, with no signs that three weeks ago he'd been shot in the chest. It did seem my brother was like a cat. He had many lives and always landed on his feet.

I kept my head down as I approached the table. The man handing out the numbers looked vaguely familiar to me but no one I knew well. Whether he'd been with us the night of the shooting, I wasn't sure.

I told myself to act completely natural, as if I belonged here instead of in the spectator stands. People milled all around. Mrs. Johnson had brought her popcorn maker. Clive and his brother had set up a stand for their sausages. Our resident candymaker, who had recently come out from the east, sold fudge from a portable table.

"I'm Cecil Barnacle. Here for the jumping competition."

The young man looked up at me. His eyes widened for a moment before he looked back at his paper with admirable discretion. "Welcome, Cecil." He sorted through a box with envelopes and pulled out one with Cecil's name on it. "Here you are. Good luck today."

"Thank you."

He smiled up at me and said under his breath, "If they ever have a shooting competition, you should do that too."

"I'll keep that in mind." I gave him a quick smile.

"Give 'em heck." He winked at me.

I thanked him again and scuttled off feeling conspicuous. Was there anyone who hadn't figured it out yet?

Never mind all that. Time to focus on the competition. I'd practiced as much as I could over the last few weeks, but the slopes and jumping area had been busy. Many of the competitors had come early to get used to the runs and jumps. Fiona had been stealthily collecting scores and so far she hadn't found anyone who could beat my fifty meters. None of the athletes from the Winter Games were here, of course, or it might have been a different story.

We had only Americans, most of them from Wisconsin and Minnesota, many of whom looked as if they could be Viktor's Norwegian cousins. Regardless, if I could clear fifty, that meant I'd beat the scores of the medalists in Chamonix. The best score had been 49.5 meters.

My family were all in the spectator stands near the jumping area. Mama and Papa and my youngest sisters stood together. Jo and Phillip had come without their children and were bundled up in a corner with Theo and Louisa next to them. Flynn and Shannon were not there. I wondered if Shannon would come this weekend at all? She had a good excuse, given the baby, but I suspected it had more to do with staying away from her husband. When Fiona had been over to bring a basket of food, she'd seen that the guest room bed had obviously been slept in.

Viktor and Fiona stood together near the railing. I pretended not to know any of them as I climbed the steps up to the drop-ping-off point, even though it would have helped my confidence to get a wink or smile from one of them. If they knew, they weren't letting on. I still hadn't confirmed if Papa knew my secret. He hadn't said anything, but I assumed Mama had told him. After I shot a man, however, I couldn't imagine he'd care too much.

There were four of us competing. I was slated to go last. Three judges, all older men, were at the bottom of the jump near the boys who would measure us. Flynn had brought them in from out of town. Apparently, they'd judged many competitions in Wisconsin and Minnesota.

I took in deep breaths as I watched the first jumper take off down the mountain. He sailed through the air with perfectly straight posture. The measurer stuck a red flag into the snow to mark his distance. From here, I couldn't tell how far he'd gone. The second, a man built similarly to Viktor, went next. He, too, had straight posture and turned his skis out slightly. Was that technique or nerves? He fell short of the first jumper. My heart pounded as the third man took off down the mountain. He was slight and probably five inches shorter than the second. His posture was the same as the others. He beat the second jumper, but not the first.

Finally, it was my turn. I took a deep breath and stepped off the platform. They'd leveled the snow to give us a place to start off from, followed by a steep decline. I skied over to the starting place. My body felt strong and ready. All those weeks of tossing rocks around had given me the muscles I needed. Scanning the stands, I panicked for a second before finding Viktor and Fiona standing next to Jo and Phillip. I made eye contact with Viktor. He placed his hand over his heart.

Gathering strength from that simple gesture, I sped down the steep slope, making sure to keep my skis only inches apart. As I approached the jumping-off point, I folded my body nearly in half.

And then I flew. As fast as an eagle, I went. For a moment, I soared. Angels were all around me, pushing me farther and farther. *Whatever happens,* they seemed to whisper, *you will have had this. No one can take it away from you.*

I landed perfectly and gracefully came to a stop. A quick glance behind me told me what I'd suspected. My jump was at least ten meters longer than the second best. The crowd roared. I raised my poles in triumph.

The judges were scribbling notes. There would be no disputing this race. I had won.

I glided over to the bottom of the platform and unhooked my skis. For the first time, I realized no one could acknowledge it was me. I would not have the congratulations of my family or fiancé in public. That would have to wait until later. As excited as I was, a small cloud of sadness hung over me. Shaking it off, I held up my hand to the still-cheering crowd.

LATER, ALL FOUR OF US WAITED ON THE PLATFORM WHERE they would bestow us with medals. I remained disguised under my face protector. No need to hide my smile, I thought, since no one could see my face.

The head judge carried three medals attached to ribbons across his arms. One would be for me. I would have it to show my children. *Do you see what your father and I did together?* I would say.

I glanced at Viktor. He was with our families, all of them smiling.

The head judge raked a gloved hand through his long white beard. "It's come to our attention that Cecile Barnacle will have to be disqualified."

A gasp went through the crowd. Had he said what I thought he'd said? Disqualified? But why?

"We have learned through an anonymous source that Cecil is in fact a woman."

Something between a murmur of dissension and shock ran through the crowd. Those in the know were not surprised, obviously, but there were enough folks from out of town that it came as a genuine surprise. I made eye contact with Viktor and then Fiona. They appeared to be frozen.

The judge stepped closer to me. "Are you indeed Cymbeline Barnes?"

Shards of ice glistened in his thick silver mustache. His eyes were as pale as a spring morning sky, with red-tinted eyelids. I hated him and his rabbit eyes.

I stared back at him, determined to pretend to be unintimidated. Inside, however, a thousand toy soldiers were storming though my stomach. How had he known? Who had told them?

He shouted theatrically. "We have no choice but to strip this imposter of her scores."

I closed my eyes. Dismay rushed through me. After all this work and courage, I would be disqualified.

"Take off your mask," the judge said.

I trembled with rage and embarrassment. *No*, I told myself. *Don't let him see how much it hurts.* I ripped my hat off my head and glared at him.

Another wave of noises came from the crowd, albeit quieter this time. The people from my own community had gone still and mute.

"Young lady, this is a serious offense," the judge said.

"Why?" I asked. "Because I beat them by a country mile?"

Laughter from those gathered around cheered me some. Still, sweat trickled down my back despite the chilly temperatures.

"Let her compete," a gruff voice called out from somewhere in the throng of people gathered around. Mr. Johnson? In my state, I couldn't be sure, but I thought it was Mr. Johnson.

"She beat 'em fair and square," someone else yelled.

"Who cares if she's a woman?" a female voice called out from the back. Nora.

From the front, a man's voice came next. "You should see her with a pistol."

I hid a smile behind my hand.

Next to me, the man who had come in second shuffled his feet. "She beat me fair and square, judge. Wouldn't be right to say different."

"I'll say what's fair and square." The judge's face turned slightly purple. "I was brought in to do a job, not manage a bunch of country ignorants."

I winced. My people would not take kindly to a statement such as that. We were proud here in Emerson Pass.

"We're not ignorant," Isak called out. "We've got one of the best schools in Colorado."

"I doubt that," the judge said under his breath. He pointed at me. "Off the stage."

I searched the sea of faces for Flynn. This was his competition, but he was nowhere to be found. Phillip had stepped forward, however, and came to stand next to the judge. He said something into his ear. The judge shook his head. "Rules are rules."

I made eye contact with Phillip. "It's all right. I'll go."

I stepped from the stage. The crowd broke into applause.

Someone started chanting, "Number one, number one."

The rest joined in. I waved to them and walked over to stand with Viktor. He put his arm around me. "I'm proud of you."

"Thanks." My vision blurred through my tears.

The judge turned to the crowd and waved his hand as if he were a conductor of an orchestra. "Be quiet," he shouted.

But the crowd continued on, undeterred. The other two judges were looking at their papers and seemed as if they'd like to fall though the bottom of the platform and disappear. My competitors were all studying their boots.

Mrs. Johnson stepped forward. She had a string of cranberries in her hands and motioned for me to come to her. The crowd hushed. Mrs. Johnson placed them around my neck. "For coming in first place at the ski-jumping contest of 1925 in Emerson Pass, Colorado, and for making fifty and a half meters. Which as far as we know, could be the world record."

Cheers and whistles. Then to my surprise, Isak and Viktor lifted me onto their shoulders. What seemed to be the entire town joined us. We marched over to the platform where the three competitors, poor men, moved out of the way. The crowd had resumed its chant of "Number one, number one," as the flock of Emerson Pass moved as one across the parking lot to the lodge. For the second time that day, I soared like an eagle above the world, this time on the shoulders of the men and women who had helped me become the woman I wanted to be.

My town. My people. They didn't care about my gender, only that I'd done what no one had done before.

Isak and Viktor set me down when we reached the lodge. Two of the staff were there to open the doors into the dining room. "Go on in," Viktor said. "It's time to celebrate."

We moved to the side to let the others come into the room. Viktor wrapped me in an embrace and kissed me. "The rest of the town can toast you all they want, but I'm the only one who gets to kiss you."

I smiled up at him. "You're the only one I want."

Everyone gathered around as Papa began to speak. "Thanks to all of you for being together today. We planned on a party to celebrate our first annual ski competition, but as a proud father, I have to say that tonight we have even more reason to celebrate. There's food and drink for all. After that, there will be music and dancing."

Papa gestured toward me. "When I dreamt of what this town could be almost twenty years ago, I hoped to foster the spirit and determination of the individual as well as the power of the collective community. Over the last few weeks, we have done what I hoped—bound together to fight for what we want this town to be. Today, my daughter has exemplified the spirit of America and of Emerson Pass. There is nothing we cannot do with hard work, grit, and a village behind us. All great accomplishments are not done alone. She could not be here today if not for many of you in this room. Thank you, one and all.

"While the rest of the world catches up, we will keep on, awarding our youth with cranberry necklaces if we have to. But we know what she did. No one can take that away from us. To Cymbeline."

Everyone cheered. When they quieted, Papa continued. "I realize she's not the only one here today who has done something extraordinary with the gifts God gave them. Your accomplishments may not be as visible as the one we saw this morning. Still, you know how hard you've fought to fulfill your dreams and destinies and how you will continue to do so. For there is great honor in the ordinary. Keeping your family fed through hard work and sacrifice. Learning a language after leaving your homeland. Starting a business with only hope for a business partner. Sending your child to college from the pennies you put away for years. These come from the best parts of us. The parts that never give up even when life sends us hardships and disappointments. But tonight, let's put aside our burdens. Tomorrow, we fight and work and pray. Tonight we eat, drink, and be merry."

The room erupted in applause, followed by the first rousing notes from Li and Fiona. I had a feeling tonight would be one I would remember all my life.

Cymbeline

That night, I danced with Viktor to the melodious music put forth by my sister and the man she secretly loved. I also danced with my father and Theo, who told me how proud they were of me. Only Flynn remained aloof. Finally, after my feet were tired, I went back to the kitchen to see if I could snag one last morsel of food, but the staff had closed down and were out dancing and enjoying themselves.

I was about to return to the party when I saw a movement out of the corner of my eye. Flynn was in the office with his feet up on the desk.

I knocked on the doorframe. He looked up from whatever paperwork had kept his attention.

"Hey, Cym."

"What're you doing back here? The party's still going strong." Or he could go home to his wife. I kept that to myself. Our relationship was tenuous at best, and I didn't want to alienate him.

"I didn't feel much like celebrating."

"Are you mad at me about the competition?" Was that why he was back here? Pouting because I'd gone ahead and done something he didn't want me to?

"Nah. I'm proud of you. Sounds like you're the town hero for that and the other thing."

I inspected the tips of my shoes. I'd changed out of my disguise into a sparkly dress and dancing shoes. Fiona had quickly fixed my hair for me, sticking a tiara into my curls. A little powder, blush, and lipstick, and I felt like a proper girl. "I guess I'm braver dressed in knickers."

"You've always been brave. Knickers or no." He pulled out a drawer and reached inside for a flask. "You want a drink?"

"No, thank you." I peered at him. "Are you feeling better?"

"Nothing to complain about." He took a swig.

"Besides my antics, the event seemed to be a success."

"We had a good day." He gestured toward the stack of receipts on his desk. "A lot of food sold. Papa paid for the party, which makes up for a night without the underground club."

I'd been surprised they'd closed the club but had been too busy all day to think about why.

"Mama asked me to shut it down tonight," Flynn said, as if I'd asked. "This seems to be the month for losing money."

"I'm sorry about everything that happened. Losing the distillery must..." What was the word? I actually didn't know at all how he felt about anything. His expression was like a "closed for business" sign.

"It doesn't matter. Nothing matters."

"What do you mean?" I asked. The bleakness in his tone filled me with a sense of foreboding.

"Shannon's still mad at me." He took another drink from his flask. "I've been sleeping here at the club."

"Oh." She'd asked him to stay away from their own home? I'd known she was miffed but figured she'd be over it by now. It had been three weeks. That was a long time to stay mad, especially at Flynn. "What are you going to do?"

He shrugged and put his feet back up on his desk. "I've no idea." He went quiet for a moment, looking up at the ceiling. "Cym, I've been lucky all my life. But I think maybe it's run out.

I've made a mess of everything, and a man like me doesn't know how to fix it."

"A man like you? You're the finest of men."

He made a noise at the back of his throat. "No, I'm not. Phillip, Papa, and Theo are fine men. Viktor and Isak, the best. Me? I'm foolish, selfish, and impulsive. Add greedy to the list too."

"You made a mistake, that's all. Everyone does. There's no reason a mistake should make you feel like a bad man."

He gave me a long look before speaking. "Do you remember how mad Jo was at me after the war? For dragging Theo over there with me?"

I nodded, inwardly cringing as a memory of their argument after Theo's breakdown came to me. I'd worried they'd never be friends again. "That was all a long time ago. Jo never thinks about it anymore."

"She might. We don't know. Regardless, I think of it. Every day. I think about how Theo could've been killed over there and I'd have never forgiven myself. The rest of you wouldn't have either. You think a secret distillery is bad? Think about if I'd come home without Theo."

"But you didn't. All's well that ends well."

"That's just it, Cym. It isn't. I've not belonged in our family since then. I can see them all thinking about what a mess I am. How poisonous I am."

"Not true. We all love you. If you'd seen how everyone fell apart when we thought we might lose you—you would never think such a thing."

"The world would be better off without me. You all would be. Shannon would have had a better life with someone else."

My stomach churned. How could he think these things? I grappled with what to say. How could I convince someone in such obvious despair that he was wrong?

His eyes filled. "What if Shannon won't take me back? I can't go on without her. She and the babies are the best part of me.

I'm without an anchor." He drank once more from his flask. When he put it down on the desk, I saw myself distorted in the metal surface.

"Flynn, listen to me. She will take you back. She's angry and perhaps not feeling too well after the baby." Our own mother had gone mad after the birth of the twins. Maybe Shannon was feeling strange too. I would ask Theo to check on her. "You and Shannon are in love. This is simply a temporary misunderstanding."

"There's no misunderstanding about it. She despises me for lying to her."

I heard footsteps out in the kitchen and turned to see Fiona, Jo, and Theo. "In here," I called out to them. Perhaps they could talk sense into him.

The three of them piled into the small office. They all had rosy cheeks from dancing and perhaps a tuck into the punch bowl someone had spiked.

"Brother, we came to pull you out to the dance floor," Theo said.

Flynn put his feet on the floor and leaned back in his chair, bringing the front legs off of the floor. "Not interested."

Jo frowned and crossed her arms over her chest. "Are you feeling sorry for yourself?"

"None of your business," Flynn said.

"He is," I said. "Shannon's still angry with him. He's been sleeping here at the club."

Fiona's hands flew to her mouth. "She's kicked you out?"

"So to speak," Flynn said.

"Well, this won't do." Jo sat in the chair next to me. "What shall we do to fix this?"

"There's nothing you can do," Flynn said.

"Nonsense, we can come up with a plan," Fiona said. "Like when we were kids. Remember, Flynn, when Cymbeline was stuck in the dumbwaiter and we all worked together to get her out?"

"This is different," Flynn said.

"She needs time," Theo said.

"No, that's not what it is," Fiona said, sounding surprisingly firm. "We need a Christmas miracle. Something that reminds her of how much she loves you."

"And that will make her forgive you," Jo said.

"Something big," I said. "So big that she can't help herself but see how you've changed."

"Have I changed?" Flynn asked. "Or am I still the same scoundrel I've always been?"

"Making mistakes and failing changes us," Theo said. "For the better."

"It makes us more humble," Jo said.

"Which I needed, apparently," Flynn said.

"I told him, everyone makes mistakes," I said. "That doesn't make you a bad person." I thought for a second before I continued. "All this time I've thought I was a problem simply because I wanted things other girls didn't seem to want. Now I see that it's just the way I am. It's the same for you, Flynn. You had ambition that led you down a certain path. Now it's time for you to veer off that course and start fresh. We can help you, right?" I looked around at the concerned faces of my siblings.

"Yes, of course we will," Fiona said. "We'll make it a Christmas that Shannon won't forget."

"But how?" Flynn asked.

No one answered.

"We'll figure it out," I said. "Just like you guys got me out of the dumbwaiter." I could still remember the close quarters that had made me feel claustrophobic. "When I was stuck in there, I was quite sure I'd never get out. And then you all left to go get help and I imagined myself in there, dying alone. All hope seemed lost. Yes, I was only eight, but it felt real."

"That's how I feel now," Flynn said. "Without hope."

"There's always hope," Fiona said.

"And love," Jo said. "We all love you very much, Flynn. With all your faults. Just as you love us with all of ours."

"Together, we'll come up with a plan," Theo said. "There's almost no problem that can't be solved if one thinks about it long enough."

"Or just jumps in to tackle it." I made a fist in the air.

"Maybe I could find a book that would give us some advice," Jo said. "Ideas for the lovelorn or something of that nature."

"Romantic music might soften her," Fiona said.

I grinned at the dear faces of my brothers and sisters. "Whatever it is, we'll do it together, like we always have."

"Not always," Flynn said. "I'm sorry, Cym, that I wasn't supportive of your dream to jump. It seems I'm the only one."

"I knew nothing about what these girls were doing," Theo said. "They kept it from me too. You're not alone."

Flynn brightened slightly. "Oh, well, that's something, I guess."

"Tomorrow marks a week before Christmas." Jo made a motion in the air as if she were writing on a calendar. "A week to fill Shannon with the Christmas spirit."

"We can do it." Fiona clapped her hands together. "I've got it. The Seven Days of Christmas. Each day Flynn can do something to win her heart back."

"Like what?" I asked. What could he possibly do to lessen her anger? This obviously wasn't the job for me.

"I don't know," Fiona said.

"We could ask Viktor for ideas." I couldn't stop the smile that spread over my face and reached into every part of my body. "He's good at wooing the worst of the worst."

"Good idea," Jo said.

"He *is* gifted at holding out hope when all seems lost," Flynn said, sounding for a moment like his cheeky self.

"But first, let's go celebrate Cym's accomplishments," Theo said. "Tomorrow is another day."

So we all traipsed out to the dining room to join the rest of our family. Fiona went back to Li and the piano. They began to play a lively Christmas tune, his violin in perfect harmony with her sweet voice.

All around us people danced and socialized and celebrated my accomplishments. They'd not minded about my deception. I still couldn't believe it, but perhaps this was what happened when you grew up in a place. The people who raise you are not just your parents. They include teachers, shop owners, bosses.

I rested my head on Viktor's shoulder as he moved me around the dance floor. Poppy and Neil danced by, staring into each other's eyes. Theo and Louisa did the same. Phillip and Jo were by the food table each with a little girl on their hips. Mama and Papa were dancing too, looking younger than they had two weeks ago. Isak and Nora, such a charming couple with him so tall and her so tiny yet mighty, had given up moving about the floor and were simply swaying to the music.

The Olofssons and the Johnsons sat together at a table enjoying punch and cookies and laughing over something. Addie and Delphia were in the corner playing jacks with their friends.

I searched for Flynn and found him over in the corner watching it all with glittering eyes. Shannon should be here. Between Jo, Fiona, and me, we would figure out how to reunite them.

"What are you thinking about in that glorious head of yours?" Viktor asked.

"Nothing really. Feeling grateful."

"Today was a good day."

I looked up at him. "Thank you for letting me be me. I hope someday I'll be able to give you the kind of joy and freedom you've given me."

"You already have, Cym. Since the day you showed up at my house willing to throw rocks around, all my dreams have come true."

"I know we said we'd wait until spring to wed," I said. "But let's get married on Christmas Eve. I don't want to wait any longer to be your wife."

"Are you sure? It's a big step. I'm afraid you'll miss your family."

"For goodness' sake, they're practically living on top of us. There won't be time to miss them."

"Isak and Nora are getting married the day after Christmas," he asked. "Do you think they'll mind?"

"I don't think so. Anyway, all I want is a simple ceremony at the church and then have a party at Mama and Papa's. We already do both those things on Christmas Eve. Unless you think your mom will mind?"

"She won't care. All she wants is for us to be happy together."

"I'll ask Papa and Mama to make sure they're all right hosting a party for us."

I hadn't realized they were close enough to hear until Papa asked, "A party? For what occasion?"

Viktor twirled me around so I had a better view of my parents. "We want to get married on Christmas Eve and have a party afterward at the house."

"What about a dress?" Mama asked.

"I have enough dresses. I can wear one of those."

Mama and Papa shared a smile. "They're like we were," Mama said. "Caring only for the marriage and not the wedding itself."

"We shall make it happen," Papa said. "Whatever you wish."

"Thank you," I said. "For everything."

Viktor danced me around the floor. He was light on his feet for such a large man. In his arms, I was a woman, content for him to take the lead. I felt beautiful and dainty in my gown with my curls and sparkle dancing with the best man in the whole world.

All my life, I'd waited for my call to adventure. I'd been so sure I'd recognize it when it came along. How mistaken I'd been to think it was as uncomplicated as a ski jump or some other physical feat. Had I loved winning today? Yes. Competition would always be in my blood. However, that was only part of my story. There was more to my life than winning a race or a jump. So much more.

All along, the grandest of all adventures had been right in front of me. Belonging to my family. Being part of a community. And Viktor.

All this time, Viktor had been my adventure. The most exciting journey of all. Love.

<hr/>

A NOTE FROM TESS...I HAVE A CHRISTMAS SURPRISE FOR YOU! Continue the Barnes family saga in a bonus novella, The Seven Days of Christmas is releasing December 24th, 2021. Will Flynn's siblings help him win back his beloved Shannon? It might take a Christmas miracle and a whole lot of love to do so! Order here and have it on your reader Christmas Eve 2021.

Are you ready for Fiona's story? Pre-order The Musician releasing May 17, 2022.

Sign up for my newsletter over at my website at www.tess-writes.com and never miss a sale or new release, plus you'll get a free ebook copy of The Santa Trial. You can also join my Facebook group Patio Chat with Tess Thompson for fun giveaways and sneak peeks.

I appreciate you helping to spread the word about my books. Thank you for sharing a recommendation with friends and please leave a review on the retailer of your choice.

Sending love from my home to yours, Tess XO

More Emerson Pass!

Are you ready for Fiona's story? Pre-order The Musician releasing May 17, 2022.

The first of the Emerson Pass Contemporaries , The Sugar Queen , starring the descendants of the Barnes family is available at your favorite retailer.

The second in the contemporary stories, The Patron is also available. Will Garth and Crystal ever find a way to leave the past behind to embrace each other and the future?

In case you've missed any of the Emerson Pass Historicals, here they are listed in order.:

The School Mistress

The Spinster

The Scholar

The Problem Child

The Musician

Sign up for Tess's newsletter and never miss a release or sale! www.tesswrites.com. You'll get a free ebook copy of The Santa Trial for your subscription.

Also by Tess Thompson

CLIFFSIDE BAY

Traded: Brody and Kara

Deleted: Jackson and Maggie

Jaded: Zane and Honor

Marred: Kyle and Violet

Tainted: Lance and Mary

Cliffside Bay Christmas, The Season of Cats and Babies (Cliffside Bay Novella to be read after Tainted)

Missed: Rafael and Lisa

Cliffside Bay Christmas Wedding (Cliffside Bay Novella to be read after Missed)

Healed: Stone and Pepper

Chateau Wedding (Cliffside Bay Novella to be read after Healed)

Scarred: Trey and Autumn

Jilted: Nico and Sophie

Kissed (Cliffside Bay Novella to be read after Jilted)

Departed: David and Sara

Cliffside Bay Bundle , Books 1,2,3

BLUE MOUNTAIN SERIES

Blue Mountain Bundle, Books 1,2,3

Blue Midnight

Blue Moon

Blue Ink

Blue String

EMERSON PASS HISTORICALS

The School Mistress

The Spinster

The Scholar

The Problem Child

The Musician

EMERSON PASS CONTEMPORARIES

The Sugar Queen

The Patron

RIVER VALLEY

Riversong

Riverbend

Riverstar

Riversnow

Riverstorm

Tommy's Wish

River Valley Bundle, Books 1-4

LEGLEY BAY

Caramel and Magnolias

Tea and Primroses

STANDALONES

The Santa Trial

Duet for Three Hands

Miller's Secret

About the Author

USA Today Bestselling author Tess Thompson writes small-town romances and historical romance. She started her writing career in fourth grade when she wrote a story about an orphan who opened a pizza restaurant. Oddly enough, her first novel, "Riversong" is about an adult orphan who opens a restaurant. Clearly, she's been obsessed with food and words for a long time now.

With a degree from the University of Southern California in theatre, she's spent her adult life studying story, word craft, and character. Since 2011, she's published over 20 novels and a five novellas. Most days she spends at her desk chasing her daily word count or rewriting a terrible first draft.

She currently lives in a suburb of Seattle, Washington with her husband, the hero of her own love story, and their Brady Bunch clan of two sons, two daughters and five cats. Yes, that's four kids and five cats.

Tess loves to hear from you. Drop her a line at tess@tthompsonwrites.com or visit her website at https://tesswrites.com/ or visit her on social media.

Made in the USA
Monee, IL
22 December 2021

86893913R00174